THE
NEW ME

BOOKS BY ELIZABETH NEEP

The New Me

Never Say No

The Spare Bedroom

Available in Audio

The New Me (available in the UK and the US)

Never Say No (available in the UK and the US)

The Spare Bedroom (available in the UK and the US)

Elizabeth Neep

THE
NEW ME

bookouture

Published by Bookouture in 2021

An imprint of Storyfire Ltd.
Carmelite House
50 Victoria Embankment
London EC4Y 0DZ

www.bookouture.com

Paperback ISBN: 978-1-80019-641-4
eBook ISBN: 978-1-80019-640-7

Previously published as *The Mix-Up*

For my sister, Rachel

CHAPTER ONE

It's hard to be yourself when you're paid to be someone else. Or not paid, in my case. I risk a glance at the other actors sat on the chairs beside me, a long line of long legs crossed and hair cascading along the corridor. I swear these people are perfect, no pretending about it.

'It went *so* well,' I hear one of them say. A sentence I've not said for years. I trace the voice back to a face so symmetrical and sparkly that it might legitimately be filtered (or at least *filled* with something). Her long brown hair shoots straight down her perfectly postured back as she holds a bejewelled phone up to her ear. 'I've got it, I swear.' She beams, as more eyes around the room turn to fix on her. She doesn't seem to mind. 'You know when you just get that feeling that the role is yours?' No. No, I categorically do not.

I search around the room for a pair of eyes to roll mine with, any pair will do. *Anyone?* But no, everyone seems far too busy with their own phones, I assume calling partners and loved ones, or agents, before jotting down addresses of their next auditions, preparing to dash off as soon as the casting agent of this apparently 'up and coming' pilot comes and puts us out of our misery. Except, no one around the room looks that miserable. Not the woman I recognise from Nike's latest ad campaign (and by woman, I mean girl, as she can't be older than eighteen). Not the dusty-blonde surf chick who seems to follow me like a shadow around the audition circuit each year. And *especially* not the sunshiny teenage supermodel singing into her phone. But then, what does she have to be miserable about? Just look at her. Oh, you already were? You and everybody else.

'I think they're going to call us back into the room any second now.'

I watch Shiny uncross her impossibly long legs only to recross them, my eyes catching on the iconic red soles of her super-cool biker boots. A thousand questions scramble for space in my mind: Louboutin do biker boots? How does an actor *afford* Louboutin biker boots? Where can I find a knock-off pair? And most importantly: do I stand a chance in hell of booking this part and being able to afford a knock-off pair of Louboutin biker boots, or... you know... *lunch?*

I reach for my phone with shaking hands. I need this job, any job. The image on my locked screen mocks me as I read the twisting typography: '*dream as if you'll live forever, live as if you'll die today.*' Well, that's all very well and good, James Dean, but you were famous by the time you were twenty-four. Okay, so... you also tragically died soon after – maybe that was a bad example – but it's hard to dream as if you'll live forever when you're surrounded by constant reminders that you're not getting any younger.

'Excuse me?' I look up to see a man standing in front of Shiny, so tall and broad that he eclipses her completely, drawn into her forcefield like an X-Men superhero (which, to be fair, he could totally play). 'I think you're really cute, can I have your number?' I hear a giggle emerge from behind the fourth Hemsworth brother. *Screw you, Shiny.* I don't hear her reply but judging from Hemmy's slump back to his seat, I assume he's been rejected. Just like I will be in T minus however many minutes. There is no way I can compete with Shiny and whatever dark magic she's thrown into her shopping bag along with those boots.

Forcing my eyes back down to my phone, I curse the fact that I can still see the quote so clearly; isn't my home screen meant to be blowing up with good luck messages from my best friend (too busy) and my flatmate (too high) and my agent (too bored)? I guess we've all seen this scene play out too many times to expect a big twist in the ending now.

'Marley?' From somewhere in the distance I can hear someone calling my name. 'Marley Bright?' I look up to see a short woman wearing glasses with colourless frames and holding a clipboard just outside the audition room. 'Marley?' She looks directly at me and, stunned, I force myself to nod. Surely, she isn't going to reject me in front of everyone. Usually, it is the successful ones who get called back into 'the room', with the rest of us thrown a brief, 'Thank you so much for coming, better luck next time.'

'Lucy?' Clipboard Lady calls into the room. Oh, maybe she just got the name wrong? I slump back in my chair, trying to act like my whole career doesn't depend on this. Trying to act, full stop. The surf chick stands and starts walking into the room, turning to me with a narrowed stare that means either 'you're my competition and you don't stand a chance' or 'your name has been called and you should stand the hell up'. I decide on the latter, forcing my shaking body to walk along the corridor and into the audition room as Clipboard calls one final name into the space behind me.

Three casting agents and one producer look up as I take a seat next to Lucy (or some desperate actor pretending to be Lucy just to get into the room). I make eye contact with each of them, trying my best to look confident. I need this job. I am a twenty-eight-year-old actor and the best role I've managed to book of late is as chief bridesmaid at my best mate's ludicrously expensive forthcoming wedding. I repeat: I *need* this job. At least I'm finally in the room. But so is Lucy. Out of the corner of my eye, I study her honeyed skin, her wavy blonde hair lopped off at her ears, an ombre that looks intentional – unlike my own, which just needs the roots doing. To my left is an empty chair. I wonder who is meant to be there?

'Sorry about that.' Shiny twinkles into the room. 'I was on the phone to my agent.' She beams at the casting panel and like magic – *her* magic – they beam back.

'That's okay, darling,' the producer says, smiling *Darling?* It's a miracle they even remembered my name. 'Take a seat.'

Suddenly, I am the freaked-out filling in a Shiny sandwich. This is unchartered territory. Are we getting called back? Are we *all* going to play the part? Am I going to be cast as Shiny's *mum*? I don't look a thing like these girls but I guess if she dyed her hair and Lucy grew hers out and I went to the gym every morning and gave up cheesy chips and you tilted your head and squinted until your eyelids were almost closed then *maybe* we could pass as related.

'Marley and Lucy.' The producer looks between us. No darlings left for us. 'The reason we have called you in here today...' What about Shiny? Is she about to get rejected in front of us? I guess she just did the same to Hemmy but that was different; this feels cruel.

'Is that you are both very promising young actors...' I swear the producer looks at Lucy when he says the 'young' part '...and we're always looking for ways to invest in upcoming talent...' Upcoming? I should have arrived by now.

'So, Sabrina here has offered to give you some pointers on how to really achieve that on-screen spark the next time you go for an audition.'

'Oh, so we didn't get—' Lucy begins, clearly not as well-versed in rejection as me.

'No, Sabrina got the role.' The producer nods at his darling as I try my best not to cry. 'Thank you so much for coming though – and better luck next time.' He trots out his spiel as Sabrina, no less than a decade my junior, tilts her head to flash me a sympathetic smile.

I knew this girl was a witch.

CHAPTER TWO

This will be okay. Everything has to be okay, I try to tell myself as I make my way out of the building and into the car park. I gulp the fresh air like it's water, drinking it deep into my lungs. Next time. There is always a *next time*. But maybe I've been at this acting game for too long already? There are only so many times you can get knocked down and get back up again – despite what that old nineties pop song taught us to chant. Now, I have a new mantra: this will be okay. Everything *has* to be okay. So what if I've just got rejected from another audition? It is just another audition. My agent will get me another one and another one, until I finally get my big break. I know that. But right now, I'm just *broke*.

I look at my phone again – not one single message – and try my best not to cry. I just need to keep putting one foot in front of the other until something better comes along.

'Hey there.' I look up to see a broad torso in front of me, up further to see the square-jaw and fringe-framed face it belongs to. If this is the something better, I will take it. I force myself to smile, tears still threatening to fill my eyes.

'Hey,' I whisper, heart picking up pace as my day finally starts to look up.

'I saw you getting called back into the room. Marley isn't it?' The gorgeous face grins, as he begins walking further into the car park. As if on automatic, I do the same.

'That's right, and you are?' I try my best to smize, channelling my inner Sabrina as we walk side by side through countless shiny cars that I don't know the name of.

'Todd,' he says, eyes fixed forward and scanning the sea of vehicles for his own. I follow suit, looking left and right until I remember I don't have a car. I don't even drive. *Shit.* We are too far into the car park for me to suddenly remember this fact now.

'So, good news?' He turns to me, slowing to a halt at what I assume is his car. Which one should I pretend is mine? Which one can I get away with lingering behind until this gorgeous stranger disappears into his day? *Stupid Marley, always pretending.*

'Not this time.' I shake my head. And none of the times before now either.

'Next time.' Todd tilts his head in the same stupid sympathetic way Sabrina had. 'Lost your car?' His eyes follow mine across the miles of metal. You could say that. I nod, eyes fixed on his, my heart hammering in my chest. As if this afternoon wasn't humiliating enough, I am now going to have to tell a perfect stranger that his perfect jaw has made me momentarily lose my mind. 'Want me to help you find it?'

'I'm actually waiting for somebody,' I lie, pulling my phone out of my pocket and wondering whether my acting skills are up to faking an emergency call. Doubtful.

'Me too.' He grins, folding his broad arms and leaning against the boot of his car. Is he waiting *for me?* Buying some time to talk to me for a little longer? If this is the universe giving me a post-rejection pick-me-up, I just wish it wasn't one that makes me feel like such a muppet. There is only so long I can pretend to look for my imaginary car. 'I could keep you company until your friend arrives?'

Oh no. Now I have an imaginary friend. I grip the phone in my hand even tighter. If I can just dial someone, anyone, I can bluff my way out of this situation.

'That's so kind of you but actually...'

'Sabrina!' Suddenly Todd's eyes aren't anywhere near me, his body stretching high as he waves over to a person fast becoming my nemesis. *Sodding Shiny.* Before I can walk (read: *run*) away, Sabrina is bounding over, throwing her arms around Todd. He lifts her into the air, and she wraps her teenage-skinny legs around his swimmer-broad body. 'I got the part.' She grins, as he pulls her back into him.

'I thought you did, baby.'

I watch as Todd twists a piece of her hair in his hand, still suspending her with his other arm. *Oh please.*

'Especially, when Marley said she didn't...'

I stare on, not knowing where to look, not knowing how to slip away.

'Who's Marley?' Sabrina asks Todd, just inches from his face.

Turns out you don't need an exit strategy when you were invisible all along.

Walking further and further into the car park, I crouch behind what I think is a Range Rover until Todd and his teenage witch have safely driven away. *Must she get every-*

thing? I think to myself as I pick myself up off the floor. Safe to say this is a new low.

Rising to my feet, my tears start to fall. I know rejection is part and parcel of being an actor, but knowing you can afford your rent feels like part and parcel of being an adult. Maybe it's time to start acting like one? Everyone else has managed to grow up by now. Like Anna, my best friend, the one getting married, the one who still hasn't called. It's not like my auditions are that hard to remember now they're so few and far between. But still, she is busy with work – selling perfect houses to perfect people. And with planning the perfect wedding, even though at times, it feels like all the planning falls on me. Pretty handy having an unemployed friend when it comes to extra womanpower. Especially when you're trying to plan said wedding in less than six months. I have no idea what the rush is if you ask me, but then no one has. Requests are usually retained to hen-party planning and leading the Bride Tribe WhatsApp group – the role that found me (and won't flipping leave me alone).

Retracing my steps across the car park, back to the building and towards the bus stop on the other side of it, I can't help the tears from falling and even though I know Anna is busy, I know she's never too busy for me. We've been best friends ever since we were thirteen (almost Sabrina's age). Swallowing my pride and my tears, I call her.

'Marley!' Anna picks up almost immediately. 'How's it going, darl?' At least I'm someone's darling. Just hearing her voice makes the floodgates open even more.

'Not great actually,' I croak, a tear tracing its way down my face as I pray to God that Todd and Sabrina aren't about to do a U-turn. I arrive at the bus stop and slump against the bench as the heavens begin to break. Nothing like a bit of pathetic fallacy to make you feel even more pathetic.

'Oh no, Marley. Why?' I hear Anna gush along with some chatter in the background – something about ceiling heights and square footage; she's clearly showing around a house. 'Sorry, I just need to take this,' I hear her whisper as I become the one in the background. She hasn't remembered about my audition or even read the message I sent to her this morning.

'I had an audition,' I say, putting a hand to my mouth to try and muffle my tears. I know Anna's getting fed up with all my drama.

'And...?' Anna's voice is injected with hope and for not the first time I question whether even she could act better than me. Anna seems to excel in every area of life.

'I didn't get it,' I say, even though I know she can fill in the blanks.

She musters a half-hearted reply – 'Next time' – and I feel my stomach sink. She could have at least remembered. 'I've been meaning to call you all day!' *Oh?* I feel a flicker of light starting to warm me from the inside as the rain begins to hammer harder. She *did* remember.

'Yeah,' she says, exhaling deeply, and it finally feels like I have her full attention. *This will be okay.* My mantra begins again. Best friends make everything feel okay.

'I was wondering whether you could do me a massive favour?' Unless the next words out of her mouth are: *I need you to come to mine and faceplant ice-cream with me whilst telling me all about your audition and the bitch who pinched your part*, consider me categorically annoyed.

I stay silent, willing Anna to say the right thing. You can do it bestie; I believe in you.

'So, there's been this last-minute cancellation at our dream wedding venue, and I have this appointment with the hotel manager tomorrow...' she begins, and I feel my stomach drop to the floor. You had *one* line. 'And, well, my dream client has just asked to look around one of my listings and well...' she says, pausing, ready to deliver the final blow. 'You don't think you could go for me, do you?'

There is it. I look down at my rain-soaked feet, not even trying to stop them getting wet – it's pointless.

'If I miss it the date will go to someone else and my name will go to the bottom of the waiting list,' Anna goes on, speaking faster and faster; the natural pace for someone who has things to do, places to be. Unlike me, sat here in the rain, waiting for the 188 to take me back to my flat share with a grown man who has just taken up juggling.

'You'd just have to meet with Cameron, take a tour of the hotel, tell them our colour-scheme and what we had in mind, which I know I've told you like a thousand times.' Anna giggles and I force myself to add my own into the mix. *Try a thousand and one.* 'Jake found the place on a work night out not long ago and it's...'

'The dream?' I snap sarcastically but Anna is oblivious.

'Exactly!' She beams as my mind searches for excuses. It's not like my diary is full but that doesn't mean I want to spend my day schmoozing some skinny Cameron Diaz looka-like at somewhere an investment banker like Jake would hang out. It's hardly my scene. I look out from my position huddled under the measly bus shelter. I guess it's not like my scene is particularly *dreamy*.

Suddenly, my phone starts to chime, and I pull it away from my ear to see my agent's name dancing across the screen. My heart leaps as a dopamine hit floods my brain –

the same way it did three years ago when she first signed me to her agency, the same way it always does when I see Billie Forester's name. Billie Forester. *My* agent.

'Anna, can I let you know in a sec?' I say, before adding (with no small amount of pride) 'My *agent* is on the phone.' Anna knows Billie's name but still, the two words 'my agent' feel like a plaster, like they could cover over any bruise to my ego and tell the world: *I still have an agent, I could still be a success...*

'Of course, of course,' Anna says speedily; these words still impress her too. 'Just drop me a text as soon as you know or I'll *have* to cancel the appointment.' Anna doesn't try to keep the disappointment from her voice. Unlike me, who's been trying all this time.

I hang up one call and without a moment's hesitation, swipe open the next.

'Hi Billie,' I say, trying my best to sound breezy. *Please* have another gig for me.

'Mary!' she sings, so loudly that I have to pull my phone away from my ear.

'It's *Marley*,' I tell her for the thousandth time, all my breeziness blowing away.

'Marley, sorry, so sorry.' Billie doesn't sound all that sorry. 'How did it go?'

'It was a no this time,' I tell her and as she talks on and on about 'potential auditions' and 'rethinking our strategy' I pull my phone away to drop Anna a quick message: *Count me in for the appointment. Just drop me the address.*

It's not like I'll have anything better to do.

CHAPTER THREE

My phone buzzes somewhere in my bed. Where the hell is it? I search the covers (not changed nearly enough) and the other side of my double bed (rarely used). Eventually, I find it nestled under the pillow I've just spent the whole night sleeping on and well, half of the morning by the looks of things. Just one look at my phone screen and I wish I hadn't found it. Not only is it ten forty-five already but there's a message from my mum, sending me a link to something. Obediently, I click it open to find not another audition, not another theatre role that she thinks I would have been *perfect* for. No, it's a link to a recruitment site. Her text may be asking me how the audition went yesterday, but her message is clear: it's time to get a *real* job. I turn over on my side, studying the shard of light forcing itself into my room and taunting me all along my bedsheets. *It's time to get up and get a real job.*

Rolling myself to the cold edge of the bed, I force my legs to swing over the side and reluctantly pull open the curtains. Light floods the room and I'm instantly reminded that there's a Saturday out there that everyone else is already seizing. Before I can think better of it, I look down at my phone again and have to shield my eyes at the sight of an aggressive yellow pop-up on the recruitment site that tells me my 'dream career is only one click away'.

I scan the jobs: a thousand executive assistant roles flash up – most of them for recruitment firms. A recruitment firm recruiting for recruitment firms. It's recruitment inception. And it's not my dream. All of a sudden, my phone jumps to life in my hand, shocking me even further awake. For a moment, the small bit of hope left inside me wills it to be Billie, calling with news of another audition, another random address for me to run over to like chasing the rainbow. Then, I see the name of the caller dancing across the screen.

'Hey Mum.' I sigh, searching my bombsite of a room for my headphones. If Mum is going to give me an earful, I'd rather do it with my hands free. At least that way I can get ready at the same time – and by get ready, I mean get *breakfast*.

'Nice to speak to you too.' My mum's voice drips with sarcasm. I get all my dramatics from her. She was once an actress herself before she became a drama teacher. Needless to say, she taught me everything I know. Which is what makes it so damn difficult to hear that even she's giving up on me now. 'Did you get the link I sent through to you?'

'Yes Mum,' I say with the exact same tone with which I picked up the phone.

'And...?'

'*And* nothing. I've just woken up...' I finally slot my headphones into the bottom of my phone just in time to hear her reply at full volume.

'YOU'VE JUST WOKEN UP?!'

Oh, for goodness' sake.

'You're twenty-eight, Marley. You shouldn't be lying-in like a teenager.'

'Need I remind you that you spent your twenties following some random bassist around the country on tour?'

'Marley, that's no way to talk about your father.'

'*Fine,*' I concede. 'But you didn't know you were going to marry the man.'

'The man can hear you!' My dad's voice rings into my ear. *Stupid speaker phone.*

'Hi Dad,' I say, managing to peel off my pyjamas (an oversized Glastonbury 2013 T-shirt) until I realise it's a bit weird to talk to your old man in the nude.

'Anyway, we're not talking about us right now, we're talking about you'

I hear my mum rant on as I scramble to put on a top (*another* oversized band shirt).

'You will take a look at the website won't you, honey?' Her voice softens and somehow this feels even worse. My parents are not just on at me, they're *worried* about me.

'I will but maybe not today, I've got something important on,' I say, pulling on some joggers, a classic sign that I have *nothing* on today, but picking up my laptop nonetheless.

'Another audition?' my dad says, somewhere between exhaustion and hope. I let a silence stretch on for far too long as I swing open my bedroom door and trudge down the small corridor of our small flat to our small living room. There I find my thirty-two-year-old flatmate Xavier doing *something* that involves Plaster of Paris. I guess the juggling career didn't take off then.

'Marley? Are you still there?' Dad asks down the line. 'An audition?'

I finally reply with a non-committal noise: *Your youngest daughter can neither confirm nor deny that her acting dreams are hanging by a thread.*

'Oh well that's wonderful, Marley.'

I slam my laptop onto the small dining room table as Xavier takes a toke of his spliff.

'Good luck,' Dad adds as I watch a piece of Xavier's Plaster of Paris fall to the floor.

Something tells me I'm going to need it.

'Dude.' Xavier nods, raising one plaster-covered hand in my direction. After watching his hobbies get more and more absurd over the last year we've lived together, I know better than to ask what he's up to. If pressed, I think his job description would land somewhere between 'freelancer' and 'unemployed'. But then, so would mine.

'Dude.' I nod back, taking a seat and opening my laptop to hide behind it. The aggressive yellow pop-up still mocks me from my phone. Maybe my parents are right. They may have spent their early twenties as a bassist and an actor respectively (well, not that respectably if the stories are anything to go by) but then they *did* become an accountant and a drama teacher. Maybe everyone's dreams have to drift into something more attainable eventually. Xavier coughs from across the room and it's like I'm staring into my weed-filled directionless future unless I do something about it, and soon. 'Plans for the day?'

'You're looking at them.' Xavier beams down at what I think will become a bowl. *That's what I was afraid of.* 'You?'

'I might start applying for some jobs.' I feel the weight of the words as I say them.

'Isn't that what you've been trying to do all this time?' Xavier asks cheerily and yet I struggle to gleam anything cheery from the words *all this time*.

'That's auditioning.' I type the URL for the recruitment for recruitment jobs site into my laptop. 'This is *applying...* for something I don't really want to do.'

'Sounds stupid to me,' Xavier mumbles. This from a grown man making a bowl.

Before I can defend the pursuit of stability any further, my phone vibrates on the table. I have no less than fifty messages (around half of them memes) from the Bride Tribe. I should probably read them, given that two thirds of its members still owe me money. I knew Anna wouldn't settle for anything less than Hollywood's depiction of a hen party, but I never thought she'd *actually* choose LA. The tenth most expensive city in the world. I'm sure when my grandma left me a nice chunk of money in her will she never expected it would be going on rent, flights and penis straws. Well, she need turn in her grave no longer because the money is almost gone.

I scan through the messages and, reading between the memes, it doesn't take long to separate the haves from the have-nots. Lauren (a friend from school) is asking whether she can buy some time to pay me back whereas Arabella (one of Anna's *Selling Sunset*-style colleagues) is posting pictures of personalised bathing suits. Swiping away a photo of a bikini with 'Best' and 'Investment' written across each of the breasts (which I have to admit is a clever nod to Jake's career), Anna's name forces its way onto the screen. I panic that the photo has been sent to the wrong WhatsApp group before I remember that even though Anna wants the hen party to be a surprise, she also gives me regular updates on *exactly* what she'd like that surprise to be. This time, the message is just to me.

Still okay to go to the appointment? You'll need to be at the hotel by twelve.

Oh crap, the appointment. I had completely forgotten. My phone buzzes again.

You've not forgotten, have you?

How could I forget!? I hit reply. No, seriously. How could I forget?

Great. I've given them your number. You'll be there at midday?

Midday. Hotel of dreams. I wouldn't miss it. I add for good measure even though looking down at my joggers, my T-shirt and the time, there's a good chance I might.

The man in front of me keeps turning around and tutting, as if me doing my make-up on the bus is akin to him buttoning up his open shirt in public. If I wasn't so flustered, I might take the time to tell him that I am in no way incomplete without my mascara on – an argument that would be much stronger if I wasn't navigating traffic lights and speedbumps just to slap some on. I look up from my compact as the bus crawls over Blackfriars Bridge, still managing to marvel at the skyline along the Thames. The man tuts again, and I wonder how many people have ever taken a public bus to the lavish

Hotel Hyde before? My guess is not many. When I arrive at the towering entrance, I adjust my bet to zero.

Two iron gates are pulled open, ivy and flowers weaving through their twisting steel panels. Behind them, two weighty wooden doors are also open, their height disappearing into the sky. I'm pretty sure people only arrive here by supercars and carriages. This place has Anna and Jake written all over it. Man, I'm glad I changed. I look down at my floor-length satin skirt and black heeled boots (Anna's), which I've paired with an off-white (a.k.a. once-white) jumper that hangs off one shoulder in a way that makes it looks intentional.

Walking through the main entrance, a gargantuan reception area unfolds around me. It's the opposite of minimalism, hinting at old money, with ceilings as high as Xavier is back home. In fact, best not to compare anything about this place to my tip of a flat share. I really don't belong here. Even as Anna's chief bridesmaid. My heels (*Anna's* heels) tap against the caramel marble floor with every step I take towards the intimidating-looking reception desk and the intimidating-looking receptionist sat behind it. She must have heard me, but she doesn't look up. I stand there like a lemon whilst I try to remember any etiquette lessons I learned from watching Rose in *Titanic*. Apart from the old 'start from the outside' knife and fork routine, I draw a blank. Surely, there was a 'don't speak until spoken to' rule?

'Can I help you?' the pretty receptionist asks, still not looking up. Maybe it's just a 'don't look them directly in the eye' sort of thing? I try my best to avert my gaze.

'No, that's okay,' I mutter, before I realise, she actually can. 'Actually... yes, I...'

'Booking number?' She says in a monotone voice that

makes me question every automated phone call I have ever received; maybe they were actually real people?

'I don't have a booking numb—'

'Rooms start from 575.' The receptionist, *still* not looking up, slides a brochure towards me; it's so beautiful that I consider taking it and gifting it to someone for Christmas.

'Fifty-seven pounds fifty. Really, for this place?' I can't hide my surprise. Finally, the receptionist looks up, fixing her perfectly lined cat-eyes on mine. I instantly look away.

'Five *hundred* and seventy-five pounds.' She accentuates the words.

'Fuck me,' I exclaim; the receptionist raises an eyebrow as if to say: *I'd rather not.*

'Can I help you?' she repeats. *Maybe she is a robot?*

'I have an appointment... a wedding venue appointment... at midday.'

She cocks her perfectly plucked eyebrow as if she can't believe someone's actually committed to spending forever with the potty-mouthed mess in front of her. I wish I could prove her wrong.

'Anna Adams?'

'*Yes,*' I say defiantly. Well, she doesn't need to know I'm not. For a moment she looks straight through me until I hear a deep voice echo her words behind me.

'Anna Adams?'

I turn slowly to find a man standing there. And not just any man, but one who looks like he's just walked right off the red carpet and into the room. Around six foot two, with freshly cut light brown hair and just the right amount of facial hair framing a curious and slightly crooked smile. My eyes linger on his, a deep dark brown. And his eyes search me, widening slightly as I realise he's just said my best friend's name for the second time. I look between the stranger and the receptionist; she's finally managed a smile for him – but who can blame her? I know I need to say something. *I'm Marley. Marley Bright.* My mind stalls on the simplest of words. I've just made out that I'm Anna, that I belong here. I'm not going to lose face now, especially not in front of one as gorgeous as the one smiling back at me.

'Uh-huh,' I mumble for want of something, *anything,* better to say.

'Nice to meet you, Anna.' He puts a big open hand out between us. I know I'm meant to shake it. *Come on Marley – or Anna – just shake it.* 'I'm Cameron.'

'Oh,' I say, forcing my hand to his, sure he can feel the sweat prickling on mine. He looks nothing like Cameron Diaz. Although, had she and Justin Timberlake gone on to have a son, I'm pretty sure thirty years on he would have looked something like this.

'Oh?' He smiles at me inquisitively. 'You sound disappointed.' Nope. There is nothing disappointing about you. Nothing at all.

'I thought you were a woman,' I blurt before I can stop myself.

'Not last time I checked,' he says, grinning, and I blush at the thought. 'Shall I show you...'

'*Pardon?*' I ask, as my palms prickle even more.

'I said, shall I show you *around?* The *hotel?* For your wedding?' Cameron looks at me like I'm a few sandwiches short of a picnic, which let's face it is more my scene than the palace he's about to give me a tour of. And like an idiot, I nod.

'Right this way, Ms Adams.'

CHAPTER FOUR

Actors don't like to be in the shadows but being in Cameron's isn't half bad. Within seconds, I'm following him into the huge lobby behind the reception foyer, a sprawling carpeted staircase dominating the space. The stairs are wider at the bottom, narrowing towards the top where a half-landing provides the perfect backdrop for photographs before the staircase splits into two, each marble ladder leading to the balcony that wraps around us from all sides. Think Hogwarts meets *Gossip Girl*.

'This way, Anna.' I hear Cameron's voice break my thoughts. 'Anna?'

Oh, right. Anna is me. I am Anna. For today, at least.

'Do you like it?' Cameron grins down at me.

'Isn't it obvious?' I laugh. Anna will love this place. And the have-nots of the Bride Tribe will love the reception area as we sure as hell can't afford to stay inside.

'Will your fiancé?' He presses on and my confusion must be palpable as he adds: 'I assume he wants a say in his wedding too – or is he leaving it all up to you?'

'No, not at all.' I grin, not knowing just how much to gush about my fake fiancé to a man I find so attractive. But then, there's something about being seen to be unavailable, taken, *chosen*, that makes me feel a little more attractive too. 'He's excited about it.'

'Can't blame him,' Cameron says with a smile that makes me feel better than I have in weeks, before leading me out of the lobby and into one of the rooms leading off it. Together we walk into what Cameron describes as the 'snug' – even though until now, the only snugs I've been in are lounges that are so small that legitimate Airbnb hosts can't get away with calling them 'living rooms'. Six huge leather sofas stretch along the length of the room, each paired off and facing one another to create three intimate spaces to relax. Trust a wedding venue to even pair off its furniture. Panels of glass stretch from floor to ceiling, framing beautiful parkland for as far as the eye can see. It's a far cry from the sea of parked cars I got trapped in yesterday. I wander towards the windows and, pressing my hands into the firm wooden window ledge, peer out across Hyde Park. I feel like I can breathe again.

'Stunning, isn't it?' Cameron appears by my side, his voice low and comforting. I bet he's trained to speak like this to invoke maximum calm as you're maxing out your credit card. I look from the park to him, one stunning view to the next.

'Yes,' I say, exhaling deeply. 'Yes, it is.' I should probably tell him I'm not really Anna now. That my name is Marley. That I'm broke. That *I'm single.* Although, I doubt he is. And if he was, would he really be interested in me? Guys like him go for girls like Sabrina. Girls like Anna. Girls who *win.* Right now, I could really do with a win.

'Anna?'

'Yes?' Damn it, Marley. You've done it again.

'Can I get you a glass of champagne?' Cameron asks, gesturing to one of the big squishy sofas and inviting me to sit down. Well, I do feel pretty tired.

'I don't know, can you?' I say and Cameron lets out another loud laugh.

'For you?' He smiles, as my legs surrender into the seat. 'Anything.'

For Anna, anything, I think as I watch Cameron's broad frame stride out of the room. But right now, after my shitty yesterday, I really don't feel like being me today.

'Anna, I won't take no for an answer,' Cameron scolds me as he tops up my glass for the third and final time, I swear. Although I swore that after the last glass and here we are again.

'Don't think I don't see right through you,' I say, fixing my narrowed eyes on him. I taste the irony along with my latest sip of champagne. 'The hotel manager trots you out here to get the brides-to-be tipsy and send their already silly minds into a financial frenzy...'

'I don't think you're *all* silly,' Cameron says with a laugh, as I remember I am also meant to be a bride. 'And I *am* the hotel manager here.'

I cough on my next sip. 'But you're so young,' I say before I can stop myself. 'That's like a pretty grown-up job.' Damn you, posh champagne.

'I'm thirty-three,' Cameron replies, nodding. 'But you're one to talk, you're getting *married*. That's a pretty grown-up move.' Yes, everyone seems to be making grown-up moves other than me. And I guess, Xavier. But that's setting a pretty low bar.

I gulp down more champagne as Cameron steers me out of the orangery – *great for canapes after the ceremony* – and on to the next room of our tour.

'It can get a little noisy in here,' Cameron says, turning to me with a grin as his hands stretch wide upon the next set of wooden doors. Please tell me we're not about to walk into the master bedroom. I'm not sure I can take it. Before my mind can drift into dreams of four-poster beds and rose petals and bubble baths, Cameron pushes against the door and the sounds of pots and pans and loud voices fill the stainless-steel covered room. This must be the hotel's kitchen. Looking across the open workspaces, I see no less than ten chefs, dressed to the nines with those floppy white hats, criss-cross one another as a thousand heavenly smells fill my nostrils. Two or three of them look up at us and I suddenly feel very aware of the half-empty champagne flute in my hand. I'm pretty sure I'm not meant to be in here. I'm not even sure if Anna is.

'Hey boss,' a male chef calls in our direction. So, Cameron really is the boss? I'm sure his success would make me feel inferior if I wasn't method-acting the role of Anna. 'Getting all the sweet things drunk, again?'

I should be offended on behalf of womankind about being called a sweet thing by a man I don't know. But three drinks in, it actually feels quite good. This whole damn day is shaping up to feel quite good. I know I still need my big break but somehow just *a break* – from real life, from myself – is managing to hit the spot. I look to Cameron who rolls his eyes, but I swear I see him blush. I was right, he does this fizz-and-flirt routine on the reg.

'This is my favourite part of the tour,' he says, leaning upon one of the counters. 'We can have as many chefs on hand as you need to make your culinary dreams come true.'

I raise my eyebrows at his clearly rehearsed lines, and he laughs. 'Okay, six. We can have six.'

'Well, that'll never do,' I say, my shock simmering with sarcasm.

Cameron's eyes widen in panic.

'Chill out dude, I was joking,' I say, instantly regretting calling him *dude*. This isn't Xavier I'm talking to – and I'm meant to be Anna.

'Unless you're going to have a Heston Blumenthal twelve-course taster menu,' Cameron says. 'I'm pretty sure six will cut it.'

'Lickable wallpaper is on the maybe list...'

'Then you're clearly not a germaphobe,' Cameron says, crossing his arms. It's the first time I notice that he's pushed his shirt sleeves up; is he relaxing into our tour? I didn't really expect this appointment to be so, well, *leisurely*. No wonder the waiting list is so long. For a moment, I think of Anna busy at work and feel bad for stealing a moment so clearly meant for her. But she did ask me to come. And I've had my fair share of crappy bridesmaid jobs thrown my way. I guess if acting has taught me anything it's that you've got to take the rough with the smooth. Maybe this is my smooth?

'So, what do you and your fiancé really have in mind, food-wise?' Cameron's voice draws my attention from his forearms.

'I'm not sure...' I say. At least that part is true.

'Is he?'

'I'm, erm... we're not very sure on the food part yet.'

'That's okay,' Cameron says, and his soothing voice

makes me feel like *everything* is okay. 'I've got an idea. Why don't we book you in for a food-tasting appointment next weekend and I can take you through some of our menu options here at Hotel Hyde?' Another well-rehearsed line, but this one sounds tasty. I risk a glance down at my phone to see whether Anna has been in touch. I'm not surprised to find she hasn't. For all she knows, I could be having a horrible time here. I'm not, but my best friend doesn't know that.

'Next weekend?' I ask, stalling for time. What will Anna and Jake be doing at the weekend? Probably working. If Anna goes, Cameron will know I'm not her. But maybe that won't matter if she doesn't choose this venue? I look around me, even the kitchen is beautiful. Of course, Anna is going to choose this venue. And she'll kill me if I pass up another opportunity for her to meet with him. I'll just swallow my pride whilst Anna – the *real* Anna – swallows five-star food. But today I get to pretend. 'Great, I'll let Anna know.'

'Huh?'

'I'll let Jake know.' I correct myself, laughing my error away. 'Sorry, long day.'

'That's okay,' Cameron says. 'We're almost at the end of our tour.' He smiles, and I can't help but feel a little sad; I don't want today to be over. 'One last stop.'

'Bye, sweet thing,' I hear the chef call as Cameron steers me back out of the kitchen.

'Ignore him,' Cameron says, shaking his head. I hate myself for not wanting to. For wanting to lap up every kind thing even strangers have to say about me. Such is the life of an unemployed millennial struggling to face up to reality. 'Anna...' Cameron says, and I'm reminded once again that today isn't for reality; it's for the dream hotel, the dream wedding venue, the dream man. 'Welcome to The Hyde Out.'

Cameron's outstretched arm beckons my eyes into another large room, dimly lit, with a colourful back bar illuminated against an exposed brick wall. An array of tables, all different shapes and sizes, are spread across the vintage-looking wooden floor while what feels like a hundred different mirrors are haphazardly hung against yet another sky-high wall. Everything is unique and yet nothing feels random, like each piece has a purpose.

'This is our hotel bar, which is also open to the public,' Cameron says, signalling to a barman who nods back at him before Cameron pulls out a chair for me at a table by the window. 'We can book it out for your guests in the evening and move the tables on this side of the room' – he points to the mirror-covered wall – 'so that the dancefloor goes there.' My jaw almost drops at the thought of how beautiful that would look, all the dancefloor lights bouncing off the mirrors and back into the bustling room.

'That would be...' I say, before the barman materialises by my side and puts yet another flute of champagne in front of me, placing a glass of something clear with a sprig of mint in it in front of Cameron. It's either vodka, a mojito or...

'Water.' Cameron looks wistfully towards my glass. 'I'm working until eleven. No rest for the wicked.' He shrugs even though from what I've seen, I would bet my bottom dollar that Cameron hasn't got a wicked bone in his body. And it would have to be my bottom dollar, given that I've spent all of my money on a wedding that isn't mine and hasn't even happened yet. I take a sip of my champagne to wash the thought away. Being Anna, even momentarily, tastes really good. 'What do you think about bands?'

'I like them,' I say as he laughs, almost spluttering his water across the table.

'I meant for your wedding.'

'Oh, yeah, I'm not really sure about that either,' I admit.

'At least you're sure about the guy.' Cameron smiles, and I offer him another non-committal *uh-huh*. He takes another sip of his water as I clock the time. Over three hours have passed and he's still spending time with me. Is this above and beyond the call of duty? Or just how successful women like Anna are made to feel every day? 'Well, we have some great live bands we could recommend to you here,' Cameron says, his grin growing wider still, the same way it did when he was talking about food.

Interests: food and music. Occupation: manager of a hella-fancy hotel. Appearance: Diaz-Timberlake love child. Is this guy for real?

'You hear this song in the background?' Cameron asks, his question reminding me that there is a whole room of people around us. I nod. 'This is Pete's band.' He points to the speakers as I hear an acoustic guitar playing over electro bass; it sounds pretty cool.

'Never heard of them.'

'No, sorry.' Cameron laughs again. 'Pete, over there behind the bar – it's his band.'

'Oh right,' I say, trying not to blush. 'And he keeps his own tunes on all day?'

'I keep his tunes on all day,' Cameron says. 'I always want to use this place for upcoming talent, whether that means blasting the staff's music from the speakers or letting writers camp out here all day or allowing actors to rehearse here...' It's only then that I realise that Cameron hasn't asked me what I do all afternoon. Not in a rude way, it just hasn't come up. And I'm glad. It's all very good defining yourself by what you do when what you're doing is going well, much harder when it's not going at all.

'That's so cool,' I say, taking another sip of champagne. So what if this drink isn't protocol? So what if I'm not Anna? Right now, no one seems to mind.

'I've had a really good time showing you around today,' Cameron says, leaning his exposed elbows onto the table, closing the gap between us just a little.

'Yeah, me too.' I smile back at him, resting my own arm upon the table.

'Hey Reese! Over here!' Suddenly Cameron is getting to his feet and waving across the room. I turn to see a beautiful, willowy figure striding towards us. In quick succession my eyes clock her tattooed olive skin, her sharp long bob, which fades from black to pastel pink, a set of strong, dark eyebrows and deep almond eyes fixed directly on Cameron. This might be the coolest woman I've ever seen. And she's about to ruin our date. 'Reese, meet Anna – she's getting married this summer.'

Oh, that's right, this is not a date. Because I'm getting married. Apparently.

'Congrats,' Reese says, revealing a perfect set of straight white teeth. She bends down to kiss Cameron on each cheek before she pulls up a chair at our two-person table. *Three's a crowd, Reese.* 'Getting suitably schmoozed?' she asks me, eyeing up my champagne flute whilst giving Cameron a jovial nudge to the ribs. I force a laugh.

'Something like that.' I smile.

'Reese is, among many things' – Cameron narrows his eyes at her playfully – 'a very talented writer.'

'You'll make me blush.' Reese laughs again but she seems

too confident and in control of herself to succumb to something as involuntary as a blush. 'What is it you do, Anna?'
There it is. The usual small-talk opener, the one that subtly
tries to work out whether your job positions you above or
below the person who has just asked the question. Well,
Anna is a hot-shot real estate agent to London's elite. But if I
say that I'll stand even less chance of answering any follow-
up questions than of the basic wedding plans I blustered my
way through with Cameron. Plus, it's never been my dream.
I've always wanted to be an actor. I still do. I just want to be
one who actually gets paid.

'I'm an actor,' I say, waiting for the inevitable follow-up
question. 'I'm in between work at the moment,' I add with a
smile that I hope is wide enough to cover the gaping holes in
my answer. Cameron smiles too, glancing in Reese's
direction.

'Well, I think I'd better get back to work.' He looks at me
kindly. 'But you guys stay here and have another drink – on
the house – unless you've got plans?'

My mind filters through all the other things I could be
doing right now: *Applying for an executive assistant role.
Waiting for Billie Forester to ring. Avoiding messages from
the Bride Tribe like the plague.* Or, I could prolong the best
day I've had in months with a super-cool talented writer.
Maybe some of her talent can rub off on me?

'I'm available.' I smile. *In every sense of the word.*

'Great.' Cameron flashes me another perfectly imperfect
smile. 'You guys have *a lot* in common.' I look at Reese's nose
ring, edgy and yet managing to be elegant. I have no idea
what me and a person like her could have in common but the
fact that Cameron thinks we do is the very reason I want my
day of being Anna to last forever.

CHAPTER FIVE

I turn to watch Cameron leave the bar and get back to work, forcing my eyes not to linger too long on his broad frame as I watch it walk away.

'He'll be back,' Reese says in a way that makes me feel sure I've been rumbled. The shock on my face must say it all as she adds: 'After he's wrapped up with work, I mean.' She smiles, and I catch another glimpse of her perfect teeth. 'He rarely leaves the hotel before swinging back to the Ho.'

'Pardon?' I croak. Am I meant to be the ho? I drain the last of my champagne.

'Sorry.' Reese shakes her razor-sharp bob. 'The Hyde Out.'

Oh, of course. I force my cheeks not to flush bright pink but after all this champagne, I can feel my control slipping away. 'Do you want another?' Reese nods in the direction of my empty flute. 'Champagne?'

For a moment, I stall. Didn't Cameron say this one's on the house? Even so, I feel like it's slightly taking the piss given that he's not here. *'Anna?'* Reese asks again and I realise that the 'taking the piss' train has already well and truly left the station.

'Sure,' I say, and before I know it Reese is up on her gazelle-like legs and floating over to Pete behind the bar and returning with not one glass, not two glasses, but a *bottle* of champagne. 'Don't worry, it's on the house,' Reese says, reading my worried expression.

'Will Cameron not mind?' I ask reluctantly as Reese pops the cork across the room.

'Of course not,' she beams before narrowing her cat-like eyes. 'Well, not if you choose Hotel Hyde for your wedding venue...' She laughs, tucking her pink-dipped hair behind her heavily pierced ears. A silence stretches between us.

Oh, she actually wants me to confirm my decision, *our* decision.

'Oh yeah... I love it. I'll just need to check with my fiancé,' I mutter into my glass; no further questions, Your Honour. *Please?*

'What does he do?' Reese asks; must she know every-body's job?

'He's an investment banker,' I say, and I see her eyes roll in their sockets. She must know the type. Maybe she even came across Jake and his work mates getting pissed here?

'I see,' she says, as her eyes drift to my empty fourth finger.

'Anyway, tell me about your writing. I want to hear all about it,' I say quickly, deflecting any attention away from my fiancé and lack thereof.

'I'm working on a new pilot for television.' Reese beams, pouring her own glass of champagne up to the rim; she may as well just neck it from the bottle. As she places it back down on the table between us, I clock the twisting letters tattooed along her olive-skinned arm: '*Dream as if you'll live forever...*' No freaking way. It's my favourite quote. I glance down at my phone background, thinking about showing her before I realise how tacky and temporary it feels in comparison to inking the sentiment into your skin. I smile weakly, taking another sip and encouraging her on.

'Thirty-minute sitcom with deep characters.' Reese speaks in ellipsis, the language of a woman who is clearly busy and booked. 'It's about two strangers in their late twenties who can't afford to get on the property ladder...'

Can't imagine what that's like, I almost say sarcastically, before I remember that I'm sat in a five-star hotel bar drinking champagne after looking around a wedding venue I've claimed I can afford.

'They meet at a bank having both had their mortgage applications rejected, one thing leads to another.' Reese's eyes light up with passion, the same passion I *used* to have for my work. 'And they decide to combine forces and incomes, buy a shit-hole and flip the place... proper *Grand Designs* meets *Selling Sunset*...'

You're thinking Anna Adams' real-life career. As if she wasn't successful enough, now even actors on television shows are pretending to be people like her. I note the irony.

'Their plan is always to sell the house,' Reese goes on, not a hint of insecurity in her voice. 'To enable them to climb the property ladder independently, but—'

'They fall in love?' I say, not meaning to cut her off, it's just – of course, the beautiful house-flippers flipping fall in love.

'Trust a soon-to-be newlywed to...' Reese begins, a stern tone in her voice. *Oh crap, maybe they don't? Clearly, I'm not edgy enough...* 'Of course, they flipping fall in love.' Her face breaks into a smile as she steals my line completely. 'Then you know, crisis, confusion, mishaps, the usual...' Reese goes on, like her idea isn't genius. Cameron was right. Reese is really talented. I would love to play that part. 'How about you, Anna?' Reese asks, reminding me once again of the current role I've taken on. Oh *crap.*

'I'm in between jobs at the moment,' I repeat, with as much confidence as I can muster.

'Sweet, what are they?'

What are they? It's a good question. I just wish I had a good answer. The truth is, my last big role was a single line on a daytime soap. And the only thing I have lined up? Well, I got rejected from that yesterday. I could just tell her the truth. It's not like I can keep this charade up forever, especially once the real Anna falls for this place. But just for today, just for tonight, it would be nice for Reese – and Cameron – to still buy the act.

My phone buzzes to life on top of the table and I pray for the caller to be anyone but Anna. It's Mum. No doubt ringing to see whether I've sent off an application to an *actual* office and not just the TV show *The Office.* And who can blame her, seeing as I've sent no less than five speculative showreels to NBC? I reject my mum's call, my mind still caught on the thought. I don't even want to move that far away, but I would, for a job...

'Do you do much work in America?' I ask, tentatively.

'Not really,' Reese says with a little shrug and I think I catch a glimpse of insecurity.

'Oh.' I smile, shamefully feeling on safer ground. 'That's where my last job was and now, well, my agent is just putting feelers out for something we're both excited about.'

Something, *anything.*

'You have an agent?' Reese asks. She sounds a little impressed, but why would she be? It's pretty standard inside our industry, one that she is excelling in. I nod and then I see Reese's slender shoulders fall, the same way mine do every time I feel inferior. *But what has she got to feel inferior about?* I think, looking around the decadent bar she clearly hangs around in. Pretending to be a part of this world, *her world*, is the most fun I've had in ages.

'I've been trying to get an agent for years.' Reese fixes her almond eyes on mine. 'I thought I'd be okay without one but it's hard having to work out everything yourself, feeling stuck in your own story without anyone to thrash it out with.'

I watch Reese drain the last sip of her champagne and begin to pour another and for a moment, I hate myself for acting up to her. I thought she had it all together, but the woman sat in front of me is turning from feisty to fragile right in front of my eyes and all I want to scream now is *me too, me too, me too*.

'Sorry, I shouldn't be moaning to you like this.' Reese sighs, shaking her head. 'Not when you've just spent the afternoon dreaming about your wedding day.'

I swallow the last of my own drink as my stomach sinks. I'm such a bitch.

'Another?' Reese asks before her beautiful features fall again. 'Or do you need to get back to your fiancé? I bet he's really missing you.' Well, *I bet* he's not real at all.

'No, no,' I say, feeling too bad to leave right now. 'I can stay for one more.'

'Anna?' Reese asks as I gaze around the bar, increasingly busy (and blurry) and not a Cameron in sight. 'One more?'

Oh right, she's talking to me. It's getting both easier and harder to be Anna the more I drink. Harder, because with every sip my pretence slips. Easier, because there is now much more of Marley added into the mix. My 'last one' should have been my last one. But somehow after Reese's hint of vulnerability and sharing *some* of my own (I owned up that I don't actually have another job lined up and I did just get rejected from one) our drinks, like the conversation, are flowing.

'It's my round,' I say, wishing I'd come clean about the fact that I'm not actually getting married to a minted investment banker before we started paying for our own drinks. Turns out it's not so easy to tell the coolest person you've ever met that you're a grown-ass woman who's been pretending to be her best friend all day.

'Thanks babe,' Reese says, and I feel a rush of warmth run through my alcohol-filled veins. *Babe. Sweet thing.* It's a lot better than being called *Mary*. 'Do you want to give me your card and I can just set up a tab for you at the bar?'

Setting up a tab at the bar sounds like the single most dangerous thing someone struggling to afford their rent can do. But still, it does sound like something *Anna* would do.

'Sure, I...' I begin, reaching for my debit card before realising it has my name – my real name – scrawled across it. 'Actually, I think I'd rather just pay as we go...' Great, now I sound like I'm buying a sim card. 'Plus, the bartender's pretty cute.'

'Need I remind you that you're getting married?' Reese winks. *Yes, yes you do*, I think as I make my way to the bar, returning with our drinks soon after.

'I shouldn't be having this, Anna,' Reese says, whilst inhaling her wine. She looks a little more human with every scrap of truth she throws my way. I wish I could give her more of mine. 'I need to finish this script. The deadline's tomorrow.'

'Can't you just ask the producer for an extension?'

'Well, that's the thing...' Reese begins slowly, repositioning an earring as she does. I catch another glimpse of her James Dean tattoo and wonder whether Cameron is right; maybe we do have a lot in common? 'I don't actually have a producer yet.'

'Then who's the deadline for?'

'Now, you probably think this is silly,' she begins, and I feel another wave of guilt wash over me. *Sillier than pretending to be your best mate?* 'But the script is for a competition that is looking for new TV talent.'

'Like *X Factor* for screenwriters?'

'Yeah, but not televised.' Reese turns up her pierced nose at the thought.

'The irony,' I say, and Reese laughs loudly, the way she has all night, the way Cameron did all day. *Maybe, I'm actually funny?* I wonder for a moment whether I'd be able to make it in comedy. But no, they think *Anna* is funny. And successful. And together.

'And it's not just for screenwriters, it's for actors too.'

Just another opportunity Billie Forester has failed to find for me.

'But it doesn't matter now anyway.' Reese sighs dramatically and I start to think maybe we are cut from the same cloth and she just got the edgy side. 'The deadline is tomorrow, and I still can't work my story out.'

'What are you talking about? Your story is *banging.*' Instant regrets about saying banging. Keep it together Marley, *Anna,* whoever you are.

'Yeah, the set-up, maybe,' Reese says. 'But I need to write a full synopsis and I'm struggling with the twist.' She takes a sip of her wine, which lingers on her stained lips. 'I've got one actor working with me, but we have quite different views editorially, hey...' Reese fixes her wide eyes on me and it's like she's seeing me for the first time. 'You don't think you could help me with it, do you?'

I don't know how much help I'll be given that I struggle to fill out the simplest of applications for the most standard jobs. But something about the way Reese is looking at me makes me feel like I might actually be of use. Or maybe it's the wine.

'Sure,' I say, feeling like I've finally passed some kind of audition.

'Oh crap, it's gone ten though,' Reese says, looking to a big clock on the wall behind me. For a moment I think she's seen Cameron walking in and my heart leaps. Then I realise how crazy it is that I'm excited by the thought of that, given that I already *have a fiancé*. 'Are you sure your fiancé won't be missing you by now?' Reese asks, perfectly on cue.

'Yeah,' I say, trying my best to hold my grin. 'I'm pretty sure about that.'

'I thought we both wanted to flip this house and be done with it,' I read from Reese's script, my eyesight dwindling with the drink but my mind now fully alive. This material is great. 'Now I'm not sure *what* you want,' I say, letting emotion course through my body, real tears gathering in my eyes.

'I want you Ella, I want you,' reads Reese; she sounds choked up and sure enough I look up to see tears threatening to pour from her own heavily lined eyes too. 'Man, you're a good actor, Anna,' Reese says breathlessly.

'And *you're* a good writer,' I assure her, drinking the niggle in my stomach away, the one that's reminding me that I should have drawn a line under this day hours ago.

'But it stops there,' Reese slurs. 'I know everything needs to fall apart, but how?'

How am I supposed to know? I see the desperation in her eyes. It's a desperation I know all too well. Okay Marley, you can do this. I look down at the script again and then at Reese's notebook, open on her scribbles. It's like reading her diary. And she doesn't even know my real name. But if this is the last time we're ever going to see each other – which let's face it, it kind of has to be – the least I can do is try to leave her better than how I found her.

'So, Ella wants to flip and sell?' I go over the basics, stalling for time. 'And Jack has fallen for Ella and knows the second they do that she's going to walk out of his life for good?'

Reese nods.

'Then he needs to stop her,' I muse, and Reese gives me a look that seems to say: *no shit, Sherlock, but how?* 'He needs to lie,' I say, ignoring that damn niggle in my stomach once again. I was just helping Anna. And now I'm about to help Reese. 'Maybe Ella has been sharing the house flip on her social media and she's started to get a following? Like all of a sudden, she's got this whole luxurious lifestyle that people want to get a piece of...' I think out loud, cursing myself for drawing from Anna's life once again. 'And she's getting loads of interview requests, getting busier and busier, so Jack offers to deal with all the potential buyers so that Ella can concentrate on her new opportunities...'

'Yes...' Reese joins in slowly. 'And so Jack deals with the buyers...'

'...of which there are plenty.'

'But he finds something wrong with all of them...' Reese says, her smile growing. '...because there's only one person he wants to make memories with there.'

'Yes!' I say, feeling creativity spark through my veins. 'Her and...'

'Cameron!' Reese shouts.

'Huh?' I say, sure I'm missing something. 'I was going to say *Jack*.'

'No, Cameron,' Reese says, pushing her short hair behind her ears. 'Over there.'

I turn around to see Cameron walking into the Hyde Out and across the room towards the bar. He chats and jokes with the barman as he reaches across the counter to pull himself a pint. There's something sexy about it. Maybe the way he owns the room? Then he turns to smile at me, and I remember that there's a thousand things sexy about him.

'Cam-err-on,' Reese says, throwing her arms wide and accentuating every syllable.

'Woah,' Cameron says, putting his hands up in defence. 'How much have you had?'

'Hey,' I say sheepishly and the fact that even this takes a bit of effort tells me the answer to his question is: too much, far too much.

'Just enough to get the creative juices a-flowing,' Reese sings again, slinging an arm around Cameron, who obediently takes a seat. It's not as if the poor guy has a choice.

'And the rest,' Cameron says with a laugh, fixing his eyes on me. 'Having fun, Anna?'

'Lots,' I say, as my stomach flips.

'I thought you were meant to be working on something.' Cameron turns back to Reese, widening his eyes, presumably to indicate the competition.

'I was,' Reese slurs, sloshing her drink onto her open shirt in the process. Why does it take speaking to a sober person to highlight just how *not* sober you've become? 'We are. Ella's been helping me with my script.'

'Ella?' Cameron asks, raising an eyebrow at the extent of Reese's drunkenness.

'Marley,' I correct, before two sets of narrowed eyes shoot to me. 'Anna,' I mutter quickly. 'Getting confused with all the characters,' I shrug. Technically not a lie.

'Anna's been helping me work out the rest of my story-line before I send it off,' Reese says, tripping up on her words. I'm reluctant to say much more for fear of doing the same.

'I figured you were a leading lady the moment I saw you giving our receptionist what-for in the lobby.' Cameron turns to me, and in the dim light his smile still sparkles.

'Why didn't I think of that?' Reese practically squeals as she throws her arm around Cameron again, sending him jumping out of his skin. 'I was going to act alongside Will myself, but this is *so* much better...'

'Who's Will?' I ask, unable to keep up with where she's going with this.

'My mate, Will,' Reese says with a coy smile as if I should know. 'The lead actor attached to the project. You'll love working with him...'

'I will?' I say, as both she and Cameron beam back at me.

'Why not?' Reese says again; she's practically buzzing with alcohol and adrenalin and I can't help but feel the same way. 'You're an actor between jobs and you've already said you love the script...' I *do* love the script. 'And anyway, it'll just be a case of throwing our hat into the ring for now. If you get any jobs in the meantime...'

That feels like a big *if* right now.

'And *if* we get through...'

Another big if.

'Then you can just let me know and I'll find a replacement.'

'Shouldn't be hard given the £100 prize money,' Cameron chips in as if this is inconsequential. But money like that could change everything. At least it could for a person like me. And then there is the script, the best thing, the best role, I've read in years.

'Give me one good reason why we shouldn't throw our hat into the ring?' Reese says, looking from me to Cameron with her winning smile. I could still really do with that win.

'I erm...' I say, my mind a blur of bubbles and booze. 'I can't think of one.'

I look at Cameron's eyes searching mine and I can't even think straight.

'Amazing,' Reese squeals again, standing up and tottering like Bambi on ice over to my side of the table to throw her arms around me. 'You won't regret this, Anna.'

No, but I have a horrible feeling *Marley* might.

CHAPTER SIX

I wake up in a cold sweat, but I'm still boiling hot. Kicking off the covers, I am surprised to find I'm completely starkers. It takes a millisecond to cover myself up again. I look around the unfamiliar room. No, no, no. Where the hell am I?

My heart starts to pound in my naked chest, my mind scrambling to find some semblance of the night before. Who was I with? Then, I remember Reese from the bar. She was beautiful, sure. But somewhere in the corner of my already banging head, I think I remember her leaving to go and meet someone in the early hours of the morning. I turn over onto my side and instantly, the room around me starts to spin. I was left there with *Cameron*.

I gaze upon the empty side of the messy-looking bed. There's no way, but just maybe we came home together. For a moment, I'm not sure how I feel about that. On the one hand, he's a gorgeous, successful hotel manager. On the other hand, I can't remember being with him here at all. I'm *mortified*. And then, my weary eyes come in to focus on the Spiderman bed sheets, before clocking the life-size cardboard cut-out of Rowan Atkinson staring back at me. It's terrifying. But not as terrifying as my next realisation: I'm in *Xavier's* room.

'No, no, no,' I mutter into the empty room. Forcing myself to stand, I try to navigate the spinning walls all the way to the door and peer into the corridor to check the coast is clear. With just a single pillow covering my nakedness, I creep like the world's worst mime artist into my room. Man, I hope the modesty is still necessary, that Xavier and I haven't got far too close already. Crap, crap, *crap*. Back in the safety of my room, I throw on the same T-shirt and joggers that I started my yesterday in. Before I went to that appointment, before I drank my day into my night and back into my morning again.

My phone buzzes on my bedside table. Okay, so my phone made it back into my bedroom. That's a positive sign, right? Then, I see who is calling, it's my dad.

'Dad.' I choke my first words of the day, trying not to vomit along with them.

'Marley!' he says in a sing-song voice that instantly makes me feel worse, even though I didn't think that was possible right now. 'How are you?'

'Erm... now's not actually a good time, Dad.' I try to sound more okay than I feel.

'What could be more important than speaking to your old man?'

Oh, I don't know, Father... finding out whether I have had sex and/or given a striptease to my Plaster of Paris bowl-making flatmate?

'Getting a job?' I lie, and it pulls back the memory of all the lies I told yesterday.

'That's my girl,' he says, and he sounds so happy that it

makes me want to cry. 'I've just sent over another of those recruitment site things your mum is always going on about nowadays.' He stalls for a second, and I hear him breathing on the end of the line. 'I know your mother may be a bit pushy with these things, Marl, but she's just worried about you.'

'Well, tell her she doesn't need to be,' I say, as a wave of sickness washes over me. I'm stood here in a T-shirt after a day of pretending to be my bestie, still unemployed, still wondering if I've just shagged my roommate, but yeah, tell her I have everything in hand.

'Right-o, Bright-o,' my dad says; it's something he used to call my sister and me – the Bright Sisters. Except only one of us has managed to sail into her bright future, my sister working as an actual real-life doctor, whilst I'm still doing dumb things. *Dumb things like Xavier?* Cue another wave of sickness. 'We love you.'

'We love you too,' I whisper down the phone. It used to be a joke of ours, using the royal 'we'. But something about my parents teaming up together to try to find me a sensible job makes me wish I was one part of a 'we' too. I guess I used to have that with Anna. Before Jake came into our lives and fell in love with her and threw our balance off completely. Love always manages to shake everything up, even when it's not you that's in it.

I know Dad's right, it's time to get a job. Yesterday was fun, really fun. But it's not like that competition is going to lead anywhere. Given how drunk Reese was when she wandered off to meet whoever she was meeting, I wouldn't be surprised if she sleeps right through the deadline. I'm not even sure we swapped numbers. I look down at my phone and type in her name, then

Cameron's, then a few rogue pseudonyms my drunken self may have stored them under: *edgy girl, manger man, man of my dreams, Cam Timberlake-Diaz*. Nothing. Probably for the best. At least now I can draw a line under yesterday. Well, almost.

Hugging the walls of our corridor, I make my way uneasily towards the living room. There, I find Xavier grooming a bonsai tree that I didn't know he had. I instantly remember I need a bikini wax. *Damn it, Marley. You didn't sleep with Xavier.* But there's only one way to know for sure. I risk a cough into the room. Xavier doesn't even look up. If he did see me naked last night, it clearly didn't have much of an impact on him.

'Xavier,' I say slowly, allowing my legs to collapse into one of the misshapen armchairs beside him. 'I've got a few questions...'

'It's a bonsai tree.' He finally looks at me with his trademark spaced-out smile.

'Yeah, I... it wasn't about that, actually,' I say, and he looks surprised that anything could be more important, the same way he had with his paper bowl and the juggling before that. 'What the hell happened last night?' I blurt, fearful of his reply.

'Oh, last night?' Xavier shrugs, a little smile threatening to turn up the corners of his mouth. He snips another branch off his bonsai. 'You came home smashed and asked me, and I just thought... well, why the hell not?'

Why the hell not? The room spins again, and my palms begin to get clammy. This can't be happening. This categorically *can't* be happening.

'Did you not think I was a bit too *drunk* for that?' I say, a sharp edge to my voice.

'I really didn't mind.' He smiles again, taking another snip.

'You really didn't *mind?*' I say, hanging my head in my hands.

'Yeah, your bed is proper comfy.'

I'm just about to hit the wall and perhaps even call the police when his words sink in. *My bed?*

'Marley, are you okay?' Xavier looks up at me now, and despite his latest spliff, he seems to clock that I'm not.

'Xavier, what *exactly* happened last night?'

'You came in smashed and I tried to steer you into your bedroom, but you just kept refusing, saying something about not wanting to be Marley anymore. I was getting tired but knew you'd feel even worse today if you woke up on the sofa, those blinds are crap.' Xavier shrugs in the direction of our grimy window as my heartbeat begins to regulate. 'So, I asked you how you'd feel being Xavier for the night instead, and well... you finally went to bed, *my* bed. You slept in my room, I slept in yours. Don't worry, I've already changed the sheets,' he says, hands in the air in surrender. That's not what I was worried about. It may be the hangover talking but right now I actually want to give him a hug.

'Thanks Xavier.' I smile, feeling embarrassed but not nearly as much as I would have been had the alternative happened.

'You're welcome,' he says, pruning another branch of his tree. 'I hope you want to be Marley again today?' He doesn't look up, but I think it may be the cutest thing he's ever said.

'Maybe once I've had some toast.'

. . .

Moving across to our little kitchenette in the corner of the room, I go in search of carbs. I need a job, a hug, a flipping gallon of water, but right now carbs top the list. With shaking hands, I grab a piece of bread and prune off tinges of mould like Xavier grooming his tree. I spread butter on it until the ratio of butter to bread is fifty-fifty and one hundred per cent shameful and plonk myself down gracelessly at the kitchen table. I don't deserve grace today.

Looking down at my mobile phone, I silence the Bride Tribe and search for messages from Anna but there's nothing. How could I spend all day pretending to be her and she's not thought about me once? In the silence, I can't help my heavy mind from drifting back to a time where we used to start our mornings together.

It would be the morning after the night before, spent at whatever club we thought was cool in the early 2010s. We'd both wake up in one of our beds and half-watch *Gossip Girl* whilst running through our own mishaps scene by scene. Those mornings would be better than the night itself; now our mornings couldn't look more different from one another.

My eyes drift from my cheap toast over to Xavier as my mind wanders to how Anna is spending her morning right now. Waking up in her four-poster bed (overkill for a London flat if you ask me, but that's Anna for you), she turns over to find her fiancé Jake already watching her sleep. 'Morning, gorgeous.' He kisses her hello, somehow managing to have perfect minty morning breath. I exhale deeply and last night's wine lingers on my tongue.

Next, Jake offers Anna breakfast, I think whilst taking another bite of my tasteless toast. I know I'm torturing myself, but I can imagine it so clearly. He jumps out of bed and begins to knock together her French toast (miraculously calorie-free) whilst Anna gets ready in the reflection of her huge diamond engagement ring, which wouldn't look out of place mounted on the Hyde Out's mirror wall. Man, it felt good to fit in there.

Are you in? Anna's message lights up my phone, and it's like I've conjured her into the room. I take another bite of my toast as my stomach churns. I can't go to another wedding appointment for her today. Yesterday was fun but it wasn't real life, and I just can't stomach perfect places and perfect people. I turn over my phone so that it faces down on the table. Today is for hiding out.

Three knocks bang at the door. I think of asking Xavier to abandon his bonsai to open it but given that the man had to deal with my tantrums and sacrifice his own bloody bed, I feel like he's already taken one for the team. It takes all my strength to drag my broken body to our front door and with my hand on the door handle, I stall. I've not ordered anything. My parents are miles away. So who could it be? For a moment, I wonder whether it could be Cameron? Or Reese from the bar? But why would either show up here? I didn't even take their numbers. Something tells me I didn't leave them with my address.

'Marley, I can see you through the glass. Open the door. Please...'

'Anna?' I say, jaw dropping as I swing the door open to find her standing there. But she doesn't look like Anna, made-up and dressed-up and ready to take on the world. No, she looks awful. And that's coming from someone who just dragged herself across the room like a zombie. My eyes search her pale cheeks, her usual contouring smudged across her face, black mascara marks making their way to her chin. Then her face crumples and she starts to cry. 'Oh, Anna,' I say, throwing my arms around her and engulfing her into me. 'What's wrong?' It's only as I ask the question that I wonder whether I might be the answer. Has she found out about yesterday? That I stole her name and flaunted it across every room of the Hotel Hyde?

'It's Jake,' Anna whispers, sobbing into my shoulder, her own shoulders heaving with the weight of the words, and I hate myself for feeling a tiny rush of relief. I like Jake, I really do. I just can't deal with my best friend being mad at me today.

'What about him?' I pull away to look at her but keep my hands on her arms, scared that if I let go her knees may buckle completely. What the hell has happened?

'I think he's cheating on me,' Anna cries even harder, putting her hands up to cover her face. You can strike the 'I like Jake' comment if this turns out to be true. *What? No? This can't be happening.* A thousand thoughts rush through my mind but only one comes out of my mouth: 'Oh shit,' I whisper under my breath. 'Come in...'

'Is your housemate in?' Anna asks, tears trickling down her face. 'I don't want anyone to see me like this.'

'Babe, he's playing with his bush,' I say softly, and Anna can't help but crack a tired and helpless smile. 'I'm sure he won't even look up.'

I pass Anna a plate of buttery toast, as she sits hugging one of my pillows to her stomach. I really hope Xavier did change the sheets. She looks down at the toast and begins to cry again. I chomp down on my second piece, trying desperately to hide my hangover before placing both plates on my bedside table. As far as Anna knows I went to the venue appointment and left as soon as the tour was done. I know I should tell her the truth about it but, clearly, she doesn't want to talk about venues right now. One look at her battle-bruised expression makes me think she may never want to again.

'Are you sure?' I ask, wrapping an arm around her and resting my head on her shoulder, trying to provide some kind of structure for her limp body and her broken heart.

'Pretty sure,' Anna says, barely audible between her cries. I watch as she pushes her ring around her fourth finger and a lump catches in my throat. Jake wouldn't do this, would he? He couldn't. They were in love. No, they *are* in love.

'How come?' I ask quietly, refusing to let my tears escape; this is Anna's moment – the one she never wanted, the one neither of us saw coming. And yet, seeing her like this seems impossible, like the shiniest person I know has just had their lights snuffed out.

'We were in bed last night,' Anna starts between sobs, and I hold my breath. 'When Jake's phone started to ring. I didn't see who called but when I asked him who it was, he just said it was no one. Why would someone call at that time? Why wouldn't he say who it was?'

'It could have been a cold call,' I say, desperately trying to look on the bright side. Something that used to come naturally to me before this season of rejection set in. But I never dreamed that *Anna* would have to experience a rejection – a betrayal – like this.

'Marley, you should have seen his face.' Anna shakes her head, fixing her tear-stained eyes on me. 'I might as well have caught him with his pants down.'

'But you didn't.'

'Not yet,' Anna says, and I feel the frost in her voice and

the hurt in her heart. 'He's been acting off for weeks. I thought it was just the stress of work and wedding planning and everything...' She stalls and I for a moment I feel horrendous for ever begrudging my bridesmaid responsibilities. 'But now I think it's more.'

'It's not. It can't be,' I say and I'm not sure which one of us I'm trying to convince. Surely, this must be some sort of mistake. Jake and Anna are perfect together, almost sickeningly so. There must be some kind of explanation for that call.

'Maybe I should have seen it earlier,' Anna goes on, her slender body shaking like a leaf. 'But I've just been so busy with work and everything.'

She collapses on my shoulder once more, looking up at me with fresh tears in her eyes just willing me to make everything okay, silently asking me the questions she is struggling to contemplate: *How could this happen to me? How do I make it stop?*

'It's okay,' I whisper, running my fingers over her hair. Now doesn't feel like the time to tell her I feel like she's been too busy for me too lately. That I've been holding my tears back from her as well. I guess in wanting a job so badly I may have forgotten that having a thriving one is pretty full-on too. And planning a wedding.

'What are you going to do about the wedding?' I vocalise the thought as soon as it pops into my mind, almost involuntarily. Anna's body stiffens at the word.

'I'm not sure.' Her tear-blotched face drains of colour.

'That's okay,' I whisper, holding her closer still, instantly wishing I hadn't mentioned it. 'You don't have to think about the wedding right now. One thing at a time.'

I reach for the plate of toast again, hoping that butter can cure her heartbreak. *Crap.* I agreed that Anna and Jake would go menu-tasting at the weekend.

'Anna, I...' I begin, and her sorry eyes look back at me pleadingly. 'I signed you up for this menu-tasting thing at the Hotel Hyde next Saturday, but I'll cancel or postpone it...' The thought makes my tummy turn over. As does imagining Cameron's face when he finds out that I'm not the real Anna.

'You don't postpone the Hotel Hyde.' She shakes her head sadly. That makes sense, I guess; it's the reason I found myself there in the first place.

'So, you want to go?' I ask, knowing I'll have to tell her all about my mistaken identity before then so that she's not blindsided completely.

'I can't,' she whispers, before more tears start to fall. I'm surprised they haven't run dry completely. 'Marley, you don't think you could...' The end of Anna's sentence is silenced by her sobs but her question rings loud and clear. I can't go back to the Hotel Hyde.

'I don't think that's...' I begin to object, her face falling further.

'I just need more time to work everything out,' Anna says, her bottom lip trembling like the rest of her. 'I mean, maybe everything will be sorted by next weekend but... Marley, are you sure you can't...' Her sentence drifts into sobs again but her question is loud and clear. I can't go back to the hotel, can I? Not as Anna. But just looking at my best friend's brokenness, I barely have the strength to say no. And maybe this will give me a chance to come clean to Cameron before he meets the real Anna.

'Do you want me to go along again and just gather all the information?'

'We won't get the information I need there.' Anna sits up

to look at me again. 'Marley, you need to help me find out the truth about Jake.'

I nod, squeezing her hand in mine as her fingers grip onto mine for strength. 'We will,' I whisper. 'There will be some sort of explanation. I'm sure of it.'

'And if you *really* don't mind going to the food thing at the weekend then that would be great, just until I work out what to do next.'

'I really don't mind,' I reply; just until I work out what to do next, too.

'Thanks, Marley.' Anna rests her head on my shoulder again. 'I don't know what I'd do without you,' she whispers, and for the first time in a long time, I actually believe her.

CHAPTER SEVEN

It's the weekend and I'm up and out before 10 a.m. Given this past week, it feels like an accomplishment. Looking out of the bus window, I watch the streets of central London begin to wake up; several joggers run along the Thames whilst huddles of tourists begin to gather in their groups. As I see two friends pose for a photo, the London Eye visible in the distance, I think of Anna. But to be fair, she's not been far from my mind all week. Ever since she turned up at my house with her broken heart.

Reaching for my phone, I pull open our messages and type: *Are you sure you don't want to come today?* I've still not told her about last weekend and as much as I wish that what happened at the Hyde stayed at the Hyde, I know my being embarrassed in front of Cameron shouldn't stand in the way of me being a good friend. *I'm sure, I'm not really in the head space for it* I read Anna's reply before proceeding to send her a thousand heart emojis. It's not enough but right now nothing is going to be, other than discovering whether Jake is cheating on her or not once and for all. Turns out it's pretty hard to look for evidence when he's always in their flat nowadays, which I would say is a *good* sign. Anna thinks he's still acting weird though they've not talked about her suspicions.

Arriving at the Hyde, my eyes delight in the entrance's décor once again. I breathe in the scent of the flowers as I pass them on the gateway. I exhale deeply. I'm going to tell Cameron the truth today. It's the last chance I'll have to do it myself before the wedding anyway. That's if the wedding happens. The thought makes my heart stop. As much as I've moaned about Jake throwing me and Anna off balance, the thought of him not being around is now the most unsettling thought of all.

I walk into the grand reception space and perch on the end of a velour, post-modern style sofa, exactly where Cameron told me to wait. It's not as comfy as it looks but something about its decadence and the twinkly music playing in the background is enough to make me relax. I allow my heavy eyes to close, remembering again how much fun it was to be Anna here. But all good things must come to an end sometime.

'Anna. *Anna?*'

I open my eyes to see Cameron has materialised in front of me. Like last time, he looks like a dream, though this time he's dressed down, his shirt replaced with a fisherman knit sweater, his hair a little less styled – he looks gorgeous.

'Yes,' I say, before I can stop myself. Damn it, Marley you have to tell him.

'Recovered from drinking with Reese?' He cocks an eyebrow, as my cheeks flush red.

'Just about,' I say, my mind running a mile a minute: I've not thought about Reese all week, not since Anna showed up at my house to interrupt the world's worst hangover. If I tell

Cameron about pretending to be Anna, then that means I have to come clean to Reese too.

'I think she's meant to hear back from that competition soon.' Cameron smiles. 'Got everything crossed for you both.' Crap. The competition. So, she actually sent the thing off?

'I'm sure £100k wouldn't go amiss, especially now,' he says. I stare back at him. He either knows I'm broke or he's heard how much I spent in the bar. '...paying for a wedding and all.'

Oh crap, that's right. Definitely time to come clean. But then, Reese should hear back from the competition soon and then we can go our separate ways without her ever needing to know that I was anyone other than who I said I was.

'Follow me,' Cameron says with his lovely jaunty smile, before walking away from the lounge area and in the direction of the exit. Huh? Where are we going?

Walking out into the early spring-time sunlight, Cameron looks down the road and then to his phone. I take the opportunity to do the same and see another message from Anna: *Please don't mention anything about me and Jake. If they doubt we're getting married, we can kiss goodbye to any more appointments.* As soon as I've read it, I look up to see Cameron staring down at me. Oh crap, did he see? His eyes fix on mine and for a moment I feel like we're the only two people in the world. Damn you, brown eyes.

'Ready to go on the tastiest adventure of your life?' He grins and my stomach leaps. I watch as a car pulls up in front of the hotel and he opens a door. I hesitate. I need to tell him the truth. I can't be Anna forever. But, on the other hand, if I am Anna for one more week then our application to that competition will be rejected and we'll have time to get to the bottom of whatever Jake is up to... 'Anna?' Cameron grins again.

'Yes,' I say. Cameron's crooked smile proves the final push. 'Yes, I'm ready.'

I watch as the streets of the city speed past, the same ones I studied just an hour ago from the bus window. Now, sitting here with Cameron in the back of a chauffeur-driven car, everything looks a little different. I feel different, confident. I feel like Anna again.

'Am I allowed to ask where you're taking me?' I turn to Cameron with a smile.

'I don't want to spoil the surprise.' I watch his eyes twinkle.

'I hate surprises,' I mutter under my breath, but loud enough for him to hear.

'Your other half must,' Cameron says.

'I don't have another half,' I say and Cameron's expression twists in confusion. Oh crap, I am meant to have a flipping *fiancé*.

'Well then, Anna,' he begins, his crinkled forehead visible below his floppy hair. 'What may I ask are we doing here?' *Well, it's a good question Cameron. One I have an incredibly simple yet really, really complicated answer for.*

'I *mean*,' I begin, thinking on my feet, 'I don't like that phrase, other half, as if we're not two wholes coming together...'

'Oh, I see,' Cameron says, a smile stretching across his face. Phew. 'Two wholes coming together. I like that. Maybe you should go into the wedding industry if acting doesn't work out.'

I burst out laughing. *If* acting doesn't work out. Good one, Cameron. I stop laughing and his expression tells me he has no idea why. But of course, he doesn't even know I'm struggling for work. He probably thinks I'm doing Reese a favour by saying I'll act in her pilot. In a wave of panic, I grab my phone and look down at the screen.

'Sorry, just saw something funny on my phone.' I explain my sudden outburst away. Cameron doesn't look convinced.

'Sure,' he says, clearly amused by the crazy woman he's about to spend his morning with. 'We're here.' Disappearing from the stationary vehicle as soon as he's said the words, Cameron reappears by my side, opening my door and offering me a hand to help me out of the car. I take his hand and look up at the big graffiti wall welcoming me to Borough Market.

'This is where we're doing our tasting?'

'It's where we get all our fresh produce,' Cameron says. 'Everyone thinks it's just for tourists but it's famous for a reason, and you're about to find out why.' And with that, he walks down a set of stone steps leading to a row of outdoor vendors. My senses are awoken immediately, by the amalgamation of scents floating through the air and the chatter of different languages slotting together like the harmonies of a score.

'I've been to Borough Market before,' I can't help but call behind him, following his broad figure as it weaves into the crowd.

'Yes, but you've never been to Borough Market with *me*.' He turns to grin at me.

'Woah,' I say, throwing my hands into the air in surrender. 'Way to back yourself.'

'Just you wait,' he whispers down at me, stopping. Confident Cameron. I like it. 'Timon!' He shouts towards one of the stalls where a short Italian-looking man soon waves him over. 'Anna' – Cameron turns back to me – 'Allow me to introduce you to my friend Timon. Timon has had a stall here for fifty years, selling the best oils and vinegars in town.'

'Try,' Timon says, forcing a cocktail stick with a generous chunk of bread pierced on the end into my hand. Behind him is an array of oil samples in every shade of a fire.

'Gladly,' I say, taking the bread and dipping it into a chilli oil greedily.

'Careful with that one,' Cameron cautions, but it's already too late.

'Wow, that's hot,' I say, breathing flames before turning to Timon. 'But great.'

He nods before disappearing to greet another customer.

'So, tell me about your fiancé, Jake, is it?' Cameron says, piercing another piece of bread and dipping it into a slightly green-looking oil. I choke on another chunk of bread.

'That's right,' I say, knowing the less I say about him the better. 'He's great.'

'But not a foodie?' Cameron asks, before adding. 'He didn't fancy this?' His forehead crinkles again and it takes all my strength not to shout *I fancy you* for all the market to hear.

'No, it's not that,' I say, thinking about what exactly *it* is. 'He's just a *workie*, too.' At least, Jake used to be. He's not been working as hard of late, which is weird given that Anna is planning a wedding to rival a Kardashian.

'Fair enough,' Cameron says, and he doesn't exactly look disappointed. 'So, what kind of food is he into?'

'All food,' I reply too quickly, too vaguely.

'That doesn't really narrow it down,' Cameron says, eyes

scanning the market as I do the same, marvelling at the hustle and bustle, the scenes and the scents.

'If it means we get to taste a bit of everything,' I say, grinning, 'I'll make my peace with that.'

I follow Cameron further into Borough's belly, trains of tourists weaving their way through the various stalls. I have to remind myself that this is not a date.

'Cheese?' Cameron slows at a counter laden with cheese and chutneys. If this *was* a date, it would be the best date ever. 'Lots of our clients like to lay out cheese and crackers for their guests in the evening,' he explains, passing me a fork with a chunk of Stilton on the end.

'Doesn't that give you bad dreams?' I ask, wrinkling my nose at the strong smell.

'Not when it tastes like this,' Cameron says, signalling for me to eat up. 'The Stilton is infused with champagne.'

I take a bite and although I thought last weekend's hangover was enough to put me off champagne for life, the cheese melts on my tongue like magic. Next, he passes me a chutney chaser, ginger and chilli, and my mouth tingles again.

'This is the one,' I say pointing to the boozy cheese, knowing that Anna would be sold on it the second someone uttered the words, 'champagne-infused.'

'Woah,' Cameron says, putting his hands in the air between us. 'Don't be hasty. You don't want to commit to the first cheese that comes along.'

'Said like a true commitment-phobe,' I say, a joke which would land somewhere between flirty and friendly if Cameron knew that I was one too.

'Maybe I've just not found the right one,' Cameron says. 'Cheese, I mean.' And with that our eye contact breaks and he steers us across the crowds towards another stall. Together we sample no less than ten more chutneys and cheeses and I start to wonder whether unzipping my jeans in public is out of the question.

'Well, now that your stomach's lined...' Cameron turns to look at me. 'Wine?'

'I erm...' I start, cursing myself for stalling. But once again I'm wasting the perfectly good weekend of a man who must have better things to do. And something doesn't feel right.

'Anna?'

Oh yeah, that's what.

'Is this, you know, standard protocol?' I say, trying to put some all-important boundaries in place. No doubt something I should have thought about before spending the entire day with him last week. And the entire night with Reese.

'Wine-tasting for a wedding?' Cameron asks, looking taken aback. 'Yeah, pretty standard,' he says, laughing. I feel like a rookie. But then, isn't that the point for most people looking to get married, that you ideally only do it once?

'In that case,' I say, trying not to melt at his smile. 'Lead the way.'

'This place,' Cameron says, coming to a stand outside a jaunty-looking building buried in a corner of the market, 'is a treasure.' Without pause, my mind starts playing Bruno Mars songs, making this moment even more rom-com worthy. 'Treasure' finishes by the time Cameron has led me to an overturned wine barrel, two twisting iron chairs pulled up beside as I try to stop myself humming 'Marry You'. Before I know it, a waiter is by our side, laying out six different-shaped wine glasses and pouring a splash of wine into each. I sip the first and the flavours hit my tongue in all the right places.

'How is this your job?' I say, catching Cameron's eye over the rim of his glass.

'A lot of hard work?' he says, with a coy smile.

'Reading between the lines,' I muse, taking another sip. 'Daddy got you the role?' Cameron almost spits out his next sip before letting out a big belly laugh.

'You're not that good at reading between the lines then, Anna,' he says. *You're not too good yourself, Cameron.* 'By a lot of hard work, I actually mean *a lot of hard work.*'

'A man who says what he means,' I say, with a grin. 'Refreshing.'

Cameron smiles but his eyes search my face, as if trying to see beneath my surface. 'Anna?' he asks earnestly. 'Is everything okay with Jake?'

Well that, Cam, is the question.

'Wonderful,' I say, my heartrate doubling in speed. 'Anyway, tell me more about this hard work.' I force the conversation away from all talk of Anna and Jake.

'Anna, this is your day, I don't want to...'

'Cameron,' I say, putting a hand on top of his and then instantly thinking better of it. 'I really want to know.'

'Well, *Daddy* could have got me a job,' Cameron says, mocking my own words. 'But he's a self-made man, and he's always wanted me and my brother to be the same. I guess he thought he was teaching us something about hard work?' The way he repeats 'hard work' again makes me think these two little words have been drilled into him for decades.

'I think it worked,' I say, as the waiter replaces our glasses and splashes in even more wines for us to try. 'What could be more successful than managing a hotel?'

'Owning one?' Cameron says, downing a sample in one go. 'Well, three.'

'Huh?' I say, now officially lost.

'My brother.'

I watch him sigh, signalling to the waiter to bring us the rest of the bottle.

'Remember that song "Anything You Can Do (I Can Do Better)"? Yeah well, that's my brother's mantra.'

'Isn't that a bit childish?' I ask, resisting the urge to put my hand on his again.

'Yeah, if it's childish to appear on the Forbes 30 under 30 list.'

'From where I'm sitting, you're looking pretty good,' I say. 'Your career, I mean.'

'Thanks.' Cameron sighs. 'But from where my dad's sitting, it's never enough.'

'I'm sorry,' I say, and this time I do reach a hand to the top of his arm. 'If it's any consolation, I know how you feel.'

Cameron raises his eyebrow as if to say: *You do?*

'My older sister is the golden girl in my family. She's a doctor who lives in the suburbs with her perfect husband and two kids. She's wonderful, but I just always feel like I'm behind.'

'Yeah, I can see how a successful actor who can afford to get married at the Hotel Hyde all before she turns thirty could feel like she's holding back the group,' Cameron says, his words dripping with sarcasm. I want to tell him how much of that's not true. Come on Marley, just say it. I look into his deep brown eyes and will him to be okay with this...

'Anyway, about the wines,' Cameron says, and like that, the time for sincerity has passed. 'I've put all of the expenses today onto your hotel account, Anna.'

Pardon?

'Of course, you already know from our website,'

Cameron continues, 'that if you choose to have your wedding at our venue, we will write off all those costs.'

'Crafty marketing technique,' I mutter, for want of anything better to say. How much has all of this cost? My stomach churns with champagne cheese. And it's on *Anna's* account.

'My idea.' Cameron grins, as if there's absolutely nothing to worry about.

'See, you're brilliant at your job,' I say, as I drain the last of my drink. How the hell am I going to afford this if Anna doesn't choose this venue? I'll have to pay her back for every penny I've wasted pretending to be her. But she *will* choose this venue. If Jake still chooses her. And then it'll be hello to real Anna and a big farewell to Cameron. I look at him now, gazing back at me with his honest eyes. I guess it was always going to be 'Farewell Cameron' from the moment 'Anna' said hello.

CHAPTER EIGHT

I look up from my laptop to gaze in Xavier's direction. I promised my parents that I'd finally send off an application for an executive assistant position today. Two weeks ago, even the thought of this would have horrified me. But given that the most productive thing I've done since my last audition is get rat-arsed with Reese (and the most I've heard from Billie is a bum dial) I think it's time to admit defeat. As my mum so helpfully pointed out: *money doesn't grow on trees.* It also doesn't come easily from Bride Tribes.

I message the WhatsApp group with the most passive-aggressive missive I can muster: *Hey girliiiiess, I hope you're all having good days. Arabella, good thinking with the bikini, babe, could you look into that for us and price up some options?...* this part is risky, given that I won't be caught dead in a personalised swimsuit, but my hunch is that Arabella is full of good ideas provided she doesn't have to organise them herself. *Also, Lauren, I know you're struggling for money darling, but I really could do with that deposit like... yester-*

day. Message me when you finally transfer. Thanks gang! The sickly-sweet tone of my message makes me feel sick.

Another message from Mum shoots onto my screen, hassling me about the job application. I'd love to see her try to complete an application whilst being serenaded by some sub-grade-one flute-playing.

'Xavier, could you please practise that somewhere else?'

'Where would you recommend?' Xavier asks, grinning back at me. He's either the king of passive aggression or he's oblivious to any tension between us. I vote the latter.

'I don't know. The park?' I say, glancing out of the window and hoping it hasn't just started pissing it down. An awkward moment hangs between us – at least *I* think it's awkward.

'Good idea.' Xavier's unshaven face breaks into a smile. 'I could put a hat out and make some money.' He's not even joking. I nod and look back to my job application, silencing the part of my brain that wonders whether I'd stand a better chance busking in the park too. I hear the door shut behind him and realise I'm not invited.

Right Marley, time to get a proper job. It's been a week since I said goodbye to Cameron, two weeks since I was drinking at Hotel Hyde with Reese. I've heard nothing from either of them and nor do I expect to. The next time I see Cameron will be at real-Anna's wedding or when I sneak into the hotel wearing a fake moustache to settle up 'Anna's account'. Wow, I need this job. I look back at the application form fields that I've filled in so far. *Name? Marley Bright.* Well, at least I've got that one right. I look down at my phone and Anna Adams's name is dancing across the screen.

'Hey lovely.' I pick up the phone immediately. We've chatted more regularly in these past two weeks than in the past two years that Anna and Jake have been together. Almost every day she's called with updates about him: he's still acting strangely, out when Anna is out, but in when she's in. 'It's like he's keeping an eye on me or something,' Anna had said. That, or he just wants to spend time with his fiancée? Either way, I know Anna needs me to be her stability, to remind her that not everything will crash around her if we find out the worst.

'Marley, Jake's gone out,' she says down the line, still in hushed tones.

'Work?'

'So he says.' The sadness is evident in her voice. But apart from one rogue phone call, a sub-par excuse and some general uneasiness, she doesn't actually have any proof that Jake is cheating on her. 'It's the first time I've been in without him since that call.'

I know Anna well enough to know where she's going with this.

'What are you up to now? Can you come round?' she asks hurriedly.

'I'm...' I start my sentence, looking at the garish yellow screen before me. *I'm meant to be looking for a job. That I don't even want.* 'Yes, of course I can come round.'

Walking towards Anna and Jake's building, I marvel at the panels of greenery built into the design. Each time I come here, I'm reminded that green spaces are a luxury in this city. And Anna's life isn't short of luxury. I reach for the intercom and she buzzes me in immediately.

Entering her building and tracing the walls of its bright white entrance into the lift, I feel proud and jealous in equal measure. Proud, because ever since we were little girls, Anna has dreamed about building a life for herself that is better than the one she grew up with. Jealous, because only one of us is living our dream. But, seeing Anna's scared face as I meet her at her door, a small part of me is fearful that her dream is about to become a nightmare.

'I'm so glad you're here,' she says, wrapping her arms around me tightly before ushering me inside. I look down the long corridor that her front door leads into and wonder again that Anna was able to afford this place all by herself. She bought the flat two years ago, a couple of months before she met Jake, and yet it still manages to smell new.

'How are you doing?' I ask as she steers me into the big open living space, the floor-to-ceiling windows inviting my eyes out to gaze over the Greenwich skyline.

'I've been better,' she says with a sigh and my heart lurches. It's been hard at times to see Anna so damn happy when I've been struggling but the one thing harder is seeing her this upset.

'I know lovely, but you can't be sure he's cheating on you.'

'I just know something's not right,' she says, putting both hands to her gut.

'Have you tried to talk to him?'

'A little,' Anna says, pushing her gorgeous long brown hair behind her back. She's make-up-less and undone but still looks far more put together than me. 'I've asked him how work is going and what meetings he's been disappearing off to, but he's being really shady about it. We used to talk about his clients and investments all the time but now every time I bring it up, he just goes quiet before changing the subject.'

I listen to my best friend attempting to process things out

loud, watching her trying to fan her anger into flames to keep the sadness from engulfing her completely. I try my best not to jump to the conclusions that I know she is. There's no way Jake is cheating on her. Admittedly, I was cautious about him in the beginning. Posh-boy investment bankers who hang out at members' clubs are hardly my type. Though *my* type of late has leaned towards struggling artists who still live with their mothers. Maybe that's why Cameron felt like such a breath of fresh air. Not that that matters now. Not that it ever mattered. Any kind of connection I felt between us was actually between him and *Anna*.

'But have you actually asked him whether he's cheating on you?'

'No!' Anna looks horrified. 'Marley, we're getting married, I'm meant to *trust* him.'

'Hmmm,' I say, allowing my eyes to gaze out at the view again. I look up to the skyline and it's only then that I notice there is a crack in the ceiling starting to show; an imperfection in Anna's life that I've never been able to notice until now.

'So, will you help me look through his stuff?'

So much for trust, then.

'Do you not think you should be able to talk to him about anything?' I ask softly. Anna looks back at me and I'm reminded that just because you love someone doesn't mean it's easy to broach the truth.

'Are you going to help me or not?' she asks again; we both know my answer is *yes*. I have a feeling this will end in tears, but Anna's mind is made up. If we find nothing, maybe it will get her out of this funk. If we find something?

Well, I'm going to *funking* kill him.

'I'll take the wardrobe, you take the drawers,' Anna turns

to me as we walk into the bedroom. It's the only bedroom in the flat but it's big enough to sleep a family of five.

'You want me to rifle through your fiancé's drawers?' I ask. We've already searched every inch of the living room, behind the bookcases, even in the pages of the books themselves. I'm not entirely sure what we're looking for. Jake is a smart guy; it's not like he's going to leave another woman's underwear in the washing basket. 'Isn't that a bit well... insane?'

Anna turns to me with a look that is *absolutely* insane before swinging the wardrobe doors wide open. In the intensity of the moment, unspoken rules come to the fore: if your best friend is heartbroken, pragmatism counts for little; it's time to feel, not think. Obediently, I open the first drawer of the bedside table by his side of their four-poster bed. The contents inside tell you everything you need to know about Jake: two sports biographies, one book on banking, hair gel, condoms, *concealer*. I lift up the latter to show Anna, 'Did you know about this?'

'What?' she says, turning around with a look of horror on her face. I appreciate I could have been clearer, given the circumstances. 'Oh yeah, he gets break-outs from time to time when he's stressed with work.'

'Let's hope that's the only thing he's concealing,' I mutter, before I realise that Anna isn't in the mood for jokes. Her face falls and I will her with my eyes to stay strong. The way she straightens out her shoulders and holds her head a fraction higher tells me our best friend telepathy, the kind that takes decades to create, is back in full force. Despite the seriousness of the situation something about sharing a mission with Anna, the way we used to, makes me feel nostalgic. We used to always come up with little plans together to find out more about the boys we liked. I swear social media has turned every woman in her early twenties into a self-proclaimed secret agent. We could team together and fight cybercrime if we weren't busy obsessing over our latest crushes. I pick up one of the sports biographies.

'Can you remember when you helped me track down that cute guy we met at the café near school back home?' I muse whilst flicking through the pages, trying my best to distract Anna from thinking about what it will mean if we do actually find anything.

'Remember?' Anna stops rifling through their wardrobe to look at me, grinning at the thought. 'I went full-on Veronica Mars,' she says with a laugh. 'The second I remembered seeing his school tie sticking out of his bag I knew which pool of boys to dive into.'

'I've never seen anyone target Facebook friends quite like you,' I say, feeling warmed by the thought; there was nothing we wouldn't have done for each other, even for the most mundane or ridiculous reasons. I discard the biography and replace it with the banking book, which falls open on a book-marked page.

'Found anything?' Anna asks, closing the wardrobe doors, a clear sign she hasn't. I look down at the book clutched in my hands and realise it's not a bookmark holding the pages open, it's some sort of branded sticky note with two words scribbled in its centre: *call me.* I turn it over and immediately wish I hadn't. There I find the doodled digits of a phone number and a lipstick kiss mark smudged in the corner. I instantly feel sick.

'I'm not sure,' I say, and quickly run through scenarios in my mind. This doesn't look good. This will break Anna's heart. Even more than it's already breaking. But she's meant to be getting married to this guy. And she's my best friend. She needs to know the truth.

'Wha-at?' Anna stammers, walking slowly across the room to join me on the bed.

'I'm so sorry, Anna,' I say, handing her the note. Her face falls and then the tears begin, slow and steady at first but followed by deep and uncontrollable sobs.

'But it still doesn't mean he's cheating,' I say, pulling her shaking shoulders into my arms, trying desperately to hold my friend and her carefully curated future together. 'He's a good-looking guy, he may have an admirer but that doesn't mean he's *done* anything.'

Together we look down at the note in her hands. If it doesn't mean anything, why has he kept it? Why hasn't he come home and joked with Anna that he's 'still got it'? I watch Anna turn the little scrap of paper over and over in her hands and I know she's going over and over the same questions in her mind. This looks bad. I look closer at the squiggly emblem at the top of the sticky note and realise I recognise it from somewhere. Then the penny drops along with my stomach: *Hotel Hyde*. My blood runs cold. Would Jake really meet up with a woman in the very same place he is considering as a venue for his own wedding?

'He's cheating on me,' Anna whispers through sobs. 'He's actually cheating on me.'

'If he is,' I say, trying to catch my breath, 'he doesn't deserve you.'

'I can't believe this is happening.'

I watch her tears fall and pray I can stop them. 'I'm so sorry,' I say, holding her closer, which seems like all the permission she needs to break down completely, sobbing and shaking and gasping for breath. And all this time I thought they were perfect. I'm just about to tell Anna about the hotel branding until I realise that this will break her even more. Right now, she doesn't need to know where it happened. She just needs to know that it did, once and for all. 'Do you want me to call the number?' I say, slowly reaching to the scrap of paper in her hands. Anna grips the note even harder, her whole body shaking as she does.

'No,' she says, looking at me dead in the eye. 'What if he's with her now?' Anna's face turns to stone and all of a sudden, she doesn't look sad, broken, fragile – she looks angry. Really angry. 'I won't give them the pleasure,' she hisses, her once-sparkly eyes narrowing in rage. 'I hate him so much for hurting me like this. After all I've done for him, after everything we've built together. And whoever this woman is,' she goes on, holding the note up in the air, her hands shaking all the more, her voice hoarse with pain, 'I hate her too.'

'Me too,' I say. I know it's not enough. Nothing I can say will make this better. 'So I'll take the note and call the number later, once we know Jake is home safe with you.'

I regret the words immediately; nothing about this dream home feels safe anymore.

'No,' Anna says again. 'This note is the only evidence we have. If I move it from where we found it, he'll claim he's never seen it before.'

'Do you really think he's that good a liar?' I ask, before Anna's look says it all. 'Okay,' I say, barely more than a whisper. 'Then what do you think we should do?'

'I'll find a night when we're both in and then invite you around...' she begins, scheming in the way we used to. This time it doesn't feel like a game. It feels absolutely awful. 'Then when you distract him, I'll call this number and finally get to the bottom of it.'

'And then what?' I ask, nodding along although I think this plan isn't necessary. Right now, Anna has a right to feel and do whatever she wants to do.

'And then we'll make him pay.'

I'm not sure which is worse: Anna devastated, or Anna deranged. Either way, my best friend's world is being turned upside down and all I can do is stand with her in the storm.

'What are you going to do until then?' I ask, tentatively. 'Do you want to stay at mine?'

'This is my home,' Anna says defiantly, 'I own it. I've worked for it. I'm not going anywhere. And I'm not going to give Jake even a hint that something's wrong until we've made a plan.'

I thought the days of me and Anna being *we* were long gone; I wish it wasn't this that has brought them back. I reach a hand to rest in Anna's and realise mine is shaking too. How could this be happening?

'Do you really think you can act like you're okay around him?'

Anna gives my hand a little squeeze. 'You might have to give me some acting tips.'

All of a sudden Anna's phone begins to ring and we look down to see Jake's name on the screen. It has three heart emojis after it, which right now feels like salt in the wound. She picks up and I once again wonder whether Anna would have made a far better actress than me. 'See you soon, honey.' She hangs up the call soon after. 'He's almost home,' she says, her voice cracking again before she steadies it, brushing any semblance of emotion from her face. I scramble to place the note precisely where I found it, closing the book and the secret away with it. I throw my arms around Anna one last time, not wanting to leave her side.

'I promise I'll be okay,' she whispers into my hair as I turn to leave her behind. She *has* to be okay. Anna was always the steady one, the settled one. Right now, I hate every inch of myself that ever resented that – but not nearly as much as I hate Jake. Walking into the corridor outside their apartment, I pray I don't bump into him coming home or emerging from the lift. Just in case, I choose to take the stairs. Halfway down to the ground floor and not *not* out of breath, my phone begins to buzz. I expect it to be Anna, telling me she's actually not okay with pretending to be okay and asking me to turn back, to not leave her alone. But instead, I see an unknown number lighting up the screen.

'Hello?' the stranger asks as soon as I pick up. 'Is that Anna?'

I'm about to reply that it isn't and then I recognise his voice.

'Cameron?' I'm so surprised it's him that I find myself sitting down in the stairwell. I never thought I'd hear from him again. I didn't even give him my number. But Anna gave the hotel mine. And he still thinks I'm *her*.

'Yes, is that Anna?'

I hear his deep voice sing into my ear, every bit as enchanting as the hours I've spent listening to it in person. For a moment, I hesitate. If Anna and Jake aren't getting married anymore and the wedding is cancelled, maybe there's a teeny chance that I can ask Cameron out and casually slip it into conversation that 'my friends call me Marley'? I instantly feel bad for even *thinking* of using my best friend's break-up to my advantage.

'This is she,' I say. Clearly, I don't mind using her name.

'Can you meet me at the hotel?' Cameron asks plainly. 'We need to talk.'

CHAPTER NINE

We need to talk. The four most petrifying words in the English language. In *any* language. Especially when spoken by someone you fancy. Not that I'm meant to be fancying Cameron. I'm meant to fancy the fiancé of my dreams (literally). Surely, that's what this is about? But after one sleepless night of wondering, I'm about to find out for sure. My stomach lurches as the bus driver pulls to an abrupt stop, sending no fewer than three small children flying down the aisle. It's safe to say that my journeys in the Hotel Hyde's private cars are well and truly over; it's the humble bus for me from now on.

Navigating my way through the packed bus and out onto the equally packed streets, I try to prepare myself for the conversation to come. So, Cameron has found out that I'm not Anna? It was only a matter of time. I sift through my options as I walk ever closer to the grand entrance of the hotel. I could just come clean, tell him that I was having a really shitty week and needed to distract myself – no, *forget* myself – for a while. That might be a valid excuse for one day, but would it really stretch to the evening I pretended to be Anna with Reese? Or an entire afternoon spent binging around Borough Market with Cameron, racking up a tab to rival a Paris Hilton shopping spree? Oh crap, that bill. The one I definitely need to pay if Anna doesn't use the Hotel Hyde as her wedding venue. Suddenly, my stomach is churning for more reasons than one; *is there even going to be a wedding?*

I look down at my phone and see a message from Anna. We've kept in constant touch since we Miss-Marpled her flat and found that note from Jake. And even though I would give anything for the reason behind our rendezvous to be different, a small part of me is enjoying having my best friend back. Sometimes you don't realise how much you've missed something until it swings right back into your life again.

What are you up to? I read Anna's message and although I know I should tell her the truth, she hardly wants to think about wedding venues right now. Or the fact that her best friend is well and truly screwing up any chance of her getting married at her dream one. My tummy flips and just like that, the hotel comes into view. It's like it's mocking me. *I bet that's nothing compared to what I'm about to receive from Cameron,* I think as I walk closer to the entrance. In reality, I already know that Cameron is not the kind to mock; he's the kind to take the high road, take my money before saying a final goodbye and meaning it. That's what makes this so hard.

Walking into the grand reception room, I feel every bit as out of place as the first time. I was never supposed to be here. Not in the kitchen with Cameron. Not in the Hyde Out with a beautiful stranger like Reese. It's a blessing we didn't swap details, really. At least that's one person who can carry on thinking I'm Anna forever now that the competition deadline has come and gone. She'll be on to a new project by now. Like I should be, too.

I move obediently over to the lounge area where I had waited for Cameron last time, back when I had good intentions of telling him the truth before he could find it out for himself. Isn't hindsight a bitch?

'Anna Adams, isn't it?' The pretty receptionist from my first visit looks down at me. The way she says it makes me sure that even she knows that's not the case. Her pinched expression and popped hip certainly scream, *if that is your real name...* I give her a non-committal nod. 'Mr. Cavill-Jones is waiting for you in the hotel bar.'

'Mr Cavill-Jones?' I ask. Is it possible that she's mistaken me for someone else?

'Cameron,' she says, turning her nose up as if I should already know that. We've only ever been on a first-name basis. Not necessarily my own. I nod again before getting to my feet. I can remember where the bar is, even if I can't remember leaving it.

Cameron Cavill-Jones, I repeat to myself as I walk towards the Hyde Out. If I didn't think Cameron was cut from a different cloth from me before – a *posher* cloth – I do now. I know Shakespeare wrote, 'What's in a name?' but somehow Cameron's makes me feel even surer that he won't have time for the messed-up make-believe of a simple 'Marley Bright'.

Emerging into the bar, shoulders low and tail already between my legs, I see him sitting there. Cameron Cavill-Jones, as gorgeous and as unattainable as the first day we met. And he isn't alone. Sitting by his side is someone equally as stunning and stone-faced. *Reese.*

'Hi Anna,' Cameron says seriously, holding a hand out to indicate the chair before them that's clearly where I'm meant to take a seat. I oblige, feeling every inch like I'm in an interview. Either that, or an interrogation. Reese looks across the table at me, her pink-dipped hair pulled back in a tiny ponytail. She doesn't look happy to see me.

'Hi guys,' I say, my eyes oscillating between them, trying to work out what to say next. I could tell them that the whole day was an investigation, that I am part of an experimental acting circle that is looking into how easily we can assume the role of another. But then I'd have to keep that lie up at Anna's wedding too – if it even goes ahead.

'We need to talk,' Cameron says, his face still unreadable. *Yes, I know Cameron. I've been driving myself mad with those words ever since you said them.* 'And I've asked Reese to join us because well, this involves her too,' he says with a sigh. 'We know who you are.'

'I can explain...' I begin, as I notice Pete, the barman from the band lurking in the distance. Out of the corner of my eye, it looks like he's holding a bottle of champagne. He's no doubt about to show me the price tag and remind me just how many times that number appears on my tab.

'Who you *truly* are,' Reese says, accentuating the word. I see a little smirk threatening to turn up the corners of her dark plum lips. Is she *enjoying* this?

'I know, I'm...' I begin, eyes darting from Reese to Cameron to Pete from the band.

'You're Ella,' Cameron and Reese say together, just slightly out of sync. I'm *who?*

'Oh man, I couldn't keep a straight face,' Reese says, her perfect teeth now out in full force as she reaches across the table to grab my hand in hers with excitement.

I look to Cameron, who is smiling too, although a little more reservedly than Reese. Not that that's hard.

'Congratulations, Anna,' Cameron says, smiling sweetly. 'This wasn't my idea—'

'No, they were *your* brilliant ideas that made it happen, Anna!' Reese interrupts.

I still have no idea what's going on. All I know is that Pete has popped the champagne and he's pouring it into two flutes before us.

'I meant, it wasn't my idea to pretend like you guys hadn't got through,' Cameron mutters but Reese is speaking at such a high frequency that his softly spoken sentence doesn't stand a chance.

'Got through?' I ask, as Pete thrusts a champagne flute into my fingertips.

'Yeah, we did it!' Reese practically hums across the table. 'Our application got through to the next round of the competition!'

Through her squeals I register the words. *We've got through to the next round of the competition. We've got a chance of winning a hundred thousand pounds.* I've got a chance of acting for money again. And they've not actually realised I've been acting all this time. I feel an unfamiliar feeling of hope filling me from the inside.

'And it was your tweaks they loved, Anna,' Reese adds, and the hope is gone. There is no way I can continue in this competition with them both still thinking I'm Anna, with them both still thinking I'm about to marry a man called Jake in a venue like this. 'I know you've got a lot on though...'

'I wouldn't say a lot,' I say, before I can stop myself.

'I meant with the wedding and everything,' Reese says quickly.

'Although, the prize money wouldn't hurt when it comes to paying for it,' Cameron adds, and my heart begins to pound in my chest. I really, really need a job. And this is the most exciting thing that has happened to me in years. Would Anna really mind if I borrowed her name a little longer? And Reese won't mind *who* I am if we win this competition. And if we don't? Well, then, it's not like our paths need to cross again in the future. As far as Reese is concerned, I could be Anna forever.

'Anyway, I'd best get back to work,' Cameron says, shooting Reese an accusatory glance. 'You've got fifteen minutes,' he says in stern tones.

'Twenty?' Reese says, looking up at him flirtatiously. What am I missing?

'Fine,' Cameron concedes. 'And only one drink.'

'Two?' Reese says, her big puppy-dog eyes looking up at him again.

'Don't push your luck,' Cameron says, but still with a smile. 'The bar will be getting busy by then,' he says, glancing over to give Pete behind the bar a quick wave. *Reese works here too,* I think, before everything starts falling into place. I had been pretending to be more successful than I was that night, but so was she. And I should have known. Contrary to what Hollywood would have us believe, not everyone can write or act or sing full-time. 'And you're not a famous writer yet,' Cameron adds with another little smile.

'Yet,' Reese says, her eyes twinkling in my direction. I gulp my drink, the same champagne that got me into this mess in the first place. But could it be that this mess might just have become my biggest opportunity?

'Just do me one favour,' Cameron says, standing up.

From my position, he looks even taller and broader than he did when he'd first cornered me in the lobby.

'Yes, you can come to the wrap party,' Reese says, rolling her eyes playfully.

'Thanks,' Cameron replies. 'But I was going to tell you to actually swap numbers this time. Something tells me this team doesn't need a middle man,' he adds with a grin. No, but as Reese hands me her phone and I key in my actual number, I worry that Cameron and Reese are already closer than I'd like. He's her boss. He sees her all the time. There's no way Cameron can find out I'm not actually Anna and Reese wouldn't discover the same.

'I've just dropped you a call so that you've got my number,' Reese says, even though I'm already distracted by Cameron's sturdy frame walking away. And Reese must notice, as she immediately adds: 'Right, now that he's gone, we need to get to work.'

'Twenty minutes, right?' I ask nervously as Reese's cheeks burn a little brighter.

'Sorry I didn't tell you I worked here,' she says, tucking a stray piece of black-pink bob back into the world's smallest ponytail. The bar lights catch on her heavily jewelled fingers, silver bands of all shapes and sizes circling all fingers but one. I look down at my own naked fourth finger and hope Reese doesn't wonder why I'm not wearing a ring there either. 'I guess I wanted to be a full-time writer for the night. Bit embarrassing really.'

Not as embarrassing as pretending to be a completely different person.

'That's okay,' I say, with a little grin. I want to tell her everything, but thoughts of Cameron and the competition stop me before I can even begin. 'I can't remember much of that night, anyway.' I try to laugh the brief memories I do have away.

'Me neither, maybe we should start from the beginning,' Reese says, and I inhale my next sip of champagne. 'The competition is called TV Talent and it's run by four people at an independent production company called Sloane Star.'

'*Wow*, Sloane Star is a big deal,' I say. It's hard to keep up with all the new companies and agencies that pop up in the industry, but Sloane Star produced a sitcom called *Out-Out* a couple of years back that I genuinely wanted to get a part in. I didn't even get an audition.

'Yeah,' Reese says, her raised eyebrow adding her silent tag-on *obviously*. 'So anyway, they've run this competition for the last five years and it's produced some amazing shows like *Out-Out* and they usually run with the main cast attached to the application.'

Maybe that's why I didn't get an audition? But why didn't I even know this competition existed? I look down at my phone, at the one missed call from Reese's still 'unknown' number, but I've not received a single call from my so-called agent in weeks.

'The concept is pretty simple,' Reese goes on. *Sure, if you know about it.* 'A team of writers and actors get together and develop a concept for a thirty-minute show, minimum three members, maximum six...'

So, she needs me? I try to convince myself but know she could have used somebody else. Although she did say my ideas were good. 'The winners get their pilot fully financed with a view to launching the entire series,' Reese says, her eyes sparkling at the thought of it and I can feel mine doing the same. This is a huge opportunity. 'And a hundred thousand pounds prize money to share between the team.'

One hundred thousand pounds? Even split *six* ways that sort of money could change everything. But split between the three of us? I could pay off my Hotel Hyde debts, I could pay for Anna's stupidly expensive hen party. I could pay for the Red Arrows to write 'my real name is Marley' in the sky and everyone would be so excited about the future that they wouldn't care about my identity mix-ups in the past. 'All those shortlisted have to perform a scene from the pilot for the producers to get through to the next round...'

'All those shortlisted?' I repeat, Reese's words bringing my daydreaming attention back into the room with a thud, my heart hammering in my chest. 'So that means... *us?*'

'Well *you*,' Reese says, and I once again remember there's only one actor between us.

'Shit,' I say, exhaling deeply, before reminding myself I can actually do this. I've loved acting since I was a little girl, back when me and my big sister would turn over the washing basket to make a stage and force our parents to pay us sweets for scenes. Back before my sister stopped playing grown-ups and actually became one. 'So, what's next?'

'I guess we have to pick which scene from the pilot you want to perform.'

'You're the writer,' I say, willing at least one of us to feel like an expert.

'Yes, and you're the one who will be standing up there in front of the producers,' Reese says with a massive grin as my imposter syndrome morphs bigger still. 'And Will.'

'Yes, I will.' I repeat like a mantra: *I can do this. I will do this.*

'No,' Reese says, shaking her head and her hooped earrings with it. 'And *Will.*'

'Who's Will?' I ask, looking around the bar before taking a final sip of fizz.

'Man, you really were wasted that night.' Reese lets out a massive laugh and I suddenly feel ashamed that I've finished my drink before her. 'Will, my erm... friend... who's an actor, the one who is going to play Jack in the show.'

'Oh right,' I say, vaguely recalling her mentioning something about him, just around the same time Cameron had walked back into the bar that night.

'I've asked him to come here so that you guys can start working through the script.'

'Haven't you got work to do?' I ask, looking to the bar and sounding like a snitch.

'Not as much as you two.' Reese winks. 'And anyway, I'll be just behind the bar,' she says, offering Pete in the band a brief wave like Cameron had. Pete looks back with a bored expression that tells me that Reese should have started her shift at least half an hour ago.

'Do you know what scenes you want us to focus on?' I ask, half wishing that I could just go back home and stare at a computer screen whilst Xavier learns how to hula-hoop; it's the life I've got used to of late. This is all so new, so complicated. But then, wouldn't £100k split between us and the chance to finally get my big break make everything seem quite simple? It's everything I've been working for, wanted since I was a little girl.

'It's between two scenes really.' Reese smiles, finally unleashing her statement hair, which hangs messily above her tattooed collarbone. 'The opening scenes, in the bank, where Ella and Jack have just been rejected from their mortgage applications and first come up with the plan to combine forces...'

I smile at the thought. It's one of these wonderful scenes that sets up the characters so well – Ella as the kind of type-A, ambitious boss of a woman I could only ever dream of being, and Jack as the good-looking but alternative thirty-year-old still holding onto his dreams of making it in a band. It's full of humour and misunderstandings and it would be perfect to perform. My heart leaps at the thought.

'Or the shower scene towards the end of the episode,' Reese says, with a knowing smile.

The shower scene I remember well – and something tells me it will leave a mark on the audience too. It's a flash-forward to later on in the storyline that leaves little doubt that the two main characters are going to get together and should leave everyone watching desperate to find out how it happens. Ella is angry at Jack for taking over the renovations and vows to fix the shower herself. Armed with a boxful of tools and no idea how to use them, she starts to hammer at a pipe that suddenly explodes, spraying water all over the bathroom. Jack rushes in to save her, even though Ella doesn't want to be saved. Soon, both characters are standing in front of each other, their clothes sopping wet, neither one of them wanting to back down, until they begin to realise how ridiculous they've been. They begin to laugh, then they begin to kiss. Until one thing leads to another and soon their clothes are left in puddles on the floor.

'How do you feel about the intimacy of the scene?' Reese asks across the table.

'It's perfect,' I say. The fact I remember it from that night says it all.

'I meant, how do you feel about *performing* it?' Reese says, her eyebrows knitted together in curiosity. 'Or should I say, how does your *fiancé* feel?'

'Oh, he's...' I begin. Engaged to someone else? Not bothered? Not real? 'Okay,' I say even though I know it's far from enough. Reese glances down at my bare fourth finger again.

'Wow, a secure man,' Reese grins. 'And he doesn't even make you wear a ring?'

'No, erm...' I begin, sure I've just been rumbled, but Reese is beaming back at me regardless. 'I've got one, it's just...'

'I get it,' Reese nods. That makes one of us. 'Women don't need to wear a piece of jewellery to mark us as available or not.' Her eyes drift off to look in Pete's direction.

'Are you...' I begin, wondering whether there could be something going on between them before Reese offers Pete a peace sign that he and I both read as: *just two more minutes.* 'Are you seeing someone?' I ask, knowing that we should probably steer clear of the subject; it'll no doubt lead to more questions about my own love life or lack thereof.

'No,' Reese says a little too quickly, before softening. 'Well, maybe... kind of... but the less said the better really,' she goes on, with a sad little smile; it still looks gorgeous on her. 'Let's just say, I have little reason to trust him.'

'Got you,' I say. I have so many more questions but if I ask them, I know she'll ask me more questions about my own mystery man.

'At least you've found someone who doesn't scare easily,' she says softly, turning our focus back to the shower scene in question. 'And you've got nothing to worry about anyway, he's a pro and I know that doesn't necessarily stop actors falling for each other...' Reese continues, sitting a little straighter, smiling a little wider. '...but Will's got a girlfriend.'

I watch as Reese gets to her feet, reaching for our two glasses and preparing to make her way back to the bar. *I've got nothing to worry about.* I roll her last sentence around my mind. What would I have to worry about with Will, anyway? If he's as professional as she says he is then our acting together shouldn't have any impact on my personal life.

'I'll leave you guys to get acquainted,' Reese says, as I turn around to follow her eyeline all the way to the entrance behind me. There, I see a guy waving back to her and walking across in my direction. He's taller and skinnier than Cameron, but carries no less presence, with his heavily tattooed arms and his long, blond hair pulled back into a tight messy bun at the top of his head. I study his bearded jawline as my own jaw drops. Now I see what I should be worried about. Even the most professional actors would be tempted by *him*.

CHAPTER TEN

Will walks across the bar like he owns the place. I immediately feel a pang of loyalty for Cameron; he might not *own* the place, but he manages it really well. But then I remember that any loyalty I have should really be reserved for my faux fiancé.

'You must be Anna?' Will says, a cheeky grin spreading across his face and dimpling his cheeks as he takes the seat that Reese has just left behind.

Must this hotel hide all the eligible bachelors? Not that this one is single. And I'm not meant to be, either. I wonder how much Reese has told him about that. I nod silently. Partly because I don't want to tie myself in any more knots than I've managed to already. Mostly because right now I'm too distracted by his dimples to be able to string a sentence together.

'Or should I call you Ella?' He smiles across the table; it's not a crooked smile, like Cameron's, but perfectly straight, like he's spent so many hours having head shots taken that he's worked out all of his angles. Though, to be fair, I can't imagine he has many bad ones.

'Ella, Anna, I answer to anything,' I say with a shrug. *But mostly, Marley.*

'Makes it easy,' Will says, lifting a tattooed arm to brush a hand through his hair until it reaches his messy man bun. My eyes search the letters inked into his skin for signs of James Dean quotes, but mostly just because I can't seem to take my eyes off them. I watch as he turns towards Reese, who is now pretending to look busy behind the bar. For a moment their eyes lock and she gives him a coy smile before averting her gaze again. I know she said that Will has a girlfriend, but she also said her 'man' isn't to be trusted.

'I guess we should get to work,' he says, pulling two scripts out of his bag. His is already annotated, whereas I'm only just getting my head around the fact that Reese isn't just a figment of my imagination. 'Reese says we're starting with the shower scene?' Will says, and he gives me a cheeky grin. If I was his girlfriend, I wouldn't let him do shower scenes. I wouldn't let him work with a woman who looks like Reese. I wouldn't let him out of my sight. For a moment, my mind jolts to Jake. The real Jake. Who may actually be cheating on the real Anna. The thought is almost too awful to comprehend. Another day of being Anna may be a welcome distraction for me, but she's stuck at home pretending to be okay with a man that she may or may not be about to marry.

'Anna? The shower scene?' I look up to gaze upon my latest distraction, sat there in all his skinny-jeaned glory. Yet another handsome man in the Hyde who is completely, undeniably out of bounds. But with this script and this scene and *his face*, winning this competition may be more in reach than I dare let myself think.

'Yes, let's begin,' I say, mustering all the professionalism I can. 'Where?'

'Here?' Will says, looking at me as if I'm a few tools short of a toolbox, which may be entirely right once we start acting as our characters Ella and Jack while they flip their flat.

'Don't we have a studio space or something we can use?' I say. I don't mean to sound entitled, I'm far from it, I just don't want to disturb any of the drinkers around the room. Plus, this scene is pretty intimate. My eyes dart from Reese to the mirror wall to the entrance into the Hyde Out before I realise I'm scanning the space for Cameron. Maybe I *am* a few tools short of a toolbox? Any connection I may have felt with Cameron was never real. 'It just feels a little strange acting here with everyone looking at us like...'

'An audience?' Will fills in the blank, his words chased with a deep, loud laugh.

'Well, yeah...' I say, realising I should be more used to this than I am. I know the reason I'm here right now isn't ideal, but I've given my time and tears to acting for years. Somewhere deep inside me the little girl I used to be feels like this opportunity is ours.

'The manager here likes to use this space for up-and-coming talent,' Will says, as I remember how wonderful Cameron is all over again. Maybe I need a distraction from him too? 'Plus, this way Reese can keep an eye on us.' He glances in her direction with a wink; Reese rolls her eyes playfully. Is Will the not-to-be-trusted guy she was talking about?

'How did you guys meet?' I ask, as Reese comes over to give us both a drink – thankfully, this time it's water.

'At Royal Central,' Will says with pride, but it's a pride I understand. I got rejected from the Royal Central School of

Speech and Drama not once, but twice. And that's before rejection became my middle name.

'Will used to follow me around all my classes,' Reese says, resting her hand on top of his shoulder and giving it a squeeze.

'You wish,' he says, lifting his hand to shrug hers away. Reese narrows her eyes at him playfully before looking towards me.

'You were a writer too?' I ask him, trying desperately to understand their dynamic – a dynamic I may have accidentally-on-purpose now become a part of.

'Oh *please*,' Reese says, her tone still playful. 'Will doesn't have the patience for that. I studied acting.'

'Before my talent forced her off the stage.'

'Or maybe it was your ego?' Reese raises her eyebrows in my direction. 'Will doesn't like to talk about it but I pipped him to the post for the role of Macbeth in our final year.'

'Positive discrimination,' Will mutters, his eyes narrowed. I *think* he's still joking.

'Best person for the job.' Reese beams at me, ignoring his comment completely. 'By then I realised that I was more passionate about writing scenes than acting in them...' If she's such a good actor, why doesn't she want to star in her own script? 'Stepping back from the stage gives me the objectivity I need to write better stories,' she adds and it's like she's reading my mind. I just hope she's not able to read all of it.

'Well, why don't you go and *act* like you work here and leave me to take Anna's clothes off?' Will says, causing me to stutter my drink across the table towards him.

'Great,' Reese says, looking down at the water marks on his T-shirt with glee. 'You're already half-way there.' My mind fills with thoughts of our characters soaked through and kissing against the bathroom wall, the broken shower sending water everywhere, as I watch Reese walk away. We can't act that scene here. Not in a posh hotel bar. There's no way.

'Anna?' Will asks, bringing my attention back into the room. 'Are you okay?'

'This is all quite new to me,' I say, sounding more and more like an imposter. 'Not acting, just practising in a public space, and with such an intimate scene...'

'I was joking,' Will says, his expression softening as he leans his elbows on the table and rests his chin on his hands. 'Reese and I play up to each other all the time, we've been competitive ever since—'

'Macbeth?' I interrupt, with a little grin. Will narrows his eyes at me for a second in fake disdain until his smile stretches across his dimpled face and I finally begin to relax.

'Ella, you don't have to have it together all the time.' Will reads the line for the thirtieth time, but it still feels like the first. He's really good.

'But if I don't, who the hell will?' I throw my arms out dramatically, knowing that in the actual scene, the shower water will be spraying all around us.

'I will,' Will says, moving one step closer to me and putting a hand to my side. My skin tingles even though, unlike my character, my clothes aren't see-through and wet. Thankfully, we've very much kept our clothes on in the Hyde Out. Though, after a good few run-throughs of the lead-up to it, we *are* going to try the first kiss for the first time. We've talked about the logistics, Will checking what I feel comfortable with, where my boundaries lie. But he's so damn gorgeous that I'm struggling to put any boundaries in place at all.

Channelling the character of Ella, I look down at Will's hand on my side with a confused look on my face. After months of banter, this is the first time Ella will actually see why Jack has been trying so damn hard to please her. She doesn't move his hand, though, she just stares at it for too long – so long in fact, that by the time she looks up, Jack is just inches from her face. Just like Will is now inches from mine. The hairs prickle on the back of my neck as I see one or two faces look up from the increasingly busy bar. Cameron is nowhere to be seen. Not that it matters. I look into Will's eyes, imagining them to be Jack's and myself to be Ella.

'You will?' I croak my line, injecting emotion into my voice, intensity into my eyes.

'I will,' Will's character says again, moving closer still. 'But only if you let me.'

It's then that Will's hand on my waist grabs at the fabric of my top a little tighter, tugging the would-be wet T-shirt further up Ella's chest. I inhale sharply and try to pass it off as acting. Next, Will puts his free hand to the side of my face and begins to close the gap between us. I knew he was going to go for it, that we wanted our characters' kiss to be passionate, but before I know it, Will's lips graze my own, gently at first but then harder, deeper, longer until his tongue parts them and entwines itself with mine. He moves the hand on my side up to caress my other cheek before moving it to the back of my neck, his fingers entangling themselves in my hair. Then, as soon as my body has surrendered into him completely, Will pulls away, my face still in his hands and his eyes still on mine.

'Wow,' Will says with a sigh, and though he might be

adlibbing, I know it's not in the script. He disconnects himself from me and steps a respectful distance away, as I look around the bar to find no less than ten sets of eyes looking our way. One set belongs to Reese.

'Woah,' she says, and I have no idea when she appeared by our side. 'You guys have chemistry.' She doesn't look entirely pleased about it. I look to Will and he's still looking at me, like he can't quite work out what has just happened.

'Yeah, that felt good,' Will says, still not taking his eyes off me. I'm not sure whether he means the kiss or the scene. I'm not sure whether it matters.

'Oh good, Cameron,' Reese says and I'm about to remind her that the man in front of us is called Will when I notice that she's looking behind me. I turn to see Cameron walking into the room, his shirt sleeves pulled up his arms, just like they were when he was with me. How long has he been standing there? My heart plummets at the thought of him watching me kiss another guy until I remember that as far as he knows, I've committed to kissing another guy for the rest of my life. Still, I can't help but feel guilty when he looks at me.

'Can I shoot off now?' Reese asks Cameron as soon as he's close enough to hear.

'Reese you started your shift half an hour late,' Cameron says, kind but authoritative.

'It's important,' Reese says, with an endearing smile.

'Big date?' Will asks, and I wonder again if there's anything going on between them.

'Something like that.' Reese smiles, standing a little taller at the thought before she looks to Cameron and realises that the importance of a 'something like a date' might not warrant getting off work twenty minutes early.

'Fine,' Cameron says, rolling his eyes. 'I'll cover for you.'

You don't have to have it together all the time. I recall Jack's lines from the script and wish for a moment that I could say them to Cameron.

'Who is he?' Will asks, his eyes searching every inch of Reese's face. He has a girlfriend, but then didn't Reese say her man can't be trusted?

'That's for me to know and you to find out.' *That's for you to drive yourself crazy thinking about.* I try to read between Reese's lines.

'How about you?' Will asks, looking from her towards me as I once again feel stuck in the middle of something I can't quite work out. 'Fancy a drink?'

I glance to Cameron, who looks for a moment like he'd be happy to host us all night.

'Sure.' I smile as Cameron does the same, his big brown eyes on mine.

'Great,' Will says, gathering our scripts up in his hands. 'Let's get out of here.'

As Will leads us out of the bar and towards the hotel exit, I turn around to see Cameron's gaze tracing our figures across the room. I have no idea where we're going or why the Hyde Out isn't good enough for Will, but I feel that pang of loyalty for Cameron again and have to remind myself that it's misplaced; it's always been misplaced.

'Where are you taking me?' I ask; it's not like I've known him for long. Not that that stopped me getting into bed with Reese that night in the hotel bar – metaphorically, of course.

'A cool little place,' Will replies, as we emerge into the fresh night air.

We've just left a cool little place, I think as he steers me down side street after side street until we are wandering into

Soho. Soon we arrive by a single door that looks entirely residential; he's not taking me back to his, is he? There is no restaurant window, no shop-front, just a brick wall rising up to three stories high. Will knocks on the door three times and before I know it, it swings opens and we're welcomed inside a dingy, dark corridor.

'My friend owns this place,' Will says and my mind once again scrambles to work out whether 'this place' is a bar or just some random guy's home. Thankfully, just a short walk down the corridor leads us to a low-lit bar area hosting two small round tables and four stools pulled close to the bar. Will pulls out a barstool for himself and I do the same. 'What are you having?' Will asks and I mentally veto all the drinks that have got me in trouble thus far: *hella-fancy champagne, ridiculously expensive wine...*

'Beer, please.'

'Two beers it is,' Will says, nodding to the petite woman standing behind the bar.

'Sure thing, dimples,' she flirts back at him and I can see from Will's easy expression that this must happen to him all the time. I wonder how his girlfriend feels back home right now whilst Will takes some random girl to some random bar? I guess it's just one drink. This kind of thing must happen in these circles all the time – circles I never quite felt on the inside of. Two pints are thrust in front of us almost immediately and I take my first sip. On any other day this would feel like a welcome break from the monotony, but not today. Today, I've done what I love with people I'm starting to like and that feels most refreshing of all.

'I never asked you how you and Reese met?' Will asks, taking a sip of his own drink and turning his body closer to me. His legs are so long that his knees almost graze my own.

In this small, mood-lit place it feels intimate, but then we have already spent the day kissing.

'Did she not tell you?' I ask, trying to work out how much he already knows about 'Anna', how much acting is still required of me today.

'Apart from the fact that your name is Anna Adams and you've done some work in the States, she's told me absolutely nothing.'

'At least you know the basics,' I say, taking another sip. Not one of those facts is true. 'Reese didn't tell me anything about you.' At least, I think she didn't. That night is still pretty hard to remember.

'Not that I'm a dashingly charming young actor?' Will says, laughing over his pint. He offers me a smile so warm that I instantly need to take my jacket off.

'Not even that,' I say, settling into my surroundings.

'Well, my name is Will Hunt,' Will begins, pressing his hand to his chest. 'I'm thirty-one, so not *that* young, and I am a professional actor...' Will continues, whilst I try to work out whether he means that in the same way Reese and I did when we said the same or whether *he* can actually afford to live off his work. I tilt my head to the side and try to place him in anything; he does look vaguely familiar. 'I have been known on rare occasions to be something like charming...' Will grins again and given how attractive his dimples and chiselled jaw are I imagine he's underestimating their power. 'And yet, despite all of that, I'm best known for being the son of someone far more famous than me.'

'Charlie Hunt!' I say, as the penny drops. 'That's who you remind me of.'

'Guilty,' Will says and he doesn't look delighted about it. I imagine by thirty-one he dreamt that it would be him who would be recognised for being a famous actor. Not acting in some TV competition with a girl who wasn't brave enough to take her top off in a bar.

'He's amazing, so good in *The Kill...*' I begin before I realise that Will must get this all the time. 'Anyway, you excited about Reese's TV show?'

'Our TV show,' Will says, taking another sip of his beer.

'I guess.' I shrug, taking a sip of my own. 'But what's a show without a writer?'

'What's a writer without their actors?' Will plays devil's advocate with a grin.

'I guess,' I repeat. But Reese's writing is something special.

'Anna,' Will says, putting a hand on my leg. I'm taken aback by the gesture, but Will looks entirely at ease. Perhaps after having your tongue in someone's throat boundaries become a thing of the past? 'You need to stop second guessing yourself,' he smiles kindly, looking into my eyes with all the intensity his character had for mine this afternoon. 'I've acted with a fair few people in my time, and you stand up to some of the best.'

'Thanks,' I say, thanking God that the room is so dark that he can't see me blushing.

'I'm serious,' he says, his hand still on my leg. 'You're really talented.'

Really talented. I repeat the words again and again in my mind. They're the kind of words I've wanted to hear from people in the industry for years. Or from my parents. Or from my friends. Just anyone who can see my dreams and believe in them after I've been chasing them for so long. I hold Will's words close to my heart as he holds my leg firmer.

'Thanks, I...' I begin, looking down at his hand on my leg

as he begins to draw circles with his fingers upon it. Is this how professional actors support one another? 'I thought you had a girlfriend,' I say, and the barmaid tries to stifle a small laugh.

'What made you think I have a girlfriend?' Will says, his bearded jaw suspended for a second in surprise. He still doesn't move his hand.

'Because Reese said you did,' I say, now my turn to be confused.

'Oh right,' Will says, lifting his hand from my leg to put it to his furrowed brow before his face breaks into laughter. 'That's just what she says to stop me screwing over her friends.' That's just what she says? Does that mean Reese and I are friends now? Does that mean Will is actually single? A thousand questions shoot through my mind at speed.

'Oh right.' I echo Will's words back to him completely, as if I can't find any original ones for myself. If I thought something might be going on between Will and Reese before, I know for sure now. Who lies about someone having a girl-friend? My mind scrambles to get to the bottom of it but then Will drains the last of his drink and puts his hand back on my leg, leaning his body towards me in the same way he had when he was pretending to be Jack.

'Definitely single,' he whispers as I remember he's not Jack anymore, he's Will.

But I'm still Anna. I hover before him, suspended in the moment. Will may be single; Reese might be too. But I'm not. At least I'm not meant to be. She and Cameron think I'm *engaged.* And even though I'm not, even though Will might have no idea about my relationship status, how can I be sure that our kiss, a *real* kiss, won't get back to them? Plus, things are already complicated, my professionalism hanging by a thread.

'I think I'm going to enjoy working with you, Anna,' Will whispers, inches from me.

'I can't do this,' I say, unsure whether I've said the words out loud. Will instantly backs away and I try my best to read his expression: not angry, just confused. 'I mean, I think maybe for now we should just keep things professional.' I have no idea why I just said the words 'for now', but it's not like I can take them back now.

There's a lot of words I wish I could take back now.

'That's cool.' Will shrugs, his ego too robust to be dented by this.

'Are you sure?' I say, not knowing what I'd do if he wasn't.

'Sure.' Will offers me a soft smile. 'I'll just look forward to kissing you on-screen. Speaking of which...' he continues, reaching into his pocket. I'm all kinds of relieved when I see his phone now clutched in his hands. 'I should take your number, to plan rehearsals.'

'To plan rehearsals,' I confirm, as I key my real number into his phone.

'I'll drop you a call,' he says, reminding me that I still haven't saved Reese's number yet. Refusing Will's offer of another drink, I make my way out of the bar and into the cool evening air. I look down at my phone to see it light up with Will's number, calling just like he said he would. I know better than to answer given that he'll ask me if I'm sure I don't want another drink again and after today, my willpower is hanging by a thread. I let the call go to voicemail before proceeding to save it in my phone. Next, I swipe to Reese's missed call from earlier and continue to do the same. I have half a mind to message her, to ask her about why she warned me off Will or to tell her, tell *someone,* that he just tried to kiss me for real. Then I remember she'll be on her 'something like a date' by now, that she might only be going on to make Will jealous in the first place. I doubt she wants to hear that he tried to kiss me.

As I put my phone back into my pocket, it begins to vibrate in my hands. I look at the screen, half expecting it to be Will but it's not. It's Anna. Shame fills my stomach as I remember again how she will have spent her day snuggling down with Jake, eating dinner across from one another, pretending to be perfect.

'Hey Anna.' I pick up; it feels strange to say her name after using it as mine all day.

'Hey Marley,' she says, and I hear her sadness down the line.

'How are you doing?' I say, and just like that the sobs come thick and fast.

'He's gone out,' Anna cries. 'And I think I know who with. It's this girl from his work...' I can't make out the rest of Anna's sentence but the message it clear: she needs me.

'I'm coming right over,' I say without a second thought. But as I make my way down into the tube station and head in the direction of her flat, I can't help but compare our lives once again. It's something I've got used to doing these past few years but never once like this. I used to imagine her perfect life in her perfect home with her perfect man standing in stark contrast to my lack of all of the above. But today, right now, her perfect life doesn't feel that perfect anymore. And my life, working on a pilot in the Hotel Hyde with Reese, being kissed by Charlie Hunt's almost-famous son, today it feels like my life is finally looking up.

CHAPTER ELEVEN

'What do you think about this one?' I say, gesturing to a rustic birch stump filled with no less than thirty white roses; I think I finally understand the word 'centrepiece' given that this would definitely be the centre of everybody's attention.

'It's okay,' Anna says, even though I'm not sure her glazed eyes are taking the monstrosity in. That was my line back when she used to take me around wedding fair after wedding fair, showing me forty iterations of the same napkins. I didn't like all this wedding stuff before, but now, not even Anna wants to be here. Not really. But she doesn't want Jake to know anything is going on, and apparently that means carrying on like normal.

'The guests might not be able to see you through the flowers,' I muse, standing on the other side of them and finding Anna's face obstructed completely.

'Is that such a bad thing?' she says and I don't need to see her to know what her expression will be; it'll be the same one she's been wearing all day, hopeless and bored. Turns out wedmin isn't as fun when you're not even sure the wedding will be going ahead.

'Of course, it's a bad thing,' I say, emerging from the rose-jungle between us to stand by her side. *Just carry on like normal,* I remind myself. It's what Anna wants. Just until we know the truth about the note. 'Everyone wants to see the blushing bride.'

'Not when the reason she's blushing is because she's just been left at the altar,' Anna says. She knows she's being dramatic but after this last week some drama feels warranted.

'He's not going to leave you at the altar,' I say, as I hope to God that's true. We'll get to the bottom of this long before they're planning to get married, I'm sure of it.

'Not if he leaves me before then,' Anna says, and tears begin brimming in her eyes. Although, can they really begin when they've rarely stopped all day?

'Anna.' I turn to face her head on and reach both of my hands up to hold her arms on either side. 'We don't know for sure that he's cheating on you.' It's a sentence I've said countless times over the last few weeks but I'm not sure it's sunk in once. I'm angry at Jake, so angry, for making Anna doubt his love for her, but exacerbating the situation isn't going to make it any better. I can't shake the memory of finding the note, watching Anna break down like that, but until she asks him about it, it's my job to keep her calm.

'I know, but at this rate, we're never going to find a time to call the number,' Anna says, reminding me of our plans; we need Jake to be in but distracted, so that we know for sure that when we call this woman, she won't be with him.

'But when we do,' I say, squeezing her arms a little harder, hoping the assurance will finally be felt. 'Then I'm sure there'll be an explanation. Things are rarely how they seem,' I say and with every moment that passes since we found the note at Anna's just over a week ago, I'm starting to believe that's true. I need to believe that it's true, for Anna. My phone vibrates in the back pocket of my jeans. I don't need to look at it to know who it's from: *Will*. He's been messaging me all week. Clearly, he doesn't know that I'm meant to be getting married.

'He's meant to be here,' Anna says, looking down at her own phone but finding no messages there from Jake. He was meant to be here today, looking around yet another potential wedding venue for their big day. But then he got a work call, something urgent that he couldn't possibly say no to. From what I know about investment banking (nothing at all) this kind of weekend emergency could totally be a thing. But from what I know about my best friend (absolutely everything) I know she's not buying it.

'I know,' I say, swiping open my latest message from Will, not meaning to smile. 'But he's busy working so that you guys can afford this thing,' I say, and instantly wish I hadn't. We both know that Anna earns just as much as Jake, if not more. 'Or at least contribute to it...' I add quickly.

Anna doesn't talk about it much, but I know Jake's job used to be quite stable before a few members of his organisation broke away to create a new start-up. The phrase 'high risk, high reward' was thrown around a lot. But given that Jake's work has become a bit of a taboo, I'd say the high risk aspect of it has been causing some pretty high tensions of late too.

'Maybe,' Anna replies, moving on to look at the next centrepiece, still far from convinced. 'What's got you so positive anyway?' Anna looks from the stack of exotic fruits heaped high in the middle of another laid table to me, and I stash my phone instantly.

'I'm always positive,' I say, looking closer at the unusual texture of the grapefruit in the centrepiece. Of course, it's covered in feathers. Anna raises an eyebrow.

'Not about the wedding,' she replies, looking me up and down suspiciously. I wish I wasn't lying to her too, but she doesn't need my drama right now, she's got enough of her own. But I guess she's right; I was never too positive about trudging around these decadent places with decadent stuff that reminded me of just how not-decadent my life had become. That was, until I lost myself in the Hotel Hyde. I can't help my mind from conjuring Cameron's face but then my phone buzzes again and Will forces himself back into centre stage.

'Yes, I am,' I say, forcing a smile. 'I've just not had all that many opinions about feather-covered fruit.' Or bridesmaid dresses, or hen party hotels, or flights that cost a bomb. But if Anna dare think I've not made an effort, I'll throw this lemon at her – a clear reminder that while my life has been giving me lemons, Anna has been too distracted by the lemonade. But not now, not since that note. 'But right now, we don't know that the note means what you think it does,' I say, the thought of the digits scrawled upon it still niggling in my mind. 'And you did say you wanted to carry on with planning the wedding until you know for sure.' I hold her hand in mine; she smiles softly at the gesture. 'So, just for now' – I reach for a mango with my free hand, black feathers covering one side of it and hold it up to her – 'I need you to tell me what you think about this mango.'

'It has a face,' Anna says, deadpan at first but then I see a hint of her smile.

'It has a *face?*' I turn the mango around and I see two delicately drawn-on eyes staring back at me. The centrepiece feather-fruits have faces. It's official: weddings in the age of Pinterest boards and Instagram feeds are well and truly ludicrous.

'This is ridiculous,' Anna says, her smile fading to show the full extent of her exhaustion. I'm not sure whether she's talking about the centrepiece or the situation. 'Let's just get out of here. Wine?'

Usually that would be the magic word, but despite everything, despite the uncertainty about her future, I really want Anna to look at this venue, to look at any venue that keeps her away from Hotel Hyde and the identity crisis I'm still yet to untangle there. I just need some time. Time to see how the competition pans out. Time to tell Reese and Cameron and Will that I'm not really the one getting married. *Not that Will seems to know that,* I think as his messages to my phone send another buzz through my body.

'Shall we not just have a look at the main function room?' I ask, and Anna's surprised face acts like a mirror to show me just how unbothered I've been about her wedmin before. 'I'm confident Jake will have an explanation and you guys will sort it out and need somewhere spectacular to tie the knot.' I smile, steering us far away from the feather-fruit.

'Well if that *is* the case,' Anna says, mustering a smile of her own as we walk past the centrepiece display the venue has laid out and into the next grandiose room. 'I'm confident we'll not be getting married here.'

'Why?' I say, allowing my eyes to gaze up at the twelve-foot high walls to the ornately decorated ceilings. This place looks like something out of *Pride and Prejudice,* the kind of place someone with a surname like Cavill-Jones would get married. I push away the thought as soon as it has floated into my mind. 'It's beautiful.'

'Yes, it is,' Anna says, walking across to the windows and gazing out of them to a courtyard illuminated by festoon lights, scattered with cute little tables and chairs. 'But it's not the Hyde.'

'But you've not even seen the Hotel Hyde,' I say, panic starting to fill my insides.

'I know, I was going to see about getting a follow-up appointment soon.'

'But their waiting list for tours is like six months long,' I say. It's the reason Anna asked me to go and check it out in the first place.

'Yeah, but now that we've looked around once,' Anna begins, as my heart hammers even harder. Not we. *Me.* 'I could chat to that Cameron...' Just hearing his name makes my stomach drop to the floor. He can't find out I'm not Anna yet, not until I've had the chance to tell him. And that can't happen until I've said my goodbyes to Reese. And that can't happen until the competition is... *oh bloody hell, Marley.*

'It's all booked up,' I blurt before I can stop myself.

'No, I mean, for the tours, there might be a...'

'Anna,' I say as I watch her face fall. 'It's all booked up on the dates you want.' I hate myself for saying it but there's a good chance that it might be true. Anna and Jake are trying to plan a wedding so quickly and places like the Hotel Hyde get booked out way in advance. Deep down I know that the only reason I've just said what I have is to keep the real Anna as far away from the venue, her dream venue, as possible – all whilst she's trying to work out whether the wedding is even going to take place. I'm officially the worst friend ever.

'Is that what they said?' Anna says, and I curse myself for causing her any more hurt than she's already feeling. But I just need time, to sort this whole sorry situation out. And Anna needs time too, to sort out whatever is going on with Jake. Once again, I don't have the strength to lie or tell the truth; I hope a simple nod will suffice.

All of a sudden, the repetitive notes of 'Here Comes the Bride' fill the room and Anna lunges for her phone, holding it in her hands so that we can both see the screen: it's Jake. For a moment, she stalls, and I see that even the need for hesitation is hurting her.

'Talk to him,' I say; I mean this in every sense of the word. We still don't know anything for sure. Except that for the past couple of years, Jake has made my best friend really happy. And I want her to be happy. I've just wanted to find my happiness too.

Anna nods and disappears into the next room to take the call. In the silence, I reach for my own phone and am surprised to find that Will hasn't replied. At first, I found his incessant messaging a little full-on, especially given his flirtation with Reese and her white lies about him, but the more I've got to know him, the more I'm enjoying it. There's something about being thrust into this competition together, this new opportunity, that feels like it is accelerating our friendship, our bond, whatever it is...

Plans cancelled tonight. Want to fit in another rehearsal?

I read the words that have just popped onto my phone and swipe to open them. I immediately think they're from

Will before I read Reese's name, now stored in my contacts. I know I should jump at the chance to rehearse after waiting so long to get my teeth sunk into a role, but right now, my best friend is standing in the next room talking to her fiancé, still convinced that he's cheating, and I also know I need to be there for her. It's the least I can do after the mess I've made with her name on.

'How was it?' I ask, as she walks back into the room, stashing her phone as she does.

'It was nice, actually,' Anna says, her smile still tired but carrying a hint of hope. 'He's going to finish work earlier than he thought and wants to make me dinner.'

'Great,' I say, wanting to add that she's got nothing to worry about, but I know the memory of the note in his drawer is still occupying too much room in my busy mind.

'Maybe,' Anna says, looking at me with earnest eyes then asking: 'Do you think I'm about to get dined or dumped?'

My phone buzzes again and I look down to read another message from Reese: *Anna?* I guess now that real-Anna has plans with Jake there's no reason why I shouldn't say yes.

'There's only one way to find out,' I smile softly. 'I'm here for you no matter what.'

'Anna, over here!' Reese shouts, as soon as I walk into the Hyde Out. I look across the bar to find her raising her ringed fingers in a wave so that I know where to look. But the gesture is completely redundant given that you couldn't miss her anywhere. Her black and pink bob is straight and sharp, popping against a long-sleeved black dress that is as shapeless as a bin bag; she still manages to look good in it. I look down at my own jeans and T-shirt, a far cry from the formal wear I wore the first time I stepped foot in here. But in my defence, I'm not trying to be someone I'm not anymore.

'Hey Anna,' Will smiles, and I'm reminded once again that that's not technically true. I look from the two of them to the people surrounding us. The bar is busy tonight. I see Pete behind the bar, but Cameron is nowhere to be seen, even though the fact Pete's band's tunes are blasting out of the speakers and into the room tells me that he can't be far away.

'You've just missed him,' Reese says, and I once again wonder whether she can read minds. Except I wasn't looking for Cameron, I was looking for...

'Will,' I say his name out loud, reminding myself once again of the task in hand: get this round of the competition out of the way, be rejected, wiggle my way out of this lie. 'Will and I have been chatting about the script.'

'Is that so?' Reese says, with a raise of her perfectly plucked eyebrow. I'm not entirely sure she's happy about this but can't work out whether it's our messaging that bothers her or us messaging about *her* script.

'I thought that maybe the shower scene could start with Jack in the bathroom?' Will says, reaching into his backpack and pulling out the crumpled script. He's wearing a grey thick-knit jumper today, pulled up to the elbows to reveal his tattooed arms. I look at his messy hair falling down to meet his equally messy beard, a dark green beanie barely clinging onto the back of his head. He still manages to look put together without even trying.

'But then how will he find Ella, waiting and wet, when he comes in?' Reese asks.

'Couldn't he just fix it for her first and then she comes in to find he's done it for her without her even needing to ask? I don't like the idea of Jack not being the kind of man that steps in to fix things,' Will says, and I can tell from Reese's crinkled forehead that she's not convinced. Nor am I, to be fair. Reese's scene captures the feisty character of Ella perfectly; she wants to do it herself; she just needs someone to turn up when things go tits up.

'What do you think, Anna?' Reese turns to me. I was scared she would ask that.

'I think there's merits to both...' I begin slowly, walking a fine line between the competitive creatives, the tension between them tangible. 'But I think we should stick to the script for now.'

Reese smiles and Will does too, only his seems to take a lot more effort.

'It was just a suggestion,' Will says, looking from Reese to me. His eyes linger on mine for a little too long; they're not sweet and kind the way Cameron's were, but hot and hungry. Either way, they're both out of bounds. But I can't deny it feels good to be wanted. I catch Reese's gaze looking from Will to her phone and back again. Has Will been messaging her all week too? Is it just something guys like him do? In any case, she seems distracted and though part of me wants to find out why, I know I need to keep my boundaries up too.

'Let's read through the scene again,' Reese says. 'I want it to be perfect.'

'What the hell, Ella?' Will says from behind me, and only one or two people around the bar look up this time. I guess they must be getting used to actors practising here by now.

'I'm fine,' I spit the words across at him, not even turning around to face him.

'Maybe Ella could turn around at that point?' Will says,

breaking character to look at Reese, still sat at the table, her annotated script laid out before her.

'What feels best for you, Anna?' Reese says.

'I like the idea that she's so into fixing the shower that she doesn't even want to turn around and look at Jack, until he says the "you don't have to have it together all the time" line,' I say, and Reese smiles broadly; we're on the same page.

'Me too,' she says, and I turn to Will who is biting his lower lip, a lip that I know I'm about to kiss for the hundredth time since I met him. Reese nods and I continue to act.

'But if I don't, who the hell will?' I say, even more dramatically than the last time I said it. I'm getting into character, and it feels good, as natural as the blood running through my veins. I forgot how much I loved to do this before agents, auditions and teenagers like Sabrina came into my life. Will, also into his role, delivers his next line and puts his hand to my side. I imagine my clothes are sopping wet. I stare at his hand, he reaches the other to my face, and I gasp even though I know it's coming. Then it's 'You will' and 'I will' and Will's lips are on mine and his tongue rolls around my own and then...

'Cut!' Reese shouts, and Will pulls away abruptly. 'That one was good.'

I watch as she smiles at us and then flips her face-down phone screen up on the table before turning it back around again; the classic sign of a woman waiting for a message.

'Another one?' Will asks, pushing a hand through his now hat-less hair.

'No, I think we're almost there,' Reese says, and I'm reminded that it's only a week until we have to perform this scene, this kiss, in front of the television producers for real.

'We can practise a couple more times before the audition but for now, I'm done.'

'Another date?' Will asks, as we watch Reese stash her script and stand up.

'Not tonight,' she replies, forcing a yawn. 'I'm just tired.' She may be tired, but she also looks gutted and I wonder again whether it's because of watching me kiss Will. I still haven't got to the bottom of why she was trying to steer me away from him. But before I can think on it any further, she turns to leave the two of us behind.

'Do you want to grab another drink, Anna?' Will asks, and his eyes almost have me convinced. But no. I'm *meant* to be engaged. And even if Will doesn't know that, is it really a good idea to entangle 'Anna' even further into this mess? As if on cue, I spy the shape of Cameron's broad frame emerging into the room out of the corner of my eye.

'No, I better be calling it a night too, actually,' I say, as I see Will's face fall. My Spidey-senses clock Cameron moving past us to stand behind the bar. Will might not know I'm 'engaged' but Cameron certainly does; it's the reason I'm here – well at least, it *was* the reason. 'My housemate Xavier will be wondering where...' I begin until I realise that I'm not supposed to have a housemate. 'My *friend*, Xavier, sorry...' I correct.

'I guess it's goodnight, then?' Will says, slinging his back-pack over his shoulder.

'I guess it...' I begin, but before I know it, Will's lips are on mine and he's holding my waist and pulling me close and I can't help but melt into him. I pull away, instantly feeling Cameron's gaze on the back of my neck. Oh crap. But as far as he knows this is just a performance. 'Will, I can't, I...' I begin, stepping back, forcing some distance between us. It *is* just a performance, right? But as I look up at Will, a man who thinks I'm single, and across to Cameron, a man who thinks I'm engaged, I know that this kiss from Will is real. And as I turn to walk out of the Hyde Out as quickly as my shaking legs can carry me, I know I'm really, *really* screwed.

CHAPTER TWELVE

I'm greeted by spring pink blossoms as I make my way out of the tube station and I can't help but feel like it's the start of a new season. Not the new season my parents would have wanted, mind you; it's not like I'm suited and booted and headed to a recruitment agency. But still, I am up early and dressed up and heading to an audition that I've actually been asked to attend by someone other than my half-arsed agent.

A nervous energy tingles down my legs as I walk away from the station and try to get my bearings. Looking down at my phone, I see my signal returning before my screen fills with all the messages I've missed underground. There's one from my parents wishing me good luck before the audition – an audition I'm not entirely convinced they actually believe I have. I've kept the details surrounding it pretty vague given all the Anna-induced complications attached to it. There's another from Reese, reminding me of the address for Sloane Star's offices. There's nothing from Anna. There's hardly been anything all week, ever since Jake cooked her dinner after we spent the day looking around that venue. *Dined or dumped?* The question hasn't left my mind, along with a thousand other questions about Cameron and Will and *that* kiss. But from the brief replies Anna has thrown my way, it seems like she's doing okay again. I type the postcode into my maps app and find that I'm less than a ten-minute walk away and still half an hour early and so decide to try to get through to her again.

'Hey Marley.' Anna picks up the phone almost immediately. I try my best to work out the sounds in the background: some low-level chatter and the clattering of pans perhaps?

'Hey, what you up to?' I ask, projecting to be heard over the central London traffic. 'It sounds like you're cooking.' My mind is instantly cast to the hive of activity in the Hotel Hyde's kitchen, and my heart lurches. What if she's there? What if Cameron has found out and Reese is about to cut me from this audition before I even step foot into the room?

'Someone is,' Anna says, and she sounds chirpier than she has in weeks.

'Jake?' I ask, looking up at Sloane Star's doorway and walking straight past with my head down before turning the corner to complete another lap of the block. I want to be just the right amount of early but at least now I know that I'm in the right place.

'No,' Anna says, and my heart stops. Have they broken up? Has she jumped into the arms of another man already? Is that why I haven't heard from her all week? I try to breathe deeply, knowing the nervous energy in my legs has made its way to my mind. 'But he's here.' She laughs, and I hear his small 'hello' in the distance. 'We're out to brunch.'

'Oh great,' I say, not knowing why I don't feel like it is.

Maybe something to do with that stupid note, the one I told Anna not to jump to conclusions about. 'So, you're all good?'

'Yeah, we're good,' Anna says. I know she can't really say anything else right now, not with Jake sat right opposite her, but she sounds genuine.

'Have you had a talk about everything? Did you ask him about the note?'

'Yes... and no...' Anna answers in ellipsis.

'How can you have talked about everything and not talked about the note?'

'Look Marley, it's fine. We're all good,' she says, her breezy tone making me feel uneasy. 'What are you up to...' Anna goes on, redirecting my concerns from her day to mine. I wonder how much I should tell her. She doesn't know anything about the competition; she's not asked about my work in weeks. At least she's asking about my day now. '... later. What are you up to later?' she repeats. 'Come round to ours? We'll make you dinner?'

Oh, so she isn't asking what I'm up to now. *Probably for the best*, I think as I hook a right back on to Sloane Star's street to see Will and Reese waiting outside the door of their offices. *Round to ours, we'll make you dinner.* I used to hate these kinds of offers, the ones that make you wonder whether you will ever have a chance to hang out with your best friend without their boyfriend anymore. For a moment it looked like these offers might be a thing of the past. Now it sounds like they're back in full force. But so long as she's happy.

But what about that note? The thought niggles through my limbs as I make my way closer towards Will and Reese, the way it did every time I told Anna that everything would be okay. But if Anna says she and Jake are good now, then they probably are. They've probably got over this blip and can continue planning their future together, right? The sinking feeling in the pit of my stomach has me far from convinced.

'Hey Anna!' Reese shouts in my direction before I can dwell on it any longer.

'Yeah?' Anna asks down the phone. 'I was waiting for you to answer.'

'Yes, yes, yours later sounds great,' I say hurriedly before she can overhear Reese or Will saying anything else.

'Hey guys, sorry about that,' I say with a smile, stashing my phone in my pocket. I wish I'd never called Anna now, something about her happy-go-lucky act doesn't sit right. But right now, I have my own act to think about.

'No worries,' Reese says, her nervous excitement matching my own. 'Ready?'

'Ready,' Will and I say in unison before looking to one another. We've been messaging about the scene all week but this time our talk has rarely strayed off topic. Maybe he's finally got the message about being professional; but then, what about that kiss? I know for a fact that kiss was real. I fear Cameron knows it too.

I watch as Reese presses the intercom on the side of the white-painted townhouse before the shiny back door swings open and one by one we step inside. This place is far fancier than any of the abandoned warehouses and town halls I've auditioned in before. A thrill runs through my body as I realise I'm actually about to perform in front of some of the best television producers in the business.

Following the two of them up three flights of stairs, I try my best not to look at Will's behind; I really don't need the distraction right now. But something about his hot then cold, personal then professional communications have got into my head. And that kiss has never left it. There's something exciting about being kept on your toes, not knowing what might happen next. Like this audition, this opportunity, the one I never ever saw coming.

We emerge into a top-storey reception area, the huge latticed windows welcoming light into the room. My eyes gravitate towards the London rooftops outside. My already nervous tummy flips at speed as my heartbeat begins to race. I breathe deeply, trying to channel some sort of calm before we get called into the audition room. At least this waiting room isn't packed full of competition, all younger, prettier and sprightlier than me. No, this audition is by appointment only. Just like the visit to the Hyde that got me here.

'It's Reese Priestley.' Reese leans against the reception desk with more confidence than I could ever muster. It's only then that I realise I didn't actually know her last name; at least I know her first. 'And Anna Adams and Will Hunt,' she continues as the male receptionist behind the desk scribbles down our names. I clock some recognition on his well-groomed features, and I remind my worried mind that's no doubt because of Will's famous dad rather than my best friend's respectable real estate game.

'Great, please take a seat.' The guy gestures to a row of velour upholstered office chairs. 'They'll call you in shortly,' he says, managing to crack a smile though it's clearly forced. This place may technically be in my industry, but I still don't feel like I belong here. Why is it that you can be a part of something for so long and yet still feel like you're on the porch whilst everybody else has been invited inside?

'How you feeling, Anna?' Will whispers, leaning his

elbow on my chair arm. It's such a simple question with such a complicated answer: nervous, excited, worried about my bestie, like all my dreams could come true. Like an actress, like a professional, like a *fraud*.

'Alright, thanks,' I say. Will doesn't seem like the kind of guy to handle complexities, but rather to take life by the balls and make any day his own. It's kind of refreshing. His face lingers close to mine and out of the corner of my eye I can see Reese looking over to us.

'Right, we're up,' she hisses as I realise that the receptionist has left his perch and is now holding open a heavy-looking door into the next room. *This is it.* For a moment, I wonder whether I should try and balls this up completely – it would be the easiest way to get out of this whole mess and just start again, begin searching for auditions, waiting for another opportunity. But I know I've started again too many times already, I've waited too long, just like Reese and Will and every other creative waiting for their big break. And if the two people I'm following into the audition room aren't reason enough, there's also another *one hundred thousand* reasons why I have to give this audition my all.

Walking into the audition room, we find four people seated behind a big, glass desk, one of whom points to the six seats opposite him. I follow Reese's lead as she sits down in one of the chairs in the middle of the row. The empty chairs on either side of us are reminder enough that our team is pretty small, but after years of being judged for me and me alone, a piece of me still feels like I'm a part of something bigger than myself.

'Right, which one of you is the writer?' a portly-looking man barks into the space between us. Reese puts up her arm, her oversized shirt sleeve falling down to reveal her tattoos.

Thankfully, this is one industry where such expressions of individuality are valued. I look towards Will and see that he's dressed up a little smarter for today, too, his trademark ripped jeans replaced with a skinny black pair which his light denim shirt is tucked into.

'And what Jerry means is, *hello*,' the one female on the judging panel says. Her long black hair falls down her sides in braids, her cold-shoulder top exposing a skinny, dark clavicle. She looks like Zoë Kravitz's sister – if Zoë Kravitz *had* a sister.

'Hello,' all three white males say in unison, and I catch Reese's eye; this woman is a legend. Her name is Tanya Moore and I know she's the reason one of Sloane Star's shows got bought by Sky. She catches my eye and smiles broadly, her teeth not the perfect veneers I've come across on women in the industry but her smile no less pretty for that.

'So, as you know...' another one of the guys sitting behind the glass table begins. He's wearing thick-rimmed glasses and a black T-shirt with a V-neck so deep that I'm pretty sure that one jaunty move would cause a nip-slip. 'Today we've asked for you to perform one scene from your pilot so we can get a feel for the talent.' He looks between us and I try not to pass out. We're meant to be the talent. *I'm* meant to be the talent. A woman whose rejection to acceptance ratio hardly falls in her favour.

'If we like what we see,' he continues, looking Will up and down as I wonder whether he's threatened or attracted by him, 'we'll invite you to another audition in a couple of weeks where we'll be taking a closer look at the pilot and the episodes to follow.'

I think he's trying to pose this as an exciting proposition, but he sounds a little menacing. Reese made the mistake of telling me that out of hundreds of applications only ten will get through to the next round and only the final two teams will get to produce their pilot. So, the chances of that being us are so slim that I try to tell myself not to worry about it; just worry about the shower scene you're about to perform with a man that one of the judges may just fancy the pants off.

'That's provided you are happy with the terms set out here,' Deep V says, pushing a handful of documents closer to our edge of the table. Clearly, he's not bothering to get out of his seat for us. Will stands up to bridge the space between us and picks up the papers before stashing them in his rucksack.

'We'll take a good look at these,' Will says, catching my eye for a second before turning towards the four producers with a kind smile. 'I'm sure they'll be fine, but any issues at all and we'll let you know.' He gives me another grin and my heart flutters; he may not be a famous actor yet, or the manager of a hotel – I force Cameron back out of my mind – but Will sure as hell has his shit together.

'Please do.' Producer Jerry nods in our direction before looking down at some more papers scattered across the glass desk. 'Great, so we've read your script,' he says, gathering the sheets in his hands as the others do the same. 'Tell us a bit about the scene.'

'The scene we're going to show you today is the climax of the pilot, a flash-forward that hints at all the tension and romance and heat to come,' Reese says, and she sounds and looks like she was born for this. 'It shows the vulnerability and authenticity of both our central characters, who have been pretending to be something they're not until now.'

'Okay, Will and Anna...' Tanya looks directly at me. 'Let's see some authenticity.'

. . .

'Guys, that was *amazing*,' Reese squeals, throwing her arms around the both of us as soon as we're out of eyeshot of the Sloane Star office.

'Are you sure?' I say, highly aware of Will's arm lingering on my side, the same way it had in the scene; why are the lines between performance and real life becoming so blurry?

'Are you kidding, Anna?' Will says, releasing our embrace to look me in the eye. 'You were the real deal. I'm feeling good about this.'

'Me too,' Reese says, beginning to walk down the street as Will and I fall into step behind her. 'We might actually stand a chance of getting through to the next round.'

I can't help the excitement of that shooting through my body like electricity.

'What are the documents that they gave us?' Reese says, turning around to look at us. Will is standing so close to my side that we may as well be holding hands.

'They're contracts,' Will replies, still walking forward. 'Setting out the terms should the pilot go ahead. I guess there's no point in getting any further into bed with them if we're not happy with what they're offering.'

I keep putting one foot in front of the other, but I feel like I'm treading through treacle. My mind on the other hand, is running a mile a minute. I had no idea this competition was such a big deal when I was drinking up a storm with Reese in the Hyde Out, but now it's feeling more and more real. And official. The last major contract I signed was to have Billie Forester represent me as my agent, something Anna and I had celebrated together for weeks. Since then, Anna has signed many more contracts than me: for her new job, her promotion, and soon her marriage certificate. The thought glues me to the spot.

'What's wrong, Anna?' Reese says, also coming to a halt on the street corner.

'Oh, it's nothing,' I say, forcing all thoughts of Anna and Jake and that note from my mind – something that was easier to do when I was kissing Will for the producers. 'I'm just not so hot on contracts. It's usually something my agent handles.'

'Of course.' Reese nods. 'Is this something she'd be able to take a look at?' Not really, seeing as she doesn't actually *know* about it.

'Don't worry about that,' Will interrupts, giving me an assuring smile. 'Why don't I ask my dad to take a look at it? It may take him a few days, but he'll know what to look for.'

'That'd be great,' I say, a little too quickly. Anything that'll buy me some time.

'Thanks, Will,' Reese agrees, brushing her hair behind her ears with her black nails.

'Great, now that's sorted,' Will smiles, casting an eye back up the street and in the direction of Slone Star. 'Who's up for a celebratory drink?'

'Yes!' Reese says, her shoulders relaxing in relief. 'I can't go home and do nothing after a day like today.' She turns to me with wide eyes, encouraging me to say the same.

'That sounds...' I begin, until I realise that I've already told Anna that I'll go around to hers tonight. It's the last thing I want to do right now, but after not seeing her all week, part of me thinks her mood-turnaround is too good to be true. I know I need to see it to believe it. 'I've actually got plans with An— another friend.'

'No worries,' Reese says a little too quickly; Will looks

more disappointed. 'We'll let you know as soon as we hear more.'

I smile, trying to hold onto today's excitement as I make my way towards the tube station. Still, as I head deeper into London's dirty Underground, I can't shift the feeling that the time to come clean is passing me by.

CHAPTER THIRTEEN

Walking through Greenwich's leafy suburbs, I try to tell myself that everything's okay. Anna and Jake are back on track, inviting me to share in their perfect life once more. Everything is exactly as it always was. But somehow that thought makes me feel even worse. Exactly how it always was wasn't exactly working for me. Nearing thirty, living in a shit-tip with Xavier and spending days waiting for the phone to ring, for anyone to call, I was barely even surviving. Today, with Reese and Will, I felt like I was thriving. Anna may have dreamt of dream homes and dream weddings, but I've always wanted more. Now it feels like I'm finally getting out of the waiting room and being invited inside. I turn the corner to Anna's flat as my phone starts to ring and I look down to see her name filling up my screen.

'Hey! I'm almost at yours,' I say, as her apartment comes into view.

'I was worried you were going to say that,' she says, and my heart drops.

'Why?' I say quickly, today's adrenalin still rushing through my veins.

'Oh no, don't worry, I'm fine,' she replies, in that same happy-go-lucky tone she used this morning. 'It's just... I got a last-minute appointment to show a client around a house. I'm on my way home now but it sounds like you've just beaten me to it.'

'Guilty,' I say, guilty and disappointed. I gave up celebratory drinks with Reese and Will for dinner with her and Jake. Not that Anna knows that. Not that she's even asked.

'Don't worry,' Anna says quickly. 'You still have your key, right?'

Oh right, I'd forgotten that Anna had given me a key the first week she moved into her flat. Probably because she asked for it back a week after that to cut a new one for Jake. It must have slipped my mind that she twisted a replacement back onto my keyring a while back.

'I do, yeah,' I say, struggling to hide the surprise from my voice.

'Well, just let yourself in,' Anna says. 'Jake says he's on his way home too but hopefully I'll beat at least one of you back to the flat today,' she says, laughing, before adding: 'But not if the Jubilee Line can help it. Make yourself at home.'

Using my spare key and making my way up to Anna's flat, I can't resist the temptation to imagine it's my own. That's one thing they definitely don't teach you at acting school: that unless you're the next Margot Robbie or Scarlett Johansson or marry someone who is, you'll probably spend a good portion of your twenties shacked up with a flute-playing, paper-bowl-making, not-entirely-employed creative. You might even become one.

As I turn the key in the door, it swings open into the

quiet, secluded space. It's not even that Anna's apartment is a little taste of luxury – which it is – it's that it's a place to call her own, where no one will tell you you're being too quiet or too loud or too little or too much. I kick off my shoes and let my socks skid across the solid wood flooring before letting my body sink into her big fluffy sofas. Reaching for a remote to rival a sound desk, I dim the lights and draw up the blinds with a single click, exposing the rooftop-scattered skyline visible through Anna's bifold doors. I'm about to work out which of these buttons turns on the television, when I hear someone speaking in hushed tones from the next room.

My heart stops as I sit bolt upright on the sofa. Who the hell is— *Jake?* I thought Anna said he was at work. Maybe, he's beaten her home, too? Not wanting to alarm him, I sneak closer to the sound of his voice. I have no idea whether Anna's told him I even have a key. Following the voice all the way to the bedroom door, I stop. It's definitely Jake, and it sounds like he's talking to someone. *No,* my stomach sinks as I wonder whether he's not been at work this afternoon at all, whether he's had better things to do. *Damn it, Jake. If you're cheating on my best friend, I'll kill you...*

Leaning my ear closer to the door, I try to make out what they're saying.

'Please, it's serious.'

I think I can make out Jake's hushed tones. I press my ear even closer, whilst pulling the door handle towards me, praying that it doesn't open, or the handle doesn't budge. I listen for a response, but nothing comes. He's on the phone.

'I need to see you,' Jake says, and this time his words are unmistakable. But he could be chatting to anyone, I try to reason, my hammering heartbeat shifting up another gear. 'Anna's is due back any second so I can't talk now, but *please,* we need to meet again soon. It can't wait. I need to see you. I need you.'

Oh crap, he's actually cheating on her. My legs begin to shake beneath me, my breath catching in my throat, my head physically hurting as I try to comprehend the one thing I've been convincing myself *can't* be happening all week.

Suddenly, I hear the front door swing open. Rushing away from the bedroom door, I throw my body onto the sofa, hitting the remote as I do. The lights switch off instantly.

'Why are you sitting in the dark?' Anna asks, reaching for the good old-fashioned light switch. There I see her perfectly made-up face beaming back at me. It takes all my strength not to blurt what I've just heard out into the room.

'Just arrived,' I say, standing up to hug her hello and holding on a bit too tight.

'I thought you said you arrived fifteen minutes ago?'

'You know me, always exaggerating,' I lie, but before Anna can press me further, Jake walks into the room and my jaw falls slack. Anna lets go of me to throw her arms around her fiancé. Her stupid, cheating fiancé. I try to keep my cool but know the second he's out of the room, I need to tell her. I watch as Jake scoops Anna into the air, making her giggle uncontrollably. It's just like before. Except it isn't. Everything has changed.

'You had a good day, sweetie?' Anna asks, and I begin to reply before I realise her question isn't directed at me. Jake is her sweetie again, and he doesn't deserve her.

'Yeah, it's been good,' Jake replies, letting go of her so that he can walk across to the kitchen at the back of the open-plan room. 'Just sorting some things out at the office.' *Liar.* 'I'm just going to grab a quick shower,' he says, grabbing three wine glasses from the cupboard and a bottle of red from their wine rack. *Washing the guilt off?* I narrow my eyes in his direction, but neither of them seem to notice. 'You guys make a start on this.'

'Thanks, gorgeous,' Anna says, accepting the bottle and another kiss from him with glee. Something in her demeanour has changed since the last time I saw her at the hotel venue. She looks happy and relaxed, as if all thoughts about Jake and that note are now a thing of the past. Like she's finally accepted my advice to not jump to conclusions. *She should know by now not to trust a single word I say,* I think, accepting the glass of wine she's offering me and taking a really big sip. Maybe I'm trying to wash my own guilt away, too?

'How's your day been?' Anna asks.

'Yeah good, thanks,' I reply. 'Anna, I...'

'You heard about any new auditions?' Anna says, and I'm almost surprised she's asking. She's not asked about my work in weeks.

'I've got something in the pipeline,' I say, knowing I need to give her something. 'But I don't really want to say more until I know for sure. Don't want to jinx it.' Or, I don't really want to say more until I know what the hell I'm going to say. *I borrowed your perfect life for a day and I think may have screwed yours up in the process?* 'Anyway, how are you feeling about Jake?' I ask tactfully, trying to find a suitable time to split my best friend's heart in two.

'Amazing,' Anna says, with a massive grin that makes me feel a thousand times worse. 'That night after we hung out, he made me dinner and it was like he'd done a complete one-eighty, like I'd got my Jake back again,' she hums, and the way she says 'my Jake' makes my heart hurt. She has no idea that she's sharing her Jake with someone else.

'But do you not want to ask about that note?' I say, lowering my voice as I do. 'Tonight could be the perfect night to call the number. He's in, he's not with her...'

'There was never a her,' Anna says with a shake of her head, smile still shining. 'We had a big chat and he's just been so stressed with work stuff. His company has made some not-so-great investments lately.' Yeah, and Jake's made some not-so-great decisions of his own. 'That's why he's been so distant lately, but things have started to turn around.'

'But what about the note?' I say, 'Surely that's the only way we'll find out the truth.'

'I trust him,' Anna says again, her hand on her heart. 'I think I was freaking out for a bit too, but after our chats and this past week I know he would never do that to me.'

'Do you not want to ring it, just to find out for sure?'

'You were the one who was saying not to jump to conclusions, Marley,' Anna says, her face falling just a little before she recovers her smile once again. 'And you were right.'

'I don't know, I may just have been distracted and...'

'It's okay,' Anna says, putting a hand to my leg. 'It's honestly okay. I'm happy.'

Yeah, but is it enough to be happy when it's founded on a lie? I can't help the highs of the last few weeks from flicking through my mind.

'I just think, maybe we should just call...'

'Jake!' Anna shouts and I follow her gaze to find him standing, hair wet and cheeks pink at the door into the room. So, when he said a *quick* shower, he really meant it. I struggle to even look into his shining, happy face and not scream liar, liar, *liar*.

'I'm not interrupting anything, am I?' he asks with a grin,

eyes scanning over my caught-in-the-act expression. It should be him who's just been caught.

'Not at all,' Anna says, clambering to her feet to stand before him and pushing her hand through his freshly cleaned hair. 'You smell nice.' She holds him closer. It was this kind of activity that made me feel awkward at the best of times, now it feels even worse. Anna thinks her perfect life is back on track, and as much as I want her to be happy, I can't let her settle for anything less than the real thing. 'Shall we get started on dinner?'

One of us needs to find out the truth about Jake, about who was on the other end of that phone call, about who wrote the number on that note hidden in his bedside drawers, and if it's not going to be Anna, it's going to have to be me. I love her too much not to.

'I'm just going to the loo,' I say, even though I'm pretty sure the love birds wouldn't even realise I'm gone. Closing the living room door behind me, I walk towards the steamy bathroom and shut the door with a bang, remaining on the other side of it. I know that any answers Anna needs are not in there, but in the bedroom, in the drawer I'm opening now, on the note I've just stashed in my pocket before anyone else can find out.

CHAPTER FOURTEEN

I toss and turn, reaching for the cold side of the pillow and instead feeling the note crumpled up beneath it. It's not like I put it there for safe keeping, but after hours of thumbing it through my fingers, trying to pluck up the courage to call the digits scrawled across it, I must have finally fallen asleep. For two and a half hours. I groan as I clock the time: *3.23a.m.* *Why the hell can't I stay asleep?* I think, but I already know the answer is buried under my pillow. Who on earth was Jake on the phone to last night? Who was he so desperate to see? And so very desperate not to get caught speaking to?

I should never have taken the note. I should have stayed out of it. But then, since when have I ever been given that option? I've been thrust into Anna and Jake's relationship ever since it started and have spent the past three months helping to plan their ludicrously expensive wedding. Even the thought of centrepieces and Bride Tribes and hen parties a struggling actor couldn't even dream of affording can't make me angry at Anna right now. All I want to do is protect her from getting hurt. Could Jake have really kept this secret forever? Doesn't the truth always come out eventually?

My phone buzzes and I look down to see a message from Reese: *Still no news.* At least someone else is awake; I can imagine any early-morning bed activities she's involved in are a lot more exciting than mine. Her message doesn't warrant a reply. It's been less than twenty-four hours since our audition. Plus, the chances of us getting through are about as slim as Reese is. *Doesn't the truth always come out eventually?* The thought floats back through my busy mind as my stomach churns; I had only wanted to be Anna for a day. The note juts into my side, a reminder to be careful what you wish for.

Another chime fills my room and I scramble to find my phone nestled deep within the sheets. For a second, I think it's Reese following up her no-news message but then I see it's light outside and notice the numbers in the centre of my screen: 9.37am. I must have finally fallen back to sleep again, but I wouldn't know it from my energy levels.

My eyes scan down my screen to find a message from Anna: *Hey Marl, thanks for coming round last night. Just having you and Jake there, my two favourite people, I felt better than I have in weeks. I'm so lucky. A x* My stomach sinks as I read the words. How can she not see that he's still up to something? But then, I've been keeping her out of my crap ever since I took that appointment for her at the Hotel Hyde. Turns out it's pretty easy to keep your loved ones out of the loop if what you're hiding would hurt them. But surely, she needs to know about Jake? Before it's too late. *And thanks for keeping me level-headed about Jake, I don't know what I was so worried about. A.*

Oh, Anna. I have a couple of ideas.

I look around for the note, panic rising within me when I realise it's nowhere to be seen. Right now, that note is the only way I can think of to find out more about Jake's secret without it being his word against mine. And as much as mine and Anna's friendship has spanned the decades, a small part of me wonders just how that *he said, she said* would play out. Forcing my legs out of bed, my feet sink into the (God only knows how old) carpet. Something hard and scratchy tickles at my toes. Before I wonder whether Xavier has got into reptiles, I look down to see the scrappy bit of paper with *that* number on it. Relief fills my body before the panic floods back in again. I have absolutely no idea what to do about it.

Reaching for my jeans and pulling on a jumper, I stumble out of my bedroom and down the corridor in search of coffee; coffee will help. As I push the door into the living room ajar, I am greeted with the familiar smell of marijuana; marijuana might help too. Through a thick cloud of smoke, I see Xavier sitting on the sofa, legs crossed, reading the paper. I marvel at the normality of the activity for a brief moment before the weed-fog dissipates and I see that he's actually reading a copy of something called *Spudman Magazine*.

'He's the most trusted journalist in the potato industry,' Xavier says, pointing to the tag line on the front cover, his bed hair messy and unkempt.

'Are you sure he's not the *only* journalist in the potato industry?' I ask, and Xavier shrugs as if my question was genuine. I don't have time to discover the source of his whimsy right now but if it results in him harvesting some home-cooked chips I'm here for it.

I sink into one of two crusty old armchairs and breathe in some second-hand smoke, still cradling the note in my hand. What the hell am I going to do? About any of this?

'Coffee?' Xavier grunts and I nearly fall off my chair; not only because one of the legs is wonky and every sit is a risk, but because he's not offered to make me coffee in the whole year we've lived here. I wasn't sure he knew how to. I nod, reluctantly as I'm *still* not sure he knows how to.

'You seem a little stressed lately,' he says, as he puts his spliff on a colourful plate in the middle of our coffee table before making his way to the kitchen. Oh man, is this to do with my drunken outpour, me not wanting to be myself? I thought I'd got away with that. I hold the note a little tighter. But can I really let Jake get away with *this*?

'Penny for your thoughts?' Xavier says, and given that he actually went busking as a first-time flutist last Saturday, I'm not sure whether I should start searching for coppers.

'I guess,' I begin, before stopping myself. Between Anna and Jake and Reese and Will, I'm confused enough as it is. Do I really need Xavier's mind in the mix? But then, I really, *really* need to talk to someone. Plus, it's highly likely that he's too high to remember this. 'I took something that doesn't belong to me...' A note, a *name*.

'My shaver?' Xavier says, heaping ground beans into the cafetiere. 'Thought so.'

'No, not your shaver,' I say, my eyes searching his overgrown facial hair for any signs of grooming and coming up short (unlike said facial hair).

'Then I guess that one remains a mystery,' he muses, and I try not to overthink what this could possibly mean – for his shaver and *our* bathroom.

'I took something because I think I might be able to help a friend with it.'

'Then what's to worry about?' Xavier says, as if everything is so simple.

'I'm worried the person I took it from will realise it's gone,' I say, remembering again how that thought had plagued me throughout the night. If I was hiding something like that, I'd check it again and again and again. I look down at the note and realise that I already am. What will Jake say if he realises it is gone? If he realises I am the one who took it?

'Then put it back?'

'But I'm also worried that if I don't use it to help my friend then she might get hurt.'

'Are you *the friend*?' Xavier narrows his eyes, moving towards me to plonk a steaming cup of coffee in my hand. I slowly take a sip and am surprised to find it's lovely.

'I can see why you'd think that,' I begin, narrowing my eyes to match his. Is this something he learnt when I found him reading *Counselling Skills for Dummies* a while back? 'But I'm not the friend,' I say, thoughts of using Anna's name rushing through my mind. Needless to say, they make me feel worse.

'Well in that case, it's simple,' Xavier says. *Is it?* 'Homer's *Odyssey*.' *Say, what now?* 'Odysseus had to choose between Scylla and Charybdis...'

'Xavier,' I say, reaching a hand to his arm. It's the first time we've touched all year – well, sober. 'In English please.' I breathe deeply for the first time since leaving Anna's last night and wonder whether it's the weed-smoke or this conversation that's calming me down.

'The lesser of two evils,' he goes on. 'Which is worse, the risk of this person finding out you took what you did or not doing the thing that may help your friend?'

My mind floods with images of Anna on the morning of her wedding day. Usually, when I let my daydreaming drift here, my emotions are mixed. Happiness for my friend and a pain in my heart for me. I once thought we'd do everything together, reach every milestone together, follow every dream together. But somewhere along the line our trains started moving on different tracks, so subtly at first that it was easy to miss, but now, a decade on, the distance between us is so stark that I sometimes wonder if it is too great to bridge. Today, I imagine her in her gown, gliding down the aisle towards a man she trusts with her whole heart, who she trusts to be there for her, to care for her, to forsake all others for...

'I need to call the number on that note,' I say, my heart throbbing at the thought.

'What number? What note?' Xavier says, reaching for his spliff again.

'Thanks Xavier.' I stand to my feet. 'You've been a big help.'

'Have I?' he says, and I'm not sure which of us is more surprised.

Rushing back to my room, I sit on the bed and study the numbers on the note for the final time. I can't believe I'm saying this, but Xavier is right. If this was one rogue number from one rogue night, I may be able to leave it alone. But whatever Jake was doing on that call yesterday evening was shady. Not that I'm one to talk. But using Anna's name was never about her – not really – it was about me. About me becoming a person I want to be. Successful, brave, courageous. The kind of woman who would mooch around Borough Market with a handsome man and enter a competition with strangers. The kind of woman who would be so happy in herself that she wouldn't think twice about backing her friend. The kind of woman that without a shadow of a doubt would call the number on this note because to ignore it might mean her best friend marries into the worst mistake of her life.

Before I can think better of it, I begin to type in the numbers on the note into my phone. Slowly at first but then with more and more speed. I need to find out who she is – who she is to Jake, what she means for Anna's happily ever after.

Reese's mobile. I read the words as they appear on my screen. I can't answer the phone to her now, can't get distracted. I delete the number and start again. *Reese's mobile.* What the hell? I try to key the number in one more time, but my phone recognises the digits again. *Reese's mobile.* The number on that note, the number that Jake was calling last night is *Reese's mobile.* But how? There's no way.

With shaking hands, I press call and wait for the person on the other side to pick up, praying for it to be anybody but her. There's got to be some sort of mistake. Reese is dating a bad boy, someone not to be trusted, someone I once thought might be Will but I never dreamed could be Jake.

With limbs trembling and heart hammering, I listen to the dial tone and then there's silence, a deep inhale and then *her* voice.

'Anna! I was just about to call you,' Reese says. I think I'm going to be sick.

'Reese?' I choke. Jake's mystery woman can't be her; it just can't be.

'You called *me*, you idiot.' Reese laughs down the line, every bit as infectious as the first time I met her at the Hotel Hyde – the same Hotel Hyde whose logo was on Jake's stupid note. So, he didn't just spend the night with someone there but with someone who *worked* there as well. 'Of course, it's me,' she goes on. *Of course, it's her.* 'What's up?'

'Nothing,' I stammer, a lump catching in my throat, my stomach sinking to the floor.

'Good, because something's happened...' Reese says.

You can say that again.

'...we got in.'

CHAPTER FIFTEEN

Shit, shit, shit. My mind curses in cue with each step I take in the direction of Sloane Star's offices. I thought walking would calm me down, but I think it's making everything worse. *Reese* is the person who gave her number to Jake that night. *Reese* is the person who has been meeting with Jake every time Anna has turned her eye. *And Reese* is the reason I've just got one step closer to all of my dreams coming true. We got in. I can't believe we got in. Well, not in but through, through to the next round of the competition. But there's no way I can carry on working with her, not now that I know she's the other woman; that my dream is wrapped up with Anna's worst nightmare. I need to tell Anna everything. But how can I without telling her that I took that note, without her thinking that I'm trying to meddle? And *what* am I going to tell her? I need to talk to Reese first. I need to find out the truth.

Walking over Westminster Bridge, I try to let the sight of the river relax me, but not even if I was back home imbibing Xavier's second-hand smoke could you calm me down today.

The producers have asked to meet with us again to congratulate us and go over the next stage of the competition. On any other day, under any other circumstances, this would be the most exciting thing to ever happen to me. It *is* the most exciting thing to ever happen to me. But it's also as Anna. It's also with *Reese*.

I look down at my phone to see Reese's name lighting up the screen, the way it had when I'd keyed in the numbers on that note for the first time. I couldn't talk to her then, couldn't find the words to tell her that she needs to stay the hell away from Anna's fiancé, but I will when I see her. I'll confront her about *everything*, I'll tell her who I really am. I want this opportunity more than anything but one damn thing: my best friend's happiness.

Quickening my pace, I make my way deeper into Westminster and look up to see a bunch of media people and paparazzi huddled outside the Houses of Parliament. Their drama is about to be nothing compared to what goes down with Reese and myself today. How dare she mess with a soon-to-be married man? My *best friend's* soon-to-be married man.

'Anna!' I hear her name being called behind me. 'Anna?' Someone shouts again before coming to pant by my side. I turn to see Cameron there, a bit out of breath, his cheeks a little pink. 'Didn't you hear me shouting your name?'

'Oh, sorry,' I say, my own cheeks flushing with colour. 'In a world of my own.' I turn to face him. 'What are you doing here?'

Cameron's eyes search me for a second, his lips lingering apart like he's about to say something and then he closes them, forcing a smile to cross his face before finally saying, 'If I told you, I'd have to kill you.'

I hold his gaze, trying to work out just how much he saw of me and Will last time we were rehearing in the Hyde Out, whether I should mention the kiss or if explaining it away would make me look even more guilty than I already do. 'Some MPs are planning to host an event at the hotel.' He nods up to the iconic building behind us, glistening bronze, yellow and orange in the sunshine, giving me yet another moment of grace. 'How about you? Off anywhere exciting?'

'Yeah actually,' I say, not knowing how much to tell him about the competition either. He probably knows everything from Reese already. 'Reese's show got through to the next round of that competition; we're just heading to see the producers now.'

'With Will?' Cameron asks, his normal confidence marred for a moment. *Shit.*

'Yes.' I nod slowly. 'I bet you've seen most of the scenes already.' I force a laugh.

'I feel like I've seen a lot,' Cameron says as my face falls to match his. How do I even begin to explain that I am not cheating on my fiancé? 'But honestly Anna,' he goes on, shaking his head as if to shake away the thought, trying to steer us back onto steadier ground, 'that's amazing. You must be so pleased.' The warmth in his smile soothes me from the inside out until his grin wavers and he adds, 'And your fiancé must be so proud.'

'Yeah, he...' I stammer, wanting to scream the truth right across the square. But what would Cameron say if I did? Here's a ruddy great tab for Anna's treats and my time? 'He is,' I force out, barely above a whisper.

'Anna, is everything okay?'

'Yeah?' I say, even though it couldn't be further from the

truth. I'm en route to confront Reese about cheating with Jake, severing my ties to the competition for good.

'I mean...' Cameron goes on reluctantly, as if he's over-stepping the mark. 'With your fiancé... and the wedding and the venue search and everything?' He brings the question back into his domain.

'Yeah?' I repeat, wishing the word didn't sound so much like a question.

'Because if it wasn't, you could like... talk to me?' Cameron says as I study his face, his beautiful jaunty smile, and hold his kindness to my heart.

'Things are fine,' I say quickly. 'We'll let you know about the venue soon.' Cameron's face falls and I feel the force field of whatever is drawing us together pop.

'Anyway, I best be getting in,' Cameron says slowly, as if swanning into Parliament is no biggie for the Cameron Cavill-Joneses of this world. 'Good luck today, Anna.'

'Thank you,' I say, feeling a sadness tightening my chest. *I'm going to need it*, I think as I walk away from Cameron and further towards Reese. Just moments ago, I was ready to explode at Reese, for my adrenalin to power my accusations, to let her know that she's a liar and a cheat. To demand the truth so that I can give it to Anna. But now, after one encounter with a man with more integrity than I have in my little finger, I hardly feel like the cover girl for candour. In fact, the quivering legs beneath me feel barely strong enough to stand on.

Loosing myself in the crowds around Buckingham Palace, I try to trace my way through the tourists. This will be okay; everything has to be okay. I don't need a stupid competition anyway, it's not worth betraying my best friend for. I may have had a pretty big dry spell since well, graduating, but I'll get another audition, another opportunity – and soon.

My phone buzzes in my pocket and I look down to see Billie Forester's name on the screen. That really was soon. My heart leaps, the way it always does when I see her name – a welcome reminder that I have at least one person still fighting for me.

'Mary! Hello!' Billie sings. Well, fighting for *Mary*.

'Hey Billie, how are you? How are things? I've not heard from you for...' I begin, my feet picking up pace on the pavement. If she's got something for me, it'll sure as hell make it easier to turn my back on Reese, Will and the competition now.

'Yes, well, that's what I was calling about, Mary,' Billie says with a sigh.

'It's Marley,' I remind her, slowing my pace to take in Eaton Square Gardens from the other side of the fencing, the private greenery reserved the higher echelons of society.

'That's what I said,' Billie replies, and this is why I don't remind her more often. 'Marley, we need to talk...'

'Are you breaking up with me?' I joke but the silence that stretches between us suddenly makes my sentence feel more serious than I intended it to.

'Sorry, Mary. I know this must be difficult for you but it's just not working out.' *It's Marley.* 'We've been trying to get you work for a while,' Billie goes on. I don't feel like I need this recap; I'm the one who's living it, who's struggling to pay my rent, who's unable to afford the hen party I'm planning. 'I just think we should bring your representation to a close so that I can concentrate on other clients...' I struggle to stop the *we should see other people* parallels from running through my mind. She *is* breaking up with me. '...and you can concentrate on other opportunities too.'

'I see,' I say, tears starting to prickle in my eyes. I've put so much on hold for the carrots she has dangled, and now she doesn't even care enough to bring out the stick. Plus, I don't have any other *opportunities*, plural. I only have one.

'Take care, Mary.'

My name is Marley.

It takes all my strength not to slump down the fence to perch on the edge of the pavement. Having an agent was the last stamp of credibility I had, my only reason for not facing the recruitment for recruitment sites months ago. I float down the street, still walking towards my original destination even though now I feel directionless. This can't be happening; it can't be over. Eventually, I turn a corner, down the final street of my journey.

'Anna,' I hear someone calling from behind me, and I see Will there, walking just a few steps behind me. 'Anna, is everything okay?' he asks, on seeing my sorry expression. And just like that, the tears start to fall. 'Oh, Anna,' he says again, throwing his arms around me and holding me close, his chin nuzzled for a moment on my neck. 'Everything's going to be okay,' Will says, even though he has no idea what's even happened. I want to tell him I'm Marley, to have him hold *me* and tell *me* everything's going to be okay. 'What's happened?'

'My agent just called,' I say, through tears, too tired to pretend. 'She dropped me.'

'Dropped you?' Will says, pulling away to look at me, his hands still on my sides.

'Yeah, said she'd stop representing me,' I sob. 'She's struggled to get me work.'

'But you're wonderful,' Will says, his smile kind and warm.

'I'm a *fraud*,' I say, fresh tears making track-marks down my face.

'No, you're not,' Will assures me, shaking his head. 'You're a smart, talented, beautiful woman,' he goes on, and I cry even harder. I feel like such an idiot. 'And you don't need her anyway, we're going to win this competition, I can feel it.'

'I...but...' I begin, knowing that Reese is going to arrive any second and start asking questions. And I've got questions for her too, questions that will put a stop to my part in this competition in an instant.

'And honestly,' Will says, an earnest expression on his face, 'I need this more than I first made out. I thought I'd have my big break by now too, we all did.'

I look at him, seeing the vulnerability on his chiselled face. He needs this. I need this. And we really don't need me screwing it up now.

'Hey guys,' Reese says from behind us and Will moves his hands from me instantly. 'Everything okay?' she asks and I draw a blank. No, everything's not okay. You've cheated with my best mate's fiancé but you're the only reason I might be able to act again. 'Ready to win one hundred thousand pounds?' And then there's *that*. As Reese walks past us to climb up the three stone steps to Sloane Star's front door, I know walking away from her, from *this*, from the money, is going to be much, much harder than I thought.

'Take a seat,' Jerry says, as soon as we've walked into the audition room. The same four producers are sitting in the very same seats we performed in front of just yesterday.

Never in my wildest dreams did I think we'd be back here so soon, that things would escalate so quickly – or even move ahead at all. Even without being dumped by my agent or sat next to the *other woman* this would be hard to take in. Right now, it feels impossible.

I look from Deep V, who I now know is called David Jones (and who is wearing another statement T-shirt, this time in bright yellow) back to portly-looking Jerry, to the strong but silent man in his sixties, and finally to Tanya Moore. She catches my eye and I swear I see her give me a little wink. She looks even cooler than yesterday, this time with half of her braids piled up high on her head, the rest cascading like a waterfall down her back.

'Will, Reese, Anna,' David continues, nodding to each of us in turn. I see Tanya rolling her eyes and I wonder whether it's because he addressed Will first – when Reese's idea is the only reason we are here. *Reese is the only reason we are here.* I glance at her again, feeling this morning's anger melting away. Just a couple of hours ago everything seemed so black and white, right and wrong. But now, it all seems grey.

'The reason we've called you in today is twofold,' David continues, gesticulating dramatically with both hands. 'Firstly, to congratulate you on getting through to the next round of the competition.' He pulls his hands together to give us a camp little clap. Tanya looks at him like he's an idiot again and I try not to laugh. 'Secondly, to go over the next stages of the process again. We could have just emailed you but...'

'That's not nearly as dramatic,' Tanya steals the end of his sentence. Reese and I both laugh whilst the rest of the room stay silent; she looks at me and smiles.

'Not nearly as *personal*,' David corrects, the tension

between them palpable. 'As we mentioned last time, we now need you to map out the first six episodes of your show in their entirety to give us a feel of the breadth and depth of the story...' He uses his hands to reach up then across as if we need the visual cues. He sounds like every person I've ever been cornered with at one of those awful industry networking events. Maybe if I went to more of them, I wouldn't have been dropped by my agent. 'And as you've no doubt seen from the contracts we've given to you, the final two groups will go on to produce their pilot so that we can see how they read on-screen,' David goes on, his veneers as blinding as his shirt.

'Provided the terms of the agreement are acceptable, of course,' Tanya chips in.

'They are,' Will replies quickly. If they are, he's not told us about them. But then, he's hardly had a chance to, not when I was drowning him with my tears. Plus, I can't imagine they'll be an issue for me. A small cut of *something* is better than no cut of nothing.

'Will, you're the main point of contact on the contract, is that right?' Jerry asks him, as if this should be obvious. Will looks from Reese to me, before nodding. 'And the two of you are happy for Will to negotiate on your behalf?' Now it's mine and Reese's turn to nod.

'You have all read the contract, haven't you?' Tanya says, narrowing her striking brown eyes at me before moving her gaze to Reese. We both continue nodding enthusiastically. At least, we will before we sign anything. 'Good, make sure you do.'

'Then if your pilot is *the one*, the prize money is yours and the future is bright,' David beams; clearly, contractual terms and commercial realities are a bit of a downer in his eyes. Why talk about money when you can be busy making it?

The future is bright. If you think you've heard that one a lot, come back to me when your surname is actually Bright. I started today wanting to get as far away from this opportunity as possible, but now, I'm drawn to it like a moth to David's bright yellow tee.

Stepping out of Sloane Star's offices and onto the street, I feel like a different woman from the angry one Cameron bumped into this morning, or the devastated one that Will found on the very corner we're all walking towards now. Against a backdrop of lies and deceit there is a chance to turn everything around, to turn my whole damn life around.

'I can't believe this is actually happening,' Reese says as soon as we're safely out of view. Nor can I. And I can't believe it's happening with *her*. 'But it's not over yet...' she continues, and I glare in her direction: *it had better be over with Jake, or else I...* What, Marley, what are you going to do? Surely, there's a way I can be loyal to Anna and still be a part of this? Just go through the motions, get the experience, the exposure, the money – money that will enable me to actually enjoy helping Anna plan her wedding without having heart palpitations about the cost. That's if there is a wedding. *Damn you, Reese.*

'Yeah, we've got some serious work to do,' Will says, giving my side a squeeze. He's trying to assure me that I'll be okay without an agent and right now I actually feel like I might be. Provided I don't kill Reese before our time in the competition is through.

'Oh, and we clearly need to look at that contract a little closer,' she says, noting Tanya Moore's insistence that we do our due diligence. 'Are you sure your agent can't take a look at it?'

'My dad's already looking over it,' Will says, saving me from having to tell Reese about my recent dumping until I'm ready. I smile at him, willing him to receive my silent: *thank you.* 'He should have everything checked over soon. And trust me, it's better that we negotiate through one person otherwise these things can get really messy.' Clearly, Will has self-elected himself as our spokesperson but it sounds like he's the best man for the job.

'Do you not think we should take a look too?' Reese says, still walking forward, weaving through the throngs of people wandering in the opposite direction to us.

'Would you know what to look for?' Will says, and Reese's face creases in objection. 'Hey!' Will says, throwing his hands up in surrender. 'I don't mean because you're a woman or anything stupid like that.'

'Good, because we women have enough to deal with without chauvinistic men telling us what to believe,' Reese says, and the way she spits the words make me feel like they're coming from somewhere else. *Jake?* I would have never classed him as chauvinistic. But then, I'd never had him down as someone who could cheat. As if I wasn't dealing with enough emotions already, my mind throws some shame into the mix: I'd just assumed that it was Reese who pursued Jake; that somehow it would be her fault. But what if she didn't know? What if he's been lying to her this whole time? *A little bit like you,* my mind berates me as I realise that I've been feeling shame about this situation since it started.

'Yeah, I definitely wasn't saying that,' Will says, as Reese begins to walk forward again. 'All I was saying is that we have a lot to do and if my dad handles that bit, and I deal with

Sloane Star, then we can concentrate on the stuff that may actually make us some money. All we'll need is our bank details and postal addresses for the studio and he can deal with the rest. Trust me, I know how much of a ball ache this stuff can be.'

'Okay,' Reese says, with a smile that suggests she feels bad for going in so hard at him. 'And you're sure you don't mind?'

'I don't mind the extra admin, but only if you guys are happy with that?'

'No, no,' Reese replies quickly; artists hate admin. 'That sounds simple enough.'

I nod even though in my case it's much more complicated. How can I give them Anna's details without getting her any more involved? Reese may even recognise Anna and Jake's address; the thought makes me feel sick. No, I'll have to give Will *my own* details; that thought makes me feel sick too.

'Now that's sorted,' Reese says, pushing her hair out of her face. 'Let's get to work.'

'I thought we were going to celebrate?' Will says, looking disappointed.

'Never heard of multitasking?' Reese says, with a little wink before disappearing through the door of a pub I thought we were just about to walk by.

'Now who's stereotyping?' Will says with a laugh as we both follow her inside.

Some days come and go exactly as you expect them to. No surprises, no curveballs. And though there's no dramatic lows, somehow the monotony can wear you down in the same way. I've had a lot of those days. Days where I've woken up and known exactly how things are going to pan out. Days that were everything I expected but still managed to leave me disappointed because the *unexpected* thing that I was hoping for didn't happen. Today was not one of those days. Today I woke up hating a hypothetical woman at the end of a very real note. Now, I'm sharing a second bottle of wine with the very real woman who wrote it. And until we know how the competition plays out, it's not like I have a choice. Is it?

'I can't believe we're actually doing this,' Reese says, looking up from the papers spread out before us, her drunken enthusiasm wearing away the last of this morning's anger.

'I can't believe it either,' I say, taking another gulp of my wine. Like, really can't believe it. If Anna knew what I was doing right now, who I was with, it would kill her. But then, didn't she ask me to help her find out the truth about Jake? *Maybe this could actually prove useful in the long run.* I try to tell myself anything that will convince me that what I am doing might be the best thing for both of us. At least I know the money will prove useful.

'What are the odds that I would walk into a bar and Cameron would be sitting there with a blushing...'

'Amateur actress,' I say over the end of Reese's sentence, before she can say *bride*.

'You're not an amateur,' Reese objects, sloshing the wine in her hand. Underneath the table, I feel Will's hand reaching for my thigh, giving it a gentle squeeze. We've not mentioned my agent – or ex-agent – since Reese has been around and I'm glad. I want to get my head around it, around *Reese,* first. I smile at him and I feel sure that I can trust him, that my big breakdown is now our little secret. 'But what are the odds?'

'Slim,' I admit, slimmer than she'd ever dare dream.

'And you've turned out to be so *nice*, Anna,' Reese goes on, her words rolling into one another. She's had at least half of the wine we've consumed tonight. *Anna* may be nice, but Marley sure as hell isn't. 'I've not really got any close female friends.'

'No idea why,' Will says, rolling his eyes playfully, poking fun at her as per usual.

'I'm s-serious,' she slurs the words. 'I'm so happy our paths crossed.'

'It's like fate,' Will says, turning to me with a smile that makes me go soft.

'Here's to fate!' Reese says, reaching her glass high into the air.

'And to the future,' Will adds, lifting his glass to clash with hers.

'To fate,' I say, a fate I orchestrated. My mind shifts to Anna's wedding. Have I accidentally befriended the reason it won't happen? How am I going to get out of this? I'm not even sure I *want* to. 'And the future,' I add; a future where I find out what the hell is going on with Reese and Jake and work out what on earth I'm meant to do next.

CHAPTER SIXTEEN

Marley, are you free today to look at flowers? Could do with a second opinion.

'What do you think, Anna?' I look up from real-Anna's latest message to see Reese's face fixed on mine, waiting for me to answer the question. It's been a week since we last met with the producers, on the day when I found out about Reese and Jake. And, I still haven't found out any more about their affair.

'Surely, you must think I'm right?' Will says, his cheeks slightly flushed. I was warned of this competitive nature between them from the off but seeing it play out before me is something else entirely. If I wasn't too embroiled in this script before, I certainly am now. Every decision they lock heads on seems to fall to me to decide. Sometimes I feel like the peacekeeper. Other times, I feel like a creative director. Mostly, I feel needed.

Marrrleyyyyyy. The flowers? I know you're just chilling.

The only problem is, I'm also needed by Anna. Not like the majority of the last few weeks, where she's needed me to vent to, to cry to, to simply sit with. But like before. Like I'm a wedding planner again, or a really niche appetisers agony aunt, or worse, like an assistant. Except now it's even more complicated because of Reese.

'The other woman?' she says, looking deep into my eyes.

'*Pardon?*' I choke.

'Do you think there should be another woman?' Reese says. 'In the script.'

'There's *always* another woman,' Will says, looking down at his own copy like it's a no-brainer. He's wearing his green beanie hat again and has just trimmed his beard; he still looks underdressed for the Hotel Hyde, though.

'That's exactly why we shouldn't write one in,' Reese objects. 'It's too cliché.'

She's one to talk, I think to myself, trying to tamp down my anger. Anna may be happy again but for how long? Until mere days before her wedding when she finds out she's about to marry a man who is cheating on her? Or worse, will she be happy until after she's said, 'I do', eventually finding out the truth when it's already too late? *You could just tell her about the note leading to Reese;* the thought rears in my mind for the thousandth time. But how can I when I was never meant to take it? When I'm scared that Anna won't even believe me? I need more information. I need the facts. I look around the Hyde Out to see some now familiar faces scattered around it, one noticeable one catching my eye from behind the bar.

'*Anna?*' Reese says again, losing patience as she loses my attention. *But does she still have Jake's?* I give Cameron a tired smile before turning back to her.

'I don't entirely see what it adds to the story,' I say, looking her dead in the eye. 'It'll make Jack less likable.' *It certainly makes Jake less likable.* 'Plus, Ella's other love interest is her social media platform, her fans – 1.8 million of them – I think that's enough of a stumbling block for their love to conquer.'

'Thank you,' Reese says, accentuating each word slowly with a hint of *I told you so*.

'Plus, it *is* cliché,' I can't help but add.

'I guess I'll have to be content just kissing you then, Anna,' Will jokes at the exact same moment that Cameron walks past carrying a tray of drinks. I think I spy him shaking his head at Will's words. I don't know why he's in here all the time when we are but a small, crazy part of me hopes it's to see me. Then, I remind myself that he thinks I'm engaged.

'Yeah.' I turn to smile at Will. He clearly doesn't think I'm taken, which is more evidence – along with Reese not knowing about my agent – that the two of them don't share everything. 'Anyone want another drink?' I say, trying to diffuse the tension.

'Two waters and a Diet Coke, please,' I say as soon as I'm at the bar, pulling up a barstool and swinging it around to face Cameron, who is busy sorting out the stock.

'You're going to have to buy something stronger if you want to keep using this as your rehearsal space,' he says, turning around to grin at me with his lovely jaunty smile.

'You trying to get me drunk, Mr. Cavill-Jones?'

'Wouldn't be the first time,' he says, with a wink, grabbing three glasses and starting to fill them up. 'But you know I'm joking. Two waters and a Diet Coke it is.'

'What brings you here?' I say, as if I'm trying out some cheesy chat-up line.

'I work here.' He grins wider still, enjoying the roleplay.

'I actually meant, why are you working behind the bar again?' I ask, leaning my elbows on the top of it. 'Don't you have a fancy-pants hotel to manage?'

'Be careful,' Cameron says, narrowing his eyes at me. 'You're beginning to sound like my dad.'

I wrinkle my nose in dramatic disgust.

'Honestly? It relaxes me,' Cameron says, his shoulders softening as he does. 'When clients and accounts and rubbing shoulders with snooty soon-to-be newlyweds and poncy politicians gets too much, I like to come in here and remind myself how far I've come.' He smiles again. 'I bet that sounds silly.'

'It doesn't.' I shake my head, taking a sip of my Diet Coke. 'Sorry if I was snooty.'

'Oh no, not you,' Cameron says, shaking his head. 'You were nothing like the other people I show around here.' I swear I see his eyes drift to Will. 'You were a breath of fresh air.'

'*Were?*'

'*Are.*' Cameron smiles again. 'How's it going?' He nods over to our table.

'Yeah good,' I say. I want to tell him everything but know my hands are tied.

'Not as much kissing this time,' Cameron says, eyebrows raised, forehead high.

'No,' I say, forcing a little smile. 'We're working through the next six episodes,' I tell him, realising that I should probably get back to them before Cameron has a chance to ask me any more questions about Will or the wedding. I gather the three drinks in my hands.

'I don't know how you balance everything,' Cameron says, shaking his head.

'You're not the only one who used to work in a bar,' I reply with a laugh, picking up the drinks.

'I meant the competition and wedding planning and everything,' Cameron says, his eyes once again searching my face for signs of something – what, I don't know. I shrug, still balancing the drinks; the less said the better. 'Does your fiancé know you spend your time here kissing another man?' Cameron tries to pass this off as a joke. I'm not sure it lands.

'It's all acting,' I say, feeling a bit sad as I do. Cameron's eyes search me again and I wonder whether that's what he's looking for, a little bit of sadness?

'Well, he's a more patient man than me,' Cameron says, with a grin. 'If you were my fiancée and I saw you kissing a man like that' – he looks across in Will's direction – 'I'd be really jealous.'

I smile, as I think it's meant to be a compliment.

'Speaking of patience,' Cameron says, and I know what's coming next. 'I can't hold the date for your wedding for much longer, so just tell me as soon as you decide what you want and we can make it official or settle up your tab with the hotel and see you on your way.'

'Sounds good,' I say, my stomach sinking to the floor. I'm not sure whether I'm going to be seen on my way or forcibly removed from here, but right now, walking back to Will and Reese sat looking over our scripts, I feel like this is the only direction that's right.

Winning this will change everything.

Ooooo and once you get this, I have some questions about the hen party.

I place our drinks on the table and make the mistake of looking at my phone. I know Anna is excited to be planning the wedding again, but it's almost offensive that she assumes that I'm chilling at home with Xavier, as if I have nothing better to do. Though, if she knew the truth about what I was up to, who I was with or where, I'm not sure that would be better. But I need to tell her about Reese just as soon as the competition comes to an end. And wouldn't it be better to be able to tell her everything? To have all the details so that Anna can decide just what the hell to do next?

'Oh good.' Reese looks up at me. 'You're back.'

'We need you again.' Will smiles. 'Well, that creative mind of yours.'

'Will thinks that we should cut the influencers' breakfast scene,' Reese says, thrusting her tattooed arm out in the accused direction.

'Why?' I say, and clearly there's a look of horror on my face as Reese's gesture once again screams: *Look, Will, I told you so.*

'Because he's not in it,' Reese says, with a sly little smile.

'That's not true, I just think it's unnecessary. We know her social media following grows from her scenes with Jack.'

I look to Reese to find her rolling her eyes again.

'Yes, but this breakfast shows what being invited into that world means and her conversations with fake friends there will highlight what a *real* relationship truly is.'

Does Reese know what a real relationship looks like? Is that what she had with Jake? Are they still sharing one together? I force my wandering mind back into the room.

'Anyway, it's staying,' Reese says, slamming her hand down on the script. Case closed. 'And I think we should call it a night. Anyone up for a real drink?'

'No hot date?' Will teases, brushing his hair behind his ears, the same way he did when Reese first disappeared on her 'date', back when I thought she was trying to make him jealous. Reese smiles coyly, her cheeks growing pinker before shaking her head. Is she thinking about Jake? Is my best friend's *fiancé* responsible for that smile? This isn't right, I should be with Anna; my loyalties will *always* be with Anna.

'I'm busy tonight,' I fib, before I'm reminded that Anna has sent me no less than ten messages about the wedding today. Maybe she needs company tonight? Perhaps she's not as okay about things with Jake as she's making out? That would make it easier to tell her what I now know, even though I'm still far from the full story. I look at Reese, gathering up her papers and hate myself for feeling a bit guilty for working out how to tell Anna the truth about Reese and Jake. What if Reese really doesn't know he has a fiancée? What if she's about to get as hurt as Anna is? Then another wave of guilt washes over me: after fifteen years of friendship shouldn't my loyalties be straightforward?

I move away from the table to find a safe space to call Anna and am about to dial her number when Cameron walks dangerously close to me on the way back to the bar. I try to look purposeful as I redirect my route towards the window.

'Hey Anna,' I whisper, knowing all too well I'm running out of safe spaces to hide.

'Marrrlllleyyyy,' she sings down the line. 'I've been messaging you all day.'

For a moment I think she's going to ask me what I've been tied up with. But, no.

'I've landed on the bridesmaid flowers; I went for the Cascading Dusty Rose Deluxe.' She says this as if it's meant to mean something to me. Anna is speaking so fast it's hard to keep up. 'They'll go perfectly with the sage silk dresses – I think I told you I've gone for silk-silk and not the silk-mix, right? They're obviously more expensive but will last you guys so much longer...' Yeah, because I've really got a thousand places to wear a hundred per cent silk floor-length dress. 'I was hoping you guys could all chip in for the price difference as you know, we're getting the flowers and everything. And I've—'

'Anna,' I snap, my tone projecting her name into the room. 'Anna,' I repeat, adjusting my volume to a whisper. 'That all sounds great... but are you... really okay?'

'Why wouldn't I be okay?' Anna replies without pause; she sounds really hyped up.

'It's just been a bit of a rollercoaster these past few weeks and I...'

'I've never been better,' Anna assures me, as I risk a glance across the Hyde Out to Reese, leaning back in her chair, completely at ease. She doesn't look like a woman with a secret – although, I'm hoping she feels the same way about me. 'Oh, and I almost forgot to say, the reason I was calling you was to tell you—'

'I called you,' I remind her; it sounds like her mind is running a million miles an hour, trying to hold everything together. I need to be there for her when everything falls apart.

'Oh right, silly me,' Anna says, not bothering to ask me why I had. I was going to ask whether she wanted me to come over tonight, whether she needed the company but every minute on this call is making me wonder whether she'd even notice I was there.

'Yes, I'm just telling her now,' I hear Anna say and

wonder who she is talking to until I hear her trying and failing to stifle an onslaught of giggles. 'Stop it, Jake.' I hear her wiggle free from his embrace. 'You know how sad we were when we found out the Hotel Hyde slot was booked up?' I try to ignore the pain in my stomach, the one that tells me again that I shouldn't be lying to her. 'Well, we've found the next best thing. We've actually booked a wedding venue! It's two months today – so just the week after the Hen like we planned – it's perfect.' Anna's squeals almost escape from the phone and across the room of her once-dream wedding venue. I don't know whether to feel guilty or relieved. At least there's only going to be one 'Anna' here – one 'Anna' who now has to work out how she's going to pay off a pretty hefty Hotel Hyde tasting tab.

'And the best part is we've booked out the whole hotel for our wedding party,' Anna goes on, forcing out the words amidst more giggles and squeals. It sounds like Jake is nibbling her neck or something. 'Your room is *amazing*,' she goes on. 'We've paid the deposit, so it's all secured.'

'Thanks, how much do I owe you?' I say, panic starting to rise within me. She should have asked me. But just like I couldn't really miss the hen party, it's not like the Chief Bridesmaid can Uber across to the venue from the nearest Premier Inn.

'We paid the seventy-five pounds deposit and don't expect it back,' Anna hums on. 'Our treat.'

'You sure?' I ask. It's a lot of money but I really can't afford anything else right now.

'Of course, we're sure,' Anna says, and I notice that all her 'I's have turned to 'we's again. 'You just need to call the venue and pay the remaining ninety per cent.'

'The room was seven hundred and fifty pounds?' I say, not even trying to hide the terror from my voice.

'Just wait until you see it.' Anna doesn't answer my question. 'It's a *steal*.'

I'm certainly going to need to rob a bank to pay for it.

'Yes, baby.' Anna's voice rings through the figures and digits filling my mind and for a moment I wonder whether she's channelling her inner Austin Powers until she says a little louder: 'Sorry Marley, I've got to go. Jake's just made dinner and it looks *amazing*.'

Everything looks *amazing* to Anna right now, safely back in her bubble of love. But after her call I most definitely need a drink, with Will and the woman who's about to burst it.

'I'm up for that drink,' I say, returning to our table to find Reese gathering up her things. She's got so much stuff you'd be forgiven for thinking she's moved in here, which for all I know she might have. I know I shouldn't, that I should keep things with Reese strictly professional until we know if we've got through to the next round of the competition but it's not like me, Reese and Will haven't had a post-performance debrief before. 'Where's Will?' I ask, searching around the bar for his trademark beanie at his six-foot-four height.

'He's headed home,' Reese says. Because he didn't think I was coming? Back when I was just Marley, I swear I never had this effect on guys – any effect really. Now as Anna, I'm actually starting to feel attractive; a by-product of being unattainable, perhaps? 'But I'm still up for one? It'll be nice to spend some time just the two of us – sober, this time.'

Before I know it, Reese is up on her Converse-clad feet and over to the bar, where I see Cameron pouring out two large glasses of wine, so not *that* sober then. This will be okay. I can just stay for one drink, unwind a little and then head back to mine and just hope that Xavier's juggling hobby hasn't evolved into him hosting a whole damn circus.

'I needed this,' Reese says, taking her first sip of wine. *You and me both.*

'Yeah, tensions seemed high today,' I say; I hope she hasn't noticed any from me. I've been trying to work out how I feel about her all day, how much she knows, whether I dare risk trying to find out more. If I know her secrets, will she try and find out mine?

'Oh, that's just how me and Will are,' Reese says, with a smile, clearly oblivious to any daggers I've thrown her way earlier today. 'We've always been competitive and well...' Reese narrows her eyes and leans forward like she's about to tell me a secret. 'Don't tell him, but his annoying little comments and questions make me better. And when it comes to the commercial stuff, I trust that man with my life.' Reese fixes her brown, almond-shaped eyes on me and they're so gorgeous that for a brief moment I can't blame Jake for falling for her. *But can I blame her?* 'I know he'll always make sure we get what he thinks we deserve.'

'I can't even tell you how much I need that money,' I say, feeling my first sip of wine sliding down my throat, soothing me from the inside and before I know it, the rant starts coming and not even the inappropriateness of my audience can stop it. 'My best friend just booked me a hotel room for her wedding that costs more than my monthly rent. I hate it when people assume that just because something's in their budget, it's in yours. We don't all have dual incomes and paying for everything on your own whilst trying not to bow out of things due to money because we're almost thirty and that's seriously uncool, it's just...'

'Woah, Anna,' Reese says, putting up her hands as if trying to slow me down.

Oh, right. I'm Anna – or at least trying to be. After her phone call today I'm not even sure I want to be. Plus, there's the tiny fact her fiancé might still be cheating on her with the woman in front of me.

'I'm not sure I'm following; you *have* a dual income right...'

'Right,' I say, hurriedly. 'I was meaning hypothetically. I have a lot of single friends.'

'That's so cool that you're even thinking about them,' Reese says, taking another gulp. 'Most people get so loved up that they can't imagine what it's like not to be anymore.'

'I *know*,' I say, instantly feeling guilty for being on the same page as her again.

'But aren't you getting married *here?*' Reese throws her inked arms out to signal the decadence around us.

'Not anymore,' I say, and I watch her face fall.

'Oh Anna, I'm so sorry,' she reaches a hand out towards me across the table.

'Oh no, I meant not *here*,' I say, before I realise that I've not told Cameron this yet. 'We've tried to make the numbers work,' I lie, and I surprise myself at how easily they are coming now. 'But realistically, I just think it's a little out of our price range. I've not had chance to tell Cameron yet though,' I add quickly.

'Don't...' Reese says, and I think she's going to finish her sentence with 'worry' but then she surprises me, for the thousandth time. 'Don't tell him.'

'What do you mean?'

'The date you're holding is in like, what? Three months?' Reese asks.

'Two and a half,' I say, with a little nod. I'm not sure where she's going with this.

'And we should know whether we've been successful with the competition before then,' Reese reasons, her expression emitting genuine empathy. Am I really in a position to judge her for her mishaps and misdemeanours when I have so many of my own? 'So then maybe if we win, you'll still be able to afford your dream wedding – and pay half for your single friends' rooms too.' Reese beams, and I wonder whether the single friends' comment is her wangling for an invite. I'm not sure she'll want to be anywhere near me when she finds out I'm Marley. And more to the point, who the real Anna is.

'Yeah maybe,' I say, and Reese smiles again; it's a smile so warm and genuine that I wonder whether she could really sleep with a soon-to-be married man and be okay with it. Maybe she really doesn't know? 'Are you still seeing that guy, *the less said the better* one?'

'Oh no,' Reese says, looking a little taken aback. 'I'm not seeing anybody, I'm fine by myself, really fine, *love it*,' she says, and the way that she's rambling on tells me she's lying. I have half a mind to press her further but know how defensive she can be. *It's staying.* I recall her words to Will about the scene earlier, the way she just shut the suggestion down because it wasn't what she wanted to hear. I can't imagine she'd want to be accused of cheating either. I'd be out of her team, this competition, quicker than you can say *Anna*.

'I seem to always find the losers and the cheaters, anyway,' Reese goes on and my stomach sinks. Cheaters like Jake? 'Have you ever cheated on a partner?'

'No, of course not,' I say, searching her face for some suggestion of shame. 'You?'

'Never.' Reese shakes her head. '*Would* you?'

'No, of course not,' I say, seemingly stuck on repeat.

'Not even with Will?' she says, eyes narrowing in accusation.

'No,' I say, managing nothing but a whisper; we're both liars. 'Of course not. Bet loads of people are cheating on their partners around here.' I deflect immediately, not knowing what I want Reese to say next. I watch as her eyes scan the Hyde Out, the same place she would have met Jake for the first time. They settle on Cameron behind the bar.

'At least there's one decent man left in the world,' she says with a laugh, taking another sip of her wine but as I do the same, it makes me feel even worse that I'm lying to him too.

CHAPTER SEVENTEEN

I take the route through the park to buy me some time, but I know it's already too late. It's been days since our last phone call and now Anna has asked me out for coffee. The butterflies in my stomach seem to know why: *I've been found out.*

Walking slowly past family members boating on the pond and lovers gliding hand in hand past the Maritime Museum, I marvel again at how Greenwich manages to make me feel like a have-not. I can't remember the last time Anna came to visit me in London Bridge. Well, actually, I can. It was the day she turned up at my front door having first suspected that Jake was cheating on her. But I know this meeting isn't about Jake, it can't be. They've been inseparable ever since their love-struck one-eighty. This has to be about me using her name. Maybe now that she knows the truth about my trip to the Hotel Hyde, I can tell her the truth about everything else: about meeting Reese, about Reese and Jake. I don't want to hurt her. I don't want her to go back to the shell of herself that arrived on my doorstep that day. But isn't the momentary pain better than a lifetime of lies?

Moving monotonously through the wrought-iron gates, I curse myself for thinking that I could get away with it. Of course, the moment that Anna said that she and Jake had found a new venue, she was going to call up the Hyde and take their names off any waiting lists for good. Just imagining Cameron's face as the real-Anna explained that she'd never once stepped foot inside his glorious hotel makes my stomach fall to the floor. As does the thought of the conversation I'm about to have right now.

Stepping into the neon-lit coffee shop, I see Anna sitting at a table for two. For once, she hasn't invited Jake without telling me. Not that I was expecting her to after sending me a single message with those four dreaded words, the words Cameron said on the phone back when me and Anna had just found the note; the words Billie Forester had uttered when she was gearing up to let me go. *We need to talk.* Only this time, I am going to be the one doing the talking, the one coming clean about everything.

'Marley,' Anna says, deadpan, no signs of standing up from her seat.

'Look Anna, I can explain everything,' I say, drawing out my own seat at the small wooden table. I don't even order a coffee first; I'm not sure how long she's going to let me stay. 'That first day I went to the Hotel Hyde, I had just got rejected and I was feeling so...'

'Lauren can't come to my hen party,' Anna blurts out across the table, out across my sentence, her face crumpling in concern as she does. *Pardon?* 'She messaged me a day ago and I've just been going crazy ever since,' Anna says, as my mind struggles to keep up with her words. 'I just needed someone to talk to about it.' *We need to talk.* This is what Anna needed to talk about? Surely, she should know those words are reserved for break-ups and bad news. 'It's *such* bad news,' Anna goes on and I realise that she really thinks this qualifies.

'I'm not sure it's the *worst* thing that could...'

'She's one of my oldest school friends and she's known about it forever,' Anna says, speaking over my sentence completely.

'Well, two months...' I begin, once again reminding Anna of the speed at which she's hurtling through milestones. I still have no idea why she's wanting to get married so soon.

'And now she says she can't afford it!' Anna says, horrified. Is she kidding? I can't afford it. Any of us with normal jobs and normal rent can't afford it. 'I just feel so let down. I want all of my friends to be there for me, for it all to be perfect.'

That damn P-word again. I used to admire Anna for it, for her determination, for her drive to build a life that was better than the one she grew up with. But now I feel like she's missing the point. She's majoring on minors so much that she can't even see the massive great mountains in the way of now and her perfect big day. I just want to get through to her, to tell her it's okay that things aren't okay, that we can face it all, together.

'I do think it's quite expensive for a hen party,' I say reluctantly – exacerbating this drama any more is only going to distract from the massive one awaiting her, the one I still haven't had the balls to blurt out.

'Are you going to drop out too?' she snaps across the table.

'No,' I say quickly, even though I have no idea how I'm going to afford it. *The competition*, I remind myself. Winning this damn competition is going to afford it. I'll just have to keep Anna out of my messed-up loop a little longer.

'Good,' Anna says. 'Because I need you there.' She reaches a hand across the table and I take it reluctantly. I search her face for signs of my best friend, the one who had last turned up at my door because she needed me, and spent the day snuggled up in my bed with me, plotting how to find out what Jake was up to. Right now, she's oscillating between a sickeningly sweet soon-to-be newlywed and a bridezilla. I'm not sure which is worse.

'I'm going to be there,' I say, giving her hand a squeeze. If there's any wedding to be at. My stomach flips at the thought. Surely, Anna knows something is still up? Or why would she be trying this hard to keep everything together? Deep down, I know I need to tell her about Reese soon. But how? And what? I've still not got the full story yet.

'And I know Lauren wants to be there too,' I begin, as I hope she's going to be able to pay me back for that deposit. Just like I'm going to have to pay Anna's new venue back for that room, and Anna's last dream venue for the costly memories I've racked up with Cameron. 'But I think the hen party is just a bit too short-notice for everyone to save up.'

'We're not teenagers saving up our pocket money,' Anna snaps again and I wonder whether she can even remember how she spent her teenage years, drinking Red Stripe lager in the park with our friends because it was the only thing she could afford. Part of me misses being those teenagers; I know a lot of me misses that girl.

'No,' I say, treading the thin line I know it will take for her to not turn her anger back at me. The last thing I need is for Anna to fall out with me now. I was going to tell her everything, but once again, now doesn't feel the right time. 'I wonder if you just slowed things down a bit,' I press on, pushing all thoughts of the competition and Reese from my mind. 'It might give everyone else time to catch up.'

That's all I've ever needed, Anna, just time to catch up with you, I think before I can push that thought away too. The competition is my chance to do just that.

'What are you saying?' Anna asks, her face like thunder.

'I'm just wondering if you could slow down the wedding plans a little, push them back a bit to buy you some more time...'

'I don't want any more time,' Anna says. 'I'd marry Jake tomorrow if I could.'

'But just a week or so ago you thought he was cheating on you,' I probe, sensitively.

'I've told you,' Anna says, her fierce eyes fixed on mine. 'I was wrong.'

No, you weren't, Anna, I think but know I can't tell her that now, not until I know more: more about what's going on with Jake and Reese, more about what's going to happen next.

'Why can't everyone accept that I'm happy?' Anna says and the fact she's on the edge of tears seems to undermine her sentence somewhat. 'I've got my dream flat and my dream job and now...'

I might be on the way to getting my dream job too, I think as I listen to Anna rattle on and on. I love her to pieces, I always have, but this is almost unbearable. I thought her happy-go-lucky turnaround was too good to be true but even that is better than this. At least when I spend time with Reese and Will they seem interested in me, interested in my life, my opinions. And not just about which of two ludicrous options I can't even hope to afford.

I look across the table at Anna, now onto her tenth 'perfect' in just two minutes and try to muster some empathy – whether she admits it or not, she's going through a lot. But here I was thinking she wanted to talk about me. She hasn't asked me about my work once, about acting jobs or otherwise. She hasn't asked about home, or Xavier or my love life or my agent. And I've been glad, as I've been trying to work out how to wiggle out of using her name without her getting hurt. But the fact she's not asked me once? Well, that really hurts too.

'Anyway,' Anna sighs, coming to the end of her soliloquy, 'I should probably be heading off now.' She looks at her chunky wristwatch. 'Jake will be on his way home now.'

'Where's he been?' I say, trying to sound casual even though by now, I'm pissed off. I thought Anna would be hurting deep down but I think she's even managed to fool herself.

'At work, I think,' Anna says, and a hint of insecurity darts across her face. I wonder about pressing her further but before I can, my phone begins to buzz on the tabletop.

Dinner later?

'Who's Will?' Anna says, her eyes widening with a curiosity long overdue. I know I should keep my answers vague, that any details could lead to disaster, but after listening to Anna rant on about her perfect life for the past hour, I really can't help myself.

'He's an actor I've been working with on a big television project,' I say, letting the pride of this confession warm me from the inside out. It's risky but it's unlikely that Anna would ever follow up with one of my 'work things' at the best of times, never mind when she has the lead role in her own wedding drama. Given how she's been going on today I might even be able to convince myself that steering her away from the Hotel Hyde was actually doing Cameron and the other employees a favour.

'Why didn't you say anything?' Anna replies, reluctantly.

Because you didn't ask. Because I'm busy being you...

'Is it like a *thing*?' Anna goes on and now I've started I can't seem to stop.

'It might be,' I say, allowing a smile to insinuate that it's much more, like Reese had when she had first mentioned his name. My stomach tumbles at the thought.

'What's he like?' Anna asks, and my face falls. The fact that Anna's interest has gone straight for the boy and not the job speaks volumes. She's listened to me talking about the next big thing, my next big break, too many times to buy it now; I'm the girl who cried wolf.

'You know Charlie Hunt?' I begin, knowing I've already said too much.

'The actor?' Anna's eyes light up; her expression reminds me of how she looked the first time I told her I had been signed to an agency, back when my acting felt ambitious and not amateur.

'It's his son,' I say, and Anna's eyes grow wider still, along with her smile.

'It's his s*on*?' Anna puts her hands to her face in glee. I feel a warmth shoot through my body as I recognise the excitable, enthusiastic girl my best friend used to be. 'Jake *loves* him.' I suspect she means Charlie and not Will, but it doesn't really matter; we're back to it being all about Jake again. 'He wants to go for dinner tonight? We *have* to double-date.'

Jake, Anna, 'Anna' and Will? There's no way. But it's too late, Anna is already swiping on her phone and putting it to her ear. *My nickname is Marley...* I try my next lie on for size, the one I'm no doubt going to have to tell Will tonight. Or I could just tell him the truth? He's not told Reese about my agent, or about our kiss; clearly, he can keep a secret too.

'Jake! You're never going to believe this.'

I look at Anna as she practically buzzes down the line, yet another mood swing to indicate how emotionally unstable planning this wedding is making her become.

'Marley's only gone and started dating Charlie Hunt's son... you know, Charlie... Will Hunt... yeah, I think he's been in some smaller things...'

Anna looks at me with a big grin as she goes on, but the way she says 'smaller things' makes me feel like once again she doesn't really get my world. Even Will's smallest roles are bigger than anything I've managed to achieve.

'Anyway, we were thinking,' Anna goes on as I mentally correct her: no, *you* were thinking. 'That we should all grab dinner tonight,' she continues, but somewhere between her excited explanations, her face starts to change. At first, from excitement to confusion. Then, from confusion to surprise. Then finally, from surprise to flirtation. 'Oh okay, baby. That sounds nice. Stop it, you're making me blush,' Anna goes on.

Eventually, she hangs up the call and I gaze across at her unclear expression, trying to work out my double-date fate. *My nickname is Marley?...*

'Sorry, Marley,' Anna says but from the look of her smile, she doesn't seem sorry at all. 'Jake says he'd rather it just be the two of us tonight.' She grins, back to her previous loved-up soonly-wed status. 'He doesn't want to share me.'

Jake might not want to share her but he's definitely

sharing himself. I try to get mad at him, to stay mad at him for what he's done, for his part in the tangle I've found myself in; stuck between his two women when he promised to be faithful to one. But sat across from Anna, having traipsed across the city to see to her for an 'emergency' only to be talked over and looked over, I know the person I'm really mad at is her. I've been driving myself crazy working out how to be there for her, how to protect her, but as she stands to leave, turning to give me one of those pat-on-the-back hugs that makes you feel even further apart than when you were standing across from each other, I wonder just when she stopped trying to protect me.

CHAPTER EIGHTEEN

I take a deep breath as I walk into the restaurant. I know I shouldn't be here, not as Anna. But, after my coffee with the real Anna earlier, after hearing her laments about Lauren, I know I need someone to talk to, someone who will actually listen to me. Plus, Jake royally rejecting a double-date has kind of made me want to prove to myself just how fun Will and I can be.

'Can I help you?' a tall, blonde woman asks me from behind a neat reception desk. My mind is instantly cast back to my first visit to the Hotel Hyde but unlike then, this woman is smiling at me. Unlike then, I could actually kid myself I belong here.

'I'm meeting someone here,' I say, letting the sentence soothe me. It's been a long time since I've been on a date. Not that this is a date.

'Name?' she asks, as another staff member offers to take my jacket.

'Marley... Anna,' I correct myself, as my cheeks pinken.

'Hmmm, there doesn't seem to be anything under that

name,' the maître d' muses, eyes scanning over her screen. No Marley Anna? Funny that.

'I think it's booked under Will Hunt,' I add, and her eyes widen in recognition.

'He's already here,' she says, face beaming. 'Let me show you to your table.'

Before I know it, the slender woman is steering me through the restaurant. As I follow in her elegant strides, two or three sets of eyes turn our way. I straighten my posture as she enters another, more private section of the restaurant; this is as close to being on the runway as I'll ever be. Gliding across the small back room, I notice the twinkling lights lining the hexagonal space are reflecting again in the glass ceiling, before I catch Will's eyes shining back at me. The maître d' nods at us before retreating back to her desk, leaving me and Will alone.

'You booked out the whole space?' I say, not even pretending to act cool about it.

'I know you don't like an audience,' Will replies, standing to his feet as I remember how nervous I'd been that first time we'd run lines together. He leans into me and for a moment I think he's going to kiss me again before he passes my lips to kiss my cheek. 'But no,' he concedes, turning to pull out my seat from the table. 'I haven't booked the space, I just asked Abs to fill up the front of the restaurant before seating people in the back.' He says this like it's no big deal, but the fact he even has the confidence to ask something like this is foreign to me.

'Thanks,' I say, taking my seat. Someone pulling a chair out for me is pretty new too. 'So, how's your day been?' I ask, my nervousness powering our small talk. *I shouldn't be here.*

'It's been good, thanks,' Will says, looking a little taken

aback by the question. It's a normal conversation starter but something tells me that after sharing salvia as much as we have, he doesn't see the need for such wooden lines. 'Yours?' he asks, lifting a bottle of champagne out of the wine cooler and reaching over the table to pour me a glass.

'Better now,' I say, looking from my champagne flute to him. He lifts his glass to mine, and I know to meet him in the middle. We hold eye contact the whole time.

'That bad?' he asks, laughing over the rim of his glass before taking a sip.

'No, not *that* bad,' I say, my conversation with Anna feeling further and further away. I look around the fairy-lit room and wonder whether she and Jake would even be welcome to join us tonight if they wanted to. It feels kind of romantic and I'm running out of reasons not to slide into the vibe. 'Just my best friend turning into a massive bridezilla,' I say, instantly wishing I hadn't. *That's* the reason I'm not letting myself go here, *Anna*. My eyes search Will's beautiful, rugged face for his reaction, a hint of a *it takes one to know one* or *are you sure your friends don't say the same about you?* But there's nothing.

'Oh, I hate that,' Will says, with a little smile. 'I'm not sure when everyone got the memo that it was time to settle down.' He shakes his head.

I wait for a moment longer, positive he's going to say something about my apparently forthcoming nuptials. But there's nothing. I think he really doesn't know.

'Tell me about it,' I say, taking another slurp of champers, my shoulders softening.

'Don't get me wrong, I'm open to meeting someone,' Will says, sending me a coy smile across the table. Does he mean *me?* 'But it's just not my priority.'

'No, me neither,' I say, as I realise that's actually true. I've spent so much of the past few years feeling like I *should* have a partner, that I *should* be settling down, that I was out of step for still holding onto my misplaced childhood dreams. Could it be that I was just trying to keep in step with the wrong people?

'So, what *is* your priority, Anna?' Will says, and my heart drops. I feel like we're connecting but on a stupid, rocky basis. *But what's in a name...*

'My career,' I say, unapologetically. It still is, that's still okay. 'You?'

'You,' Will says as my heart starts throbbing in my chest. 'And Reese, and this competition,' he adds, and I take another gulp of my champagne. Will soon tops me up. It's only then that I notice the cuffs of his sleeves, that under his thin black jumper he's actually wearing a shirt. 'Sorry if I've been coming on a bit strong.'

The kiss? The one Cameron definitely saw. I curse his face for coming into my mind again. The only reason we met was because he was showing me around 'my' wedding venue. But Will seems to think I'm single. Either that or he doesn't care. I drain my flute again. After today, I'm not sure I want to care tonight either.

'That's just how Reese and I can get sometimes...' Will continues, and I stall on the words. What is he talking about? 'With the script,' he confirms, clocking my confusion.

'Oh right, yeah, it was tense,' I say, accepting another glass. Will looks remorseful at the thought. I want to tell him that him and Reese arguing was the least of my worries, that I have my own reasons for having tension with Reese.

'I know it's her script,' Will goes on, topping up his own glass of champagne and turning the bottle neck-down in the cooler with a nod to the nearest waitress. I really hope he's paying for this. 'But I do think that as the people who are performing it, we know what feels right.' He rests his bearded chin in his hands and smiles across the table at me.

This feels right. But no, it can't. Will thinks I'm Anna. Though, given where her attention is right now, I'm not sure she'd ever find out. I'm not even sure she'd care.

'And contrary to what she thinks,' Will says, a little smile turning up the corners of his mouth, a mouth I already know so well, 'Reese isn't always right.'

Well, I know that much.

'The contract's almost sorted by the way,' Will goes on, and the knot in my stomach reminds me that I'm not in the right either. 'I still need your bank details and postal address though.'

I may have been able to fib my way into this competition, but I know I can't lie about this. Not on a contract. Not when I really, really need the money to be *mine.*

'Why did you really think we should cut out the influencer's brunch scene?' I say, ignoring his question completely, trying to steer the conversation back onto steady ground. I'll work out what I'm going to do about the contract soon, I have no choice not to.

'Oh I...' Will stutters, stalling on my sudden change in conversation. 'It won't date well,' he continues. 'If our pilot gets picked up, it will take a while to produce and get to market and by that point, people might be over the whole Instagram thing.'

'Over Instagram? Do you really think that?' I ask, remembering Reese's words about him simply wanting more screen time. Will fixes his kind eyes on me and I realise that unlike her, unlike *me*, he's given me no reason not to trust him.

'I do,' he smiles. 'Take Facebook for example, that's already getting less popular amongst millennials. And there's always something new around the corner. Our generation always seems to want something *more*,' he muses, and I have to admit he's right. I could have never seen this, the competition, *him*, coming and now that they have, I'm struggling to let the promise of more not overrule my reason. 'I just want us to be one step ahead.'

As if on cue, a waiter appears holding two large platters in our hands. 'I ordered for us,' Will says. *One step ahead.*

'There's so much food,' I say, eyeing up the colourful array of tapas from the steaming *patatas bravas* to the salt-scattered Padrón peppers.

'Life's too short not to try everything,' he says, that same glimmer of mischief shining in his eyes. It may be the champagne talking, but I'm beginning to think that Will's philosophy of trying everything might even extend to him being okay with me 'trying' to be Anna. And though I told myself I'd keep my guard up, that I wouldn't let myself get any more mixed up in the mess I'd made, after two more courses and another bottle of wine, I'm running out of reasons not to surrender. Will is great, and he's single. And he likes me, and *I'm* single. And...

'Anna...' Will says, reaching across the plate-scattered table to take my hand. 'Can I be real with you for a second?'

'Please,' I say, heart beating faster as I feel the warmth of his hand on mine.

'When Reese first told me she met you in the Hyde, I thought you might just be like every other girl I meet there,' he says, looking into my eyes intently as my heartbeat goes into overdrive. 'But when I met you, when we first started acting together, you were like a breath of fresh air.' *You were like a breath of fresh air, still are...* Cameron's words from the other day at the bar rush through my mind and I force them away. Cameron is off limits, he always has been, always will be. And Will is here. Inches away, so very close. 'And then when you let yourself be so vulnerable with me, so real about your agent...'

'Yeah, thank you for that,' I say, my voice barely above a whisper, his 'real' comment weighing heavy on my heart. I'm being far from real with him. 'You haven't told...'

'Reese?' Will fills in my blank. 'No, don't worry. Reese is great but...' *She can't be trusted*; my own thoughts now splurge into his spaces. 'Anything you tell me will stay with me,' Will says, giving my hand a little squeeze in his. 'Anna, I like you.'

'I like you too,' I say, knowing I should move my hand, knowing I should leave.

'No, I *like* you, like you,' he says, accentuating the word, his eyes growing wider still.

'No,' I whisper as I watch his face fall. I have to tell him; trust him. 'You like *Marley*.'

'Pardon?' Will says, reluctantly letting go of my hand.

'I can explain...' I begin, almost waiting for him to stand up and leave, but he doesn't. He just sits, staring across at me, eyes narrowed in my direction. 'But you can't tell anyone.'

'What have I just said?' Will says, leaning a little closer. Okay Marley, time to find out whether that's true. For the competition, for the contract.

'This is going to sound crazy, but my name isn't actually Anna, it's Marley, and I'm not engaged,' I say, waiting to feel something, maybe remorse, possibly relief.

'You're *engaged*?' Will says, glossing over the name-thing

entirely. So, he really didn't know? That bodes well for what I'm about to tell him next.

'No, I'm not,' I say, every sentence another bomb that I expect will scare him off. 'But Reese thinks I am,' I admit, before telling him everything: about my audition, about Sabrina in the car park, about real-Anna and her perfect wedding, and the perfect day I had pretending to be her. About the night Cameron introduced me to Reese and we entered the competition together. 'I never dreamed we'd get this far,' I say, almost close to tears. 'And I've tried to tell Anna, I've tried to tell Reese...but each time...'

It feels good to finally tell someone the truth, but I stop short at telling Will about Reese and Jake, not until I find out what's actually going on. Will leans back in his seat and takes another sip of his drink. Somewhere in the midst of my confession he's ordered another bottle. I'm not even sure we're going to remember this conversation tomorrow.

'I'm going to tell her,' I say. 'I just need to find the right time.'

'I see,' Will says, taking another sip, his expression still too hard to make out.

'Please don't tell her before I get the chance to,' I say, daring to lean in a little closer to him. 'I am going to tell her everything, I am.' I remind myself of that truth. Even if Reese is a homewrecker, even if we don't get through this next round, I know I need to tell her now. Before Will can. I look at him across the table, leaning onto his elbows, moving closer to me.

'Your secret is safe with me,' he says, smiling for the first time in ages. 'Marley.'

As soon as the waiter comes to clear our plates, Will is settling up the bill and getting up to his feet. For a second I wonder whether he's going to turn and leave, go straight to Reese and tell her everything, but then he comes to stand closer to my side and I feel his fingers reach for mine, interweaving within my own.

'What do you want to do now?' he says, his voice lowering to a whisper as he looks down from our fingers to my face, his face now just inches from my own.

'I don't mind,' I say, as his eyes search me, leaving me feeling excited and exposed.

'Well, I don't know about you...' Will grins, leaning down to kiss me on the lips softly, pulling away slowly. 'But I'd like to get to know you a little more, *Marley*.'

The Uber ride back to Will's passes in a blur of alcohol and anticipation and before long, he is opening the door into his small apartment, stopping to kiss me on the staircase as I try to steady myself on the hard, cold wall behind me. But it's hopeless. My heart lurches and my limbs tremble as his fingers feel through my hair before reaching down to my hand to lead me further and further up the stairs towards the door into his bedroom. In the safety of his room and the secrecy of this moment, I let his mouth search new parts of me. First my neck, then my clavicle, then my chest, him clearing the way with each and every layer he peels off. 'You're beautiful, Marley,' Will whispers, his eyes taking me in. And then I let myself go completely.

Afterwards, I lie looking at the ceiling just waiting for the magic to wear off. I look around the room, from the stacks of books climbing up from his floor to the bust-up old diary, held open by a Sharpie upon his bedside table. Then, I feel

Will's fingers reach for mine, until we're laying hand in hand, side by side.

'I hope this doesn't make things complicated,' I say, my breath still heavy.

'Oh, I think you've already made things complicated, Marley,' Will says, his tone playful as he turns his body to face mine; I turn into him and he kisses the bridge of my nose.

'I know.' I sigh. 'But I'll straighten everything out, I promise and until then...'

'Our secret,' Will says, turning onto his back as I mirror his motions.

'Speaking of secrets,' I say, after a comfortable silence lingers between us. 'You keep a diary?' I nod towards the diary on the table beside me.

'Guilty,' he says with a grin, before reaching his naked body across mine to hold the book in his hands. 'I find it helps to get all my thoughts out onto the page.'

So maybe he wants to be a writer after all? I think, remembering all of his notes on Reese's script. I study his fingers as he removes the pen from the pages of his diary to hold it in one hand, flicking through his scribbles with the other.

'Marley,' he says, almost to himself, still holding the diary in his hands. It feels good to hear him saying my name, my real one. 'It's a cool name.'

'I never used to like it,' I say, laying a palm back onto his bare chest. Anna thought it was cool though; she even used to pretend it was her middle name in secondary school.

'Really?' Will looks to me in disbelief. 'It sounds like a celebrity name to me.'

'Not quite.'

'Not *yet*.' Will stares at me, his diary now held to his chest. 'Will Hunt is so basic.'

'You said it,' I say, my words stained with sarcasm.

'I used to always pretend my name was Horatio,' Will says and I can't help my laugh from escaping into the room. *I used to pretend my name was Anna.* 'Horatio Hunt, that's a great celebrity name, everyone would want *his* autograph,' Will says into the space between us. 'Confession,' Will continues with a smile; we both know it won't be as big as the one I've made today. 'I used to practise my autograph all the time.'

'Me too,' I say, as Will pushes himself up to sitting, opening his diary on a blank page. Like my confession earlier, it feels like a fresh start.

'Can I have it?' Will jokes, thrusting the Sharpie in my direction.

'What?' I laugh, pushing myself up to sit beside him, clutching the sheets to my chest. 'Your autograph?'

'Huh?'

He leans down to kiss me lightly on the lips. 'For when you are famous.'

I look into his eyes, the champagne wearing off but the heat between us burning strong.

'Sure,' I say, taking the pen from him and pressing in onto the blank white page. I let the nib of it savour the space, carefully inking the words I've been holding onto for too long: *Marley Bright.* 'But what are you going to give me in return?' I say, feeling confidence rush through me as Will takes the diary from me and discards it onto the bedroom floor, using his hands to take me in for the thousandth time as he whispers my name again.

CHAPTER NINETEEN

Marley. *Marley.* Almost a week has passed, and I can still hear Will whispering the words. I look down at my phone to see a message from him: *Can't wait to see you tomorrow.* It's almost enough to drown out the noise of dread that keeps reminding me that even though I've come clean to Will and he's okay with it, it doesn't mean that Reese is going to be. Or Anna. Or Anna *and Jake.* The thought of it all makes my brain hurt. That, and the sound of Xavier strangling cats down the corridor.

'Xavier, *please,*' I say, as soon as I've opened the door into the living room. There, I find Xavier without said cat and holding a pair of bagpipes; I'm not sure which is worse.

'Sorry, is it too loud for you to concentrate?' he says, looking down at the pages in my hand. It's the script for the read-through tomorrow, when we'll run through some of the scenes from later on in the show for the producers, and when I'll get to kiss Will all over again. And he'll have to pretend I'm Anna for just a while longer.

'It's too loud for me to flipping think,' I say, and Xaiver's face falls.

'Something came for you,' he says, pointing to a manilla envelope lying on the coffee table, as if his safe retrieval of it will be suitable compensation for my latest noise complaint.

'Whatever happened to the flute?' I ask, almost nostalgic for the marginally less squeaky sound.

'Sold it for these.' Xavier shrugs with a smile for his beloved bagpipes, looking every inch like the cat who got the cream (still holding the 'cats' about to be strangled).

'I see,' I say, whilst ripping the envelope open. My eyes explore the formal-looking documents inside. The first page is a cover letter from Sloane Star and the second part is a contract, between Will Hunt, Reese Priestly and Marley Bright. Oh shit. I message Will instantly and he replies back just as quickly: *I had Reese's copy sent to me too.*

I relax a little upon seeing Will's message, and his next one telling me not to worry and to leave the commercial stuff to him. Reese did say she trusts Will with her life when it comes to this kind of thing. Plus, we have time to sort everything out just as soon as we've got through tomorrow's read-through. I stash the contract back in the open envelope and return it to the coffee table, picking up the script for the sixth and final episode of our show.

I begin to read from the top just as Xavier hits another high note. I have half a mind to ask him to go busking again but it's raining outside, and this house is as much his as mine. Possibly even more than mine, seeing as he's covered this month's rent for both of us. I pull up my banking app to be greeted by angry red digits. All the more reason to concentrate on the competition. The sooner we know whether we get through to the final stage or not, the closer we are to the money or me finally having the time to get another temp job.

I look at Xavier now, content to be creative, and wish I could say the same. How he has the money to cover all of our rent this month is beyond me. Maybe his stint flute-busking was more lucrative than I thought. Or more likely, he doesn't just smoke weed but sells it. Either way, ignorance is bliss. I reach into my back pocket for my headphones and try to drown out his noise completely before another 'ping' interrupts my playlist.

I've been thinking about the hen party again. Shall we all offer to split the price of Lauren's flight ticket? I really want all my favourite people together x

I read Anna's message and feel my body tighten more than it already is. Yes, she may want all her favourite people together but Anna suggesting this is going to get her in everybody's bad books, more than she already is. Well, with the 'have-nots' of the Bride Tribe at least – Arabella may actually feel buoyed by the opportunity to 'give back'.

I'm not sure. Let me sound out a few people in the...

I begin typing whilst the sound of Xavier's bagpipe-playing drowns everything out.

Anna, can I come over to...

I start typing another message before stopping my sentence short again. It's one I've written many times before when house sharing got too much. Back when the thought of

Anna being on the property ladder was a novelty and not a hint that I should be closer to that rung too, not left behind on the first unsteady step. When a win for Anna felt like a win for me. I know that same caring bestie is still there somewhere. It's not like I've been perfect either.

I'm not sure. Let me sound out a few people and we can talk about it. Actually, can I come over now? I'm trying to read my script for this television thing I'm working on and I could do with a quiet space x

A quite space, a safe space; the best space with my best friend.

Sorry. With Jake. Maybe chat later? X

I read her message, the speed at which she replied adding more salt into the wound. The 'maybe' in her sentence tells me that she's not going to ring, unless she has another wedding drama. Why is she being so weird? I wonder, whilst Xavier's bagpipes add more confusion into the mix. Jake being at hers never stopped her from inviting me over before. Until we found that note and Anna then told me to drop it. Maybe she knows I've not let it go yet. Perhaps she knows that if I spend too much time with them, I'll see that she's not dropped it either. And with good reason. My phone begins to ring, and I pick up instantly.

'Anna?' I ask, part of me hoping that she's changed her mind. I need to get out of here and another part of me wants to tell her just how fun my date was in the end.

'No, *Reese*,' Reese says down the line and I pull the

phone away to see that it's her name on the screen again. 'Do you always answer the phone with your own name?'

'Never,' I say at speed. 'I'm just distracted...'

'I can tell that,' Reese says again. 'What the hell is that?'

'My housemate playing the bagpipes,' I say, before realising again that as far as Reese is concerned, I still live with my investment banking fiancé. 'Old housemate, sorry.'

'I don't care how old he is,' Reese says, laughing my stupidity away. 'That sound should be illegal.' I think in some public spaces it probably is. 'Are you free?'

My eyes shoot to Xavier, bearded as ever but still managing to be red in the face. I really don't feel like seeing Reese right now. It's the day before our next meeting with the producers and speaking to her now will be an actual minefield. *You're sleeping with my best mate's fiancé.* Boom! *I slept with your university friend Will.* Boom! *My name isn't Anna and I'm not getting engaged – oh and please don't tell your boss.* Boom, boom, boom!

'No, sorry. I'm just running through the script for tomorrow,' I say.

'Yeah, it's about that,' Reese says slowly, and I swear I hear a croak in her voice. Has Will told her about me? Has she found out the truth about Jake? Shit, shit, *shit.*

'Oh yeah?' I say. I can't meet her today. I just *can't.* 'Everything okay?'

'Yeah, everything's fine,' she says, and I know from the way she says it that she's holding back tears. 'It's not really a work thing. It's just like a... I need a friend thing.'

Oh crap, she thinks we're friends, I panic before recalling the past weeks we've spent together. She's invited me in, made me welcome, made me feel like part of the team. We've worked together, created together, drunk together, laughed together.

'I didn't know who else to call,' Reese says. 'I just need a safe space, a sounding board.'

I need that too. Just with anyone other than her. Then I hear her muffled cries down the phone, and I know we're about to be the kind of friends who cry together too.

I see Reese sitting on the park bench from a mile away, her pink hair drawing the eye in, her legs going on for days. I know I need to tell her everything, just not today. I just need twenty-four more hours for us to get in front of the producers, perform to the best of our ability, before giving up my Anna performance for good. But as soon as she knows who I am, will she be able to link me back to the real-Anna? Have she and Jake talked about her, about me? It's not like there's that many Marleys in the world. My mind shoots back to being in bed with Will before Reese looks up at me.

'Hey Anna,' she says, and I try to force Will from my mind, sure she can read me.

'Hey,' I say, coming to sit on the bench beside her. 'Are you okay?' And with those three simple words, Reese begins to crumble before me. I can't help but throw my arm around her, pulling her into my side. Like watching a tough guy break down in tears, it's not so much that she shouldn't be crying right now but more that I didn't know she knew how.

'I'm not who you think I am.' She turns to me, tears making tracks down her face. What? Who is she? Is she about to tell me about Jake? 'I've made you think I'm this strong, confident feminist who has it all together,' Reese goes on, and I realise our performances aren't in the same vein, they're not in the same ballpark. 'But I'm so anxious about tomorrow. I feel like this is my last shot.'

'Why would it be your last shot?' I say, feeling a lump catch in my throat because in reality, all I want to say is *me too*.

'I'm tired,' Reese says, looking me dead in the eye and I feel every word. 'I've been trying for so long, trying to keep going and this is the closest thing I've got to an open door in months.' Try *years*, I want to add but I know Reese needs me to listen right now. What's more, I actually *want* to. 'And it's not so much the writing that's exhausting, it's the hoping.'

I watch her pretty face crinkle at the forehead, worry etched into her brow and realise that my hand has started to stroke her back. It's instinctive, like the way I couldn't help touching Will, some actions are just impossible to fight. Some relationships don't take effort, they kind of just happen.

'It's the constantly telling yourself that it's going to be okay, that it's okay that everyone else seems to be thriving, that social media is their highlight reel anyway,' Reese goes on, and I'm still surprised to hear her speak like this. But maybe that's the point; I've only seen her highlight reel too. 'But all the positive talk, all the getting back up, all the *keep on keeping on*... It's all just exhausting, I'm exhausted. Do you know what I mean?'

'I really do,' I say, feeling a tear run down my face; I wipe it away before she can see.

'And now, it feels like things are finally happening,' Reese continues, her eyes once again fixed on me. 'And I'm scared it's all about to go away again,' she cries. 'That it's all too good to be true.'

It takes all my strength not to look away. *I'm too good to be true.*

'I've sacrificed *everything* for this,' Reese says and against my better judgement I ask her to go on. 'His name was...'

Jake? Jake. *Jake.*

'Corey,' Reese says, as I realise that she said 'was'. If she was talking about Jake, wouldn't it be 'is'? My stomach turns at the thought. 'I met him a few years back and we fell in love,' Reese continues. 'He was an actor too.' She shakes her head at the thought, as if it was inevitable that he would end up hurting her, like we all lie for a living. I wish I could prove her wrong. 'And he got a big job in America, just when I got what I *thought* was a big opportunity here. So, he went, and I stayed and well... that job was like chasing the wind.'

'Oh Reese...'

'He would have married me, Anna,' Reese says, and I feel a little sick; sick for her, sick for me. 'He even said he was planning to propose on our anniversary, that he wanted to tie the knot on the same day a year later, tenth October, ten, ten. I could have had my big dream wedding too. But I picked writing.'

'Do you regret it?'

'No, not when it's going well,' Reese says, with a sad smile. 'But I'm scared that if we don't get through this next round, if something goes wrong, if someone lets me down...' I gulp at her words. 'Then none of the sacrifice will make sense, you know?'

I nod. I've never been in love, at least I think I haven't. But I've loved and lost my passion for acting a thousand times over. And I know how it feels to lose hope.

'It's probably why I end up screwing up with guys I don't have a future with,' Reese goes on. *Maybe try shagging someone who isn't engaged to someone else?* I think, but there's no force to the thought. Reese is broken, just like I'm broken, just like everybody else. We all make mistakes and right now, stood on the verge of everything Reese has dreamed of and fought for, I feel like I've made the most.

'It hurts to hope sometimes,' Reese says, brushing a stray tear away, her mascara smudged under her eyes; she still looks gorgeous – even more so for her vulnerability.

'Yes,' I say, holding her closer to my side. 'But the only thing that hurts more,' I whisper, remembering how I felt before the day I met her, 'is not holding onto it.'

CHAPTER TWENTY

I turn down the corner to Sloane Star's offices to find Will walking a few steps in front of me. My anxiety shoots into overdrive.

'Will?' I call, and he turns around instantly, his smile beaming back at me.

'Marley!' He grins, opening his arms to scoop me into a hug. I try not to act weird but it's the first time I've seen him since we were lying together in his bed, naked. Plus, he's just called me by my proper name for the first time in public.

'You can't call me that,' I say, lowering my voice to a whisper, my eyes scanning the space around us for Reese. 'I haven't found a good time to tell Reese yet.'

Yesterday might have been a good time until I was reminded of just how much this means to her, how much it means to all of us. I need to hold this together, for everybody.

'That's okay,' Will says. 'As far as she knows the contract is still just with me. And David knows I'm taking the lead on it. He's being really helpful actually, showing loads of flexibility for our *unique circumstances*.' Circumstances such as the fact one third of our team doesn't know my real name? 'He must know who my dad is.' Will rolls his eyes.

'Yeah, that.' I smile, ignoring my shame about lying to Reese for the thousandth time, reminding myself that she's lying to me too. 'Or he fancies the pants off you.' I try not to blush but we both know I fancy the pants off him too.

'Either way, he seems to be giving me loads of bargaining power, not letting the red tape of the legal department get in the way.'

'Any increase on the one hundred thousand pounds?' I joke.

'That part, he isn't budging on,' Will says, laughing. That doesn't matter. A third of one hundred thousand pounds is more than enough, now that it's going to 'Marley Bright'.

'You've got my details, right?' I ask, still in hushed tones.

'Yes, safe and sound.' Will smiles down at me, his hand holding the top of my arm.

'I feel bad for keeping secrets from her,' I say, as I try to remember she's still keeping secrets from me; but she doesn't know I'm Anna's best friend. Or at least, I used to be.

'I know,' Will says, though we both know keeping the contract away from her is concealing a much bigger reveal. 'But from where I'm standing, you're doing the right thing. You made a mistake and you're going to clean it up but just giving us a good shot at this.' Will wanders the few short steps down the street, slowing outside the Sloane Star sign, bold and mounted on the stone wall. I stand on the first step and Will grabs my hand from behind, spinning me around to face him and holding my hips as he does.

'You look gorgeous, Marley,' he says, moving an inch closer towards me.

'You need to *stop* it,' I say, pushing his hands off me playfully but I know there's a sharp edge to my voice. Things feel like they are hanging by a thread and it will only take one more mistake to see them fall completely. 'What if... Reese!' I say on seeing her appear behind us. She looks every inch the star, with half of her hair pulled up in a small ponytail, the rest of her pink tips reaching to her severe shoulder blade. She looks like the powerhouse I had first met in the Hotel Hyde, but I know from her little wink cast in my direction that everything has changed. There is nothing like shared imposter syndrome to form a bond.

Together we walk into the studios and up the stairs until we are in the familiar reception room once again. This time, I'm the one sat in the middle; Reese on one side of me, her trembling hand held in mine, Will sat on the other, my hand wanting to reach for his. I nervously check my phone for messages but know that the two people who I now keep in touch with the most are right beside me. Anna knows about today and hasn't messaged once. The only thing that's surprising about this is that I'm still surprised. And maybe the fact that next to Reese – more real somehow after yesterday – and Will, who seems to like the real me, Anna forgetting to be there for me is beginning to hurt less.

'Will.' David pokes his head out of the audition room to beckon us in. One by one we walk into the room to see the remaining three producers sitting behind the desk. Tanya Moore smiles at me as I take a seat in front of them; I let it warm me from the inside out. She looks incredible in black leather leggings and an oversized cashmere sweater and I feel proud for taking a leaf out of her book and wearing all black.

David takes his space beside her, walking the long way around to his seat so that we can all marvel at his lime green trousers and oversized black T-shirt layered over the top. I think the strut is mostly for Will's benefit but looking at him now, wearing black jeans and a fresh white T-shirt that makes his muscular arms look even more tanned, I can't really blame David for trying. Or giving Will's word so much weight.

'Thank you for sending through your outline and sample scenes for the next episodes of your show,' David says, every bit as flamboyantly as the first time we met him. 'As you know, we'd like to just get another taster of the chemistry, the sexual *tension*, between the main characters, as it's such a key element to the show.'

I look at Will and he flashes me a wink so slight I might have dreamt it. For a moment I wonder whether our chemistry will be as strong now that some of the tension between us has been relieved.

'We wanted to see the scene *after* the shower scene you teased us with last time,' David says, looking directly at Will. I gulp. It's another intimate moment between the characters, not entirely dissimilar from the one Will and I shared in real life last week. My pulse starts to pick up pace, unsure as to whether Reese will notice a change in our dynamics, whether now Will knows I'm Marley, knows me *personally*, she'll see our professional relationship for what it really is – a line-crossing, blurry mess.

'We also wanted to see the scene where Ella is at the influencers' breakfast.' Tanya looks between me and Reese, her sentence carrying a sense of defiance, like maybe she's had to fight to keep this scene in too. What is it about influencers that most men get to pass off as irrelevant when they're clearly not immune from their influence? 'I thought the scene was such a strong social commentary on the fact that a love rival doesn't always have to be a man; it can also be a mission.'

I look to Reese who is momentarily beside herself, then to Will who looks like he's been put in his place. Reese catches my eye: *Tanya gets it.*

'We'll start with the post-shower scene first though,' Jerry says.

Both Will and I get to our feet and stand in the space between the chairs and the desk. The scene before this has concluded with our wet clothes piled on the floor, the rest of the shower scene thankfully left to the imagination. I know by now that Reese thinks that it's the things that the audience doesn't see and have to work out for themselves that can really keep the viewers engaged. Sex may sell but imagination keeps them invested.

'Ella, I...' Will begins, morphing into the character of Jack, but not nearly enough for my liking; it's all a bit too close to home. Surely, I can use these feelings to my advantage.

'Don't worry, Jack,' I say, looking him in the eye, using the space around me to walk away from his side, pretending to clamber for my clothes to cover my nakedness. 'This won't change anything...' I say slowly, searching Jack's face for signs of panic. Ella thinks this is what Jack will want, for everything to stay on track with their plan to flip the flat when all Jack really wants is Ella. It's an emotionally charged scene that picks up from the shower scene just gone that will surely have the audience screaming at their screens.

'It won't change *anything?*' Will looks at me, trying to hide the wobble from his character's voice in a way that makes it clear to everyone else that a change in their shared circumstances is exactly what Jack wants. 'But I thought you wanted—'

'I want what you want, Jack.' Ella's sentence cuts over his own dramatically. 'I want what we both wanted when we met in the bank, to flip this house so that we can both finally get on that damn property ladder,' I say, throwing my hands out in exacerbation. Ella, true to form, is putting her guard up again, but I know Jack is about to bring it down once more...

Will takes a step towards me, his eyes searching my own as we play out what we've rehearsed countless times before.

'Is that all you really want?' Will asks, taking a step closer.

'You know it is,' I say, taking another step closer to him too.

'Are you sure about that?' Will looks down at me, bridging the gap further still.

'Yes,' I reply, Will now so close that I can feel his breath on my face. Then, he puts his hand to the back of my head and pulls me into him again. I know it's coming but I still gasp for real; I do every time. I feel his lips graze my own and mine open to him and then...

'Cut!' David shouts, slamming his hands down on the table as he does. 'Next scene.'

I look down at Reese's hand clutched in mine, back in the waiting room where today started. The next scene went as well as the first, although I was acting on my own this time, as Ella, feeling every line that Tanya fed to me from across the table.

'Don't worry, you were really good,' Will whispers to me from my other side.

'Thanks.' I smile as Reese squeezes my hand tighter in hers and I follow her gaze back to the closed door to the audition room where we know the producers are discussing our script. In just a few short moments we'll know whether we've got through or not. Whether we can hold onto our last hope for a bit longer or we'll have to go away and lick our wounds and find the energy to hope again. Either way, I need to find the courage to come clean to Reese or walk away from our friendship completely. I thought that might be easy to do once I found out about her and Jake but now, I'm not so sure.

'We're ready for you.' Tanya pops her head around the door and my heart lurches. Reese stands first and I swear I see Tanya giving her a quick nod. Quick nods have to be a good thing, surely? 'We won't keep you any longer,' Tanya continues as soon as we've sat down in our usual seats. 'We're pleased to say...'

'You got into the final two!' David throws his hands out dramatically, stealing the end of Tanya Moore's sentence; she looks annoyed for a second but recovers her smile shortly after. Reese lets out a squeal and stands up, Will shooting out of his chair too. I remain seated, my legs shaking and my teeth chattering as I do. I can't believe this is actually happening, that one rogue appointment of Anna's has led to the biggest opportunity I've ever had in my life. And now it's so close I can almost touch it. With a man I fancy (and have slept with) and a woman who fancies Anna's fiancé (and who might have slept with him too).

'Anna?' Reese turns to me now. *And it's all got Anna's name on it.*

'Mar... Anna!' Will turns to me too. Well, it's got her

name on *for now*. Now we've done the audition, now we've got through to the final round, I *have* to tell her the truth.

'We did it!' Reese says, trying to work out why I'm not jumping up and down.

'I can't believe it.' I smile up at her, knowing I've never meant anything more.

'The next step,' Tanya says, her smile saying *well done*, but her tone saying *simmer down*, 'is filming the pilot episode in its entirely. All of the terms for that are of course, set out in the contract.' Her eyes dart between the three of us again and Reese and I look to Will.

'Yes, that's all under control,' he says back to her confidently; at least, it will be once we've shown the final copy to Reese and explained why *Anna's* name isn't at the top. I wonder once again how much Jake has told her about the real Anna, if anything at all. Has he mentioned that his fiancée is in real estate? That she has a best friend who is in Reese's industry too? A best friend called *Marley?*

'Great,' Jerry says, speaking over Tanya's next line of enquiry again; this time, I'm kind of glad for the cut-off. 'We look forward to seeing your finished pilot.'

As soon as we're out of Sloane Star's offices, I know it's time. Maybe Reese will be so high on today that not even my confession will deter her from the final hurdle. After all, there's still countless reasons this competition is important to her, to all of us. *One hundred thousand reasons.* I pinch myself again. But, as soon as we're walking around the corner and out onto the safety of the busy street, Reese and Will explode with plans and excitement.

'So, I've got a studio and a vacant house booked on standby, I'll confirm that tonight and we can begin shooting it next week,' Will says, his long legs striding at speed as both Reese and I struggle to keep up.

'A studio? A vacant house?' Reese repeats, her energy palpable, her confusion even more so. 'Doesn't Sloane Star sort all of that out?'

'They gave some suggestions in the appendix to the contract,' Will explains, as Reese and I fall into step on either side of him. He turns into the pub nearby, the same one we celebrated in last time. Neither one of us objects, we clearly have a lot to talk about.

'Yeah, we still need to look at that properly,' Reese says, taking a seat at a table by the window as I offer to get us a bottle of wine.

'We'll get the contract to you soon,' Will says, as I ditch my bag under the table and begin to walk to the bar, catching Reese's reply as I do.

'*We?*' she asks, and I dare look back to see her eyes looking from Will to me. I knew she wouldn't be able to watch us perform our scene today without noticing some sort of shift.

'But who's going to pay for all of this?' I hear Reese say as soon as I'm back at our table with a bottle of wine and three glasses in my hands. Maybe if Reese has enough, I'll be able to tell her the truth about me and she won't even remember.

'Sloane Star have got that all covered,' Will says, smiling from ear to ear. 'We film next Friday,' he goes on as Reese's face shows her trying to make sense of what she's hearing. 'So, can we just trust that everything's taken care of, that everything's going to be okay?'

Reese forces a smile. Now I know why she finds it so hard to trust that, everything makes a bit more sense. Well, almost everything.

'Reese, I...' I begin, mustering all the courage I have to begin my confession, even if I don't know where it will end, but she's still looking at Will.

'You're right,' she says back at him, not hearing or choosing to ignore my sentence completely. 'We've all waited so long to get an opportunity like this.' Reese recovers her smile. 'I'm sure as hell not going to let anything get in the way of us enjoying it now.'

CHAPTER TWENTY-ONE

I reach for my script from the top of our coffee table, ignoring the open manilla envelop entirely. Will says he's got it sorted, that we'll tell Reese together as soon as we shoot the pilot, as soon as we find out whether it's getting picked up. He reasoned that our third of one hundred thousand pounds on signature may soften the blow. That, and all her dreams coming true. *Not all of them,* I had thought, remembering again our time in the park together, what she told me about Corey and the wasters she's spent her time with since then, just protecting herself from getting hurt. Still managing to hurt my best friend in the process.

I try my best to concentrate on my script, but the sound of Xavier's bagpipes refuses to be confined to his bedroom. Trust this to be the one hobby he sticks with for longer than a week. If this was several months back, I would be over at Anna's in a flash, finding solace and silence over in leafy-green Greenwich. And yet, ever since Anna decided Jake wasn't cheating, our chats have remained wedding-based only. It's almost as if her talking about their love is sustaining it, that if she were to stop consciously conjuring it in her mind it might all drift away. But a made-up romance is just a fairy tale. Anna deserves more than that.

Somewhere between reading the same line for the thousandth time and Xavier's fifth rendition of what I *think* is 'Sweet Child of Mine', complete with a kick drum that has me wondering whether he is launching a one-man-band, I decide to go to Anna's. I never used to wait for an invitation, back when I actually remembered I had a spare key to her apartment: 'my case is su casa,' she used to joke in broken Spanish, to which I'd always reply: 'Who's Sue?' I miss when it was just us; I even miss when it was me, her and Jake sometimes, back when I believed they were happy, even if it did sometimes remind me that I wasn't.

With every tube station the train passes through, I wonder whether this is a bad idea. *Bermondsey*. It's not like Anna has been gagging to spend time with me lately, always keeping me at arm's length; but haven't I been doing the same to her? *Canada Water*. But I know what I'm trying to hide; what is she? *Canary Wharf*. If she and Jake are out, I can drop her a message and read my script in peace. If she and Jake are both in, then I can just read my script in the next room. If Anna is in alone maybe we can finally really talk, not just about the wedding plans but about how she feels about it. And, if Jake is in alone, or with Reese, I... well, I don't know what I will do but at least I'd know what was going on for sure.

Walking up the stairs to Anna's apartment, I try to tell myself that this is no big deal – she gave me that spare key for a reason, didn't she? But now, everything feels different, *distant*; like our friendship is hanging by a thread. I turn the key in her door slowly, pushing it ajar. Her reaction when I used to call round unexpectedly was always one of joy. Whether she was celebrating something, hoovering in her underwear or crying on the sofa, there was nothing that was off limits, nothing she wouldn't let me see. *Or hear.* I stop still as I clock the raised voices coming from inside.

'Jake, what the hell? You have to tell me.' I hear Anna's voice force itself my way.

'Anna, I'm allowed to go to *work*,' Jake spits his reply. *Liar.* 'I don't know about every open house you're showing around or every time you go into the office.'

'I just don't get why all of a sudden your clients need you all the time, now that we're planning a wedding. I just need some help with it. I have a full-time job too, you know?'

I stand behind the slightly ajar front door, not knowing whether to step further inside.

'I know,' Jake says, with a heavy sigh. 'But did you ever think the reason I'm working all these hours is all for the God-damn wedding?'

'So, it's the *God-damn* wedding now?' Anna shouts back and I wince at the words. 'It's meant to be the happiest day of our lives, Jake.'

'Our lives, or *your* life, Anna? Because I sure haven't had much input.'

'I'm *trying* to get you to give your input,' Anna screams back and my heart hurts. She's been an absolutely nightmare with this wedding, but I am starting to see why. And it's no excuse for Jake to cheat and lie; there's never an excuse to... I catch the thought before it forms; I know there's no moral high ground underneath my feet.

'Look Anna,' I hear Jake saying, and I feel his voice moving closer. I slowly push the door so that it's almost closed again. 'I need to go to this meeting, it's important. But

I'll be back soon. I love you, okay?' With that I hear footsteps walking towards me and duck into the stairwell. Running down a flight of stairs, I take the next door onto the landing below and hide, out of breath and out of sight. I knew things couldn't be as good as Anna was making out. Maybe now we can talk about it for real.

After a good twenty minutes of pacing up and down someone else's corridor and praying that they don't call the police, I make my way back up to Anna's floor. Knocking on the door this time, I wait for her to materialise, every inch the mascara-stained woman that turned up on my doorstep all those weeks ago. Back when she'd first suspected Jake was cheating. I look down at the script in my hand and suddenly my reason for being here feels redundant. Now this afternoon is about finding out how Anna *really* is, seeing her open up.

'Marley?' All of a sudden, the door swings open and Anna is standing there, not messy and upset like I was expecting, but made-up, perfectly pieced together, smile pinned on her face. 'What are you doing here?' She says this politely, but I can tell she's put out.

'I've not seen you in ages,' I say, *since that awful coffee we shared.* 'And I wanted to see how you're getting on with everything.' I stash my script by my side as best I can.

'Great, I was actually just about to do some wedmin,' Anna says, and I feel my empathy for her slipping away. But no, I need to see underneath this façade.

'Oh goodie,' I say, and I know Anna is oblivious to any tension. 'How are you doing?' I ask, as she welcomes me into her pristine apartment, no less than three big wedding folders open on her coffee table.

'Yeah, the planning's going well thank you,' Anna says, as

I doubt the words I've just said. I thought I asked her how *she* was, not how the wedding was. 'Almost there now.'

'Good,' I say, trying to navigate this tricky terrain as best as I can. Anna doesn't look like someone who has just fought with her fiancé; her long dark hair is bouncy, her skin is tanned, her white leisure wear is spotless. 'But, how are *you? In yourself?*' It feels like the kind of question grown-ups ask their friends over a catch-up coffee; I never thought Anna and I would be the kind of friends who needed to catch up when our lives were so in sync.

'Yeah, I'm good, thanks,' Anna says, pouring two cups of coffee from a freshly brewed cafetière. She couldn't know I was coming, but she always seems prepared. 'But I've been thinking...' Anna goes on, coming to sit beside me and offering me a hot mug. It's the first time she's looked me in the eye for more than a second, and I finally feel like she's here again, *present*. 'I think we should do a London-based hen party...' So maybe she's not opening up but *wising* up to the fact that her wedding is bleeding everyone dry. '...as well.'

'*As well?*'

'Yeah, so, you know, Lauren and some of the people who I didn't want to invite to the America one can come as well,' Anna goes on, her smile shining. I love her and I want the best for her, but this is unbearable. I have half a mind to perform a bridezilla-exorcism.

'This is ridiculous,' I mutter under my breath, but Anna doesn't hear. 'I don't think you need two hen parties,' I say, louder this time, but softly – trying not to awake the beast. Though, to be fair, even that would feel more real than this. 'And so close to the wedding.'

'But I just want everyone to know that...'

'You've got nothing to prove,' I say, daring to move a hand to her leg.

'...Jake makes me so...' Anna's sentence darts across my own before my words register in her mind. 'I'm not trying to prove anything,' she looks at me accusingly.

'I know,' I say, still keeping my voice slow and steady. 'I don't know why I said that...' I try to retreat, but I know I can't just let this go, can't let Anna go on pretending that everything's perfect when it is so far from that. I heard that much half an hour ago. 'Anna, are you okay?' I ask for the third time. 'It's just, this wedding is getting really big and it's *soon* and not so long ago you turned up at my house thinking Jake was cheating on you.'

'I told you,' Anna replies, quickly. 'I was being stupid.'

'But what it you weren't?' I say, thoughts of Reese filling my mind.

'I never should have doubted him.' Anna shakes her head, unable to hold my gaze. 'I trust Jake,' Anna reminds herself. 'I *love* Jake.'

'I know you do,' I say, my hand still on her leg, tucked up on the sofa. 'But what about that note?' I risk steering her attention to the one thing I never should have taken, well... apart from her name.

'He's thrown it away,' Anna says. 'It was nothing.'

Oh no, does that mean Jake's noticed it's gone?

'But what if it *was* something?' I say, trying to get her to open up, trying to see just a hint of the insecurity that I know is inside her, that I overheard mere moments ago.

'But it wasn't,' Anna says sternly. 'I even feel bad for *thinking* it.'

But you shouldn't, you were right, I almost want to

scream across the room. But how can I tell her that without sharing everything else? I need her to get there on her own.

'Where is he now?' I probe. 'Has he been acting shifty at all?'

Come on Anna, you can tell me anything, I think before noting the irony.

'Look Marley,' Anna snaps, pushing my hand off her leg in the process. 'I know we had a blip before, but can't you just let us be happy?'

'I want you to be happy,' I say. 'I'm just not sure you are.'

'Well, I *am*,' Anna spits but the tears gathering in her eyes tell me otherwise. 'In fact, Jake will be home any second now,' she goes on, lying through her pained smile. 'And we're going to spend some quality time together so...'

'It's okay,' I say, even though nothing feels okay. 'I've got to go anyway.'

As soon as the door to Anna's apartment has closed behind me, I feel sure that she will be starting to cry on the other side. Even now I want to hold her, to tell her it's okay, that everything is going to be okay. But clearly, I don't get the privilege of seeing the real Anna anymore. She's not letting her guard down; she's not even listening.

As I walk into the fresh air, my mind runs wild with thoughts. If only I hadn't taken that damn note, I could tell Anna everything. But I still don't know what *exactly* there is to tell. That Reese is a man-stealer? That she's an innocent party in all this? I never thought my loyalties to Anna would wane, not for anything or anyone, but lately Reese has been more of a partner to me than Anna has been in years. But still, if Reese is with Jake now Anna needs to know, before it's too late. I dial her number.

'Hey Anna,' Reese picks up quickly. 'You okay?'

'Hey, yeah,' I reply, trying to sound breezier than I feel. 'What are you up to?'

I keep walking forwards, waiting for her response, for any hint of Jake's voice in the background, but all I hear is faint music and nondescript chatter.

'I'm at the hotel, just finishing my shift,' she says. 'Only one more hoop to jump through with Sloane Star and this could be my last one.'

I gulp, struggling to find the words to reply. I never thought I could feel sorry for the *other woman*, especially not Jake's, but here we are: two liars who need each other. But I need to find out the truth about this, for Anna to find out the truth about Jake.

'Fancy grabbing dinner?' I ask.

'Yes, I'm erm just finishing up...' Reese begins, and that's when I think I hear a man's cough in the background. 'How quickly can you be at the hotel?'

'Forty-five minutes?'

'That's fine,' Reese says, along with a sigh of relief. 'I'll meet you there.' I thought she already was there? 'I think I owe Cameron a bit of overtime,' Reese adds.

I think I owe him a bit more than that.

I arrive at the Hotel Hyde almost exactly an hour after speaking to Reese, an hour after leaving happy-go-lucky Anna behind. I drop Reese a message from outside, not even wanting to go in. I still haven't told Cameron whether we're taking the venue or settling up the tab and going somewhere else. But soon I'll be able to pay for everything.

'Anna?' I look up from my phone to see him standing in front of me, as broad and beautiful as the first day we met. Of course, he'd be walking into the hotel now.

'Hey Cameron,' I say, smiling back at him, my heart in my throat.

'Alone again?' He looks at the wall I'm leaning on, to the empty space beside me.

'I'm just waiting for Reese,' I explain quickly, sure he doesn't believe in my fiancé.

'No Will today?' Cameron crinkles his nose at the mention of his name.

'Just us girls,' I say, searching his face for reasons he might not like him. Cameron looks put out; tired and exhausted and like he can't quite relax. I hope he's okay, but it's not my job to worry about him. 'Reese is just finishing her shift.'

'I didn't think she was working today?' Cameron says, more confused still. My stomach drops as I realise that Reese is clearly covering up for something. 'Any news on...?'

'Soon,' I say quickly, knowing I'm covering up too. 'It's just been full-on.'

'You're okay though?' he asks, concern written across his brows, his body taking what looks like an involuntary step towards me.

'Never better,' I say, a little too quickly, feeling very much like Anna again, pretending to be perfect.

'And your fiancé? Anna, why is he never here?'

'He's...' Busy. Invisible. Non-existent. Reese appears from the entrance, saving me from Cameron's latest line of questioning, saving me from having to finish my sentence. She looks between Cameron and me, not sure what to make of the tension brimming between us.

'You ready to go?' Reese says, glancing from Cameron to me one last time. I nod. 'Be good,' Cameron shouts behind us and for some reason, it sounds like a warning.

From our starters to our main course, I chew through Cameron's final words. *Be good.* I still don't know what he meant by that, whether he was talking to Reese or to me, whether she was actually at work today or not. I study her face closely, trying to work out whether I want her to confide in me about Jake. If she does, I can tell Anna everything. But if I tell Anna everything, Reese will also find out everything about me.

'What do you know about the pilot filming?' Reese says, her eyes darting to her phone, laid on top of the table; is she waiting for a message from someone? Jake?

'Other than the address and the date, not a lot.'

'And you've not seen the contract?' She narrows her eyes at me suspiciously.

'Will says it's all in hand,' I respond, sidestepping the full truth. Reese looks down at her phone again nervously. 'How's the not-to-be-trusted guy?' I ask as she looks up at me, caught in the act, before turning her phone face down on the table.

'Still trying to work him out,' Reese says, with a little shrug and a flick of her hair. So, it's definitely still going on? Suddenly I'm not sure I can stomach desert. I sure as hell can't afford it. Thank God for credit cards. Thank God for this competition. I can't ask her about Jake now. Not until after we film the pilot. What would Will say?

'I'm just going to pop to the bathroom,' Reese says. 'Do you want to get the bill?'

'Sure,' I say as Reese gets to her feet. I don't want to pay for it though. I watch Reese's slender figure walk away and I signal for the bill. It's only when I put my soon-to-be maxed-out credit card (another one) onto the table that I notice that Reese has left her phone there, still face down. I look at it for a second. If I could just glimpse her messages from Jake, maybe I might find *something* – a photo, a location – just something I could use to warn Anna not to marry Jake without *me* needing to tell her or needing to ask Reese.

Without another thought or any other ideas, I reach for the phone and turn it over in my hands. There on the screen, I see the start of a message from an unknown number.

Hey bella, I really need to see you...

Bella? I know I shouldn't read any more, but somehow, I feel like this is the piece of the puzzle I am missing. And today, more than ever, has made me see that Anna needs to know what is going on. I swipe across the screen and the passcode pad comes up. I look up to see whether Reese is coming back to the table and then begin to try different combinations, *1111. 1234.* Then, I remember the reason she'd be messaging someone she wouldn't have a future with anyway. Corey. And their would-be wedding date had Reese not chosen her career over him. *10-10.*

The screen floods with light and I see the rest of the message.

Hey bella, I really need to see you. Stop trying to push me away. I know neither one of us saw this coming, but you have to let me take care of you, you have to let someone take care of you. J x

I study the sign-off before swiping away the message. There are countless others from the same unsaved number interspersed with message after message from Will.

Will: I'll tell you everything soon...

Will: Just trust me...

Will: Reese, please. It's not like that...

'Anna?' I freeze upon hearing Reese's voice. *Crap.* 'Anna? What are you doing?' I look up from her phone, still cradled in my hands.

'I erm...was looking for...' I begin, my voice barely audible above the throbbing of my heart. I know there's no coming back from this.

'Anna, tell me,' Reese says, too angry to sit down. 'What the *hell* are you doing?'

'I know you're cheating with a guy called Jake,' I blurt out, unable to stop myself. Reese glares back at me, hands on her hips, as I relinquish her phone.

'I didn't...' Reese stutters, trying to work out how I would know, why I would even care. 'That was just...' she tries to cover up again.

'I know his fiancée,' I say. *I am his fiancée,* or at least pretending to be.

'Oh.' Reese's face falls. 'I didn't... you have to believe me.'

'I'm not sure I do,' I say, looking from the surrendered phone to her sorry face.

'Well, even if I had,' Reese goes on, finding her fight. 'You're one to talk.'

'What's that supposed to mean?' I say, my voice croaking, my cheeks flushing red.

'I know you cheated on *your* fiancé with Will,' Reese spits, looking me up and down.

'Yet another man you're sleeping with?' I shout back at her. 'Wasn't one enough?'

'What the hell are you on about?'

'I've just seen your messages from him. From *Will*...'

'The ones you never should have been looking at in the

first place.' Reese narrows her eyes and her nostrils flare. 'I can't believe you're accusing me like this after what you've done. Do you know why I befriended you that night in the Hotel Hyde?'

'Because your boss made you?'

'Because I thought you were different,' Reese hurls the words at me. 'But no, you're just another silly girl using people to get what you want.'

'Reese I...' I begin, stung by her words but before I can find the rest of my sentence, she's picking up her phone, throwing on her jacket and preparing to leave.

'Save it,' Reese says, putting her hand up to stop me from following her. 'Planning the perfect wedding whilst cheating on your fiancé...' she shakes her head, now red in the face. 'You're as bad as the rest of them, *Anna.*'

Right now, listening to her say that name again, the name I never should have taken in the first place, I think I might be worse.

CHAPTER TWENTY-TWO

'Are you 'k?' Xavier asks through a cloud of weed smoke as soon as I'm through the door. Even through the haze, I can see that he's wearing a cape. And no, I'm not *k*. I'm so far from *k* right now it hurts. How dare Reese accuse me of cheating on my fake fiancé when she's sleeping with my best friend's real one?

'We're filming our pilot soon,' I shrug, trying to explain away my stress before another rush of adrenalin flowing through my body reminds me that this might be the most stressful fact of all; we've all pinned too much on this to turn our backs on it now.

'You're filming a pilot?' Xavier mumbles, barely visible through his latest puff of weed. I can't really blame him for not keeping up, it's not like I've let him in. Plus, the fact that his eyes keep drifting down to the sloppily placed sofa cushions below him suggests he's not really listening anyway. I study his cape, willing him to be the superhero I need right now and not the thirty-two-year-old waster I see before me wearing a flipping cape.

'Yeah, with my...' I stop myself short of saying 'friends'. Reese and I hardly feel like friends anymore. Will and I are clearly more than that.

'Isn't that, like, really expensive?' Xavier interrupts me, still eyeing up the cushions.

'We've got a production company helping us.'

Xavier's almost comatose face still manages to look impressed. And why wouldn't he be? He's wearing a *cape*. And this is a big deal. The biggest deal to happen to me in a really long time. To happen to any of us. Reese may hate me right now. I might hate her for what she's done too. But there's no way she's going to miss the filming next week, that we're not all going to give this our very best shot. Not when there's one hundred thousand pounds and the chance of getting our pilot made and picked up on the table.

'Look, I need to rehearse,' I say, heart still racing, my thoughts attacking me from all sides. Xavier nods and takes another toke. Why did I try to be Anna when I could be like him – so chilled he's horizontal, so checked-out that it's hard for him to care? But I do care, I really do. I don't want to check out from society like him, I want to be someone society celebrates. I reach down onto the coffee table to pick up the latest iteration of our pilot script.

'Did you tell your friend about the thing you took?' Xavier says just as soon as I'm about to leave the room. I'm surprised he's even remembered.

'Not yet,' I say, the thought of all of Jake's messages to Reese filling my mind. *And what about those messages from Will?* They will have surely been about the contract, buying us some time, *me* some time. *But Reese knows about us now,* the realisation reverberates around my mind. Why does she care so much? How can she after what she's done? 'But I will,' I assure Xavier and myself at the same time. 'I'm going to tell her everything.'

Back in my bedroom, I try to read through my lines. I should know them off by heart by now, but somehow my heart is occupied with other things. As I read the dialogue between Ella and Jack, I can't help but see imprints of Reese and Will on every page.

Ella: But I thought we were just friends.

Jack: Men and women can never just be friends, not without one fancying the other.

Ella: So, do you fancy me?

Jack: If I did, I'd never give you the satisfaction of finding out.

I read the words from the pilot, the scene following their first encounter in the bank, where they head to a nearby coffee shop and lay out the rules for the house flip. But we all know what happens next. I guess some rules are always made to be broken. I skim on and on, reading over every annotation and amendment scribbled onto the script until I find my way to the final scene: the flash-forward to that fateful shower-fixing moment. As I read out Ella's lines to Jack, I imagine Will stood before me, taking step after step closer to me. And then I remember him kissing me on the stairway at his house; him almost pushing me into his bedroom, hungry for more; him lying next to me, promising me that one day people will want my autograph.

Then the script ends. I flip the page over in my hands to check the reverse for the final lines. We have rehearsed this one so many times that I shouldn't really need it but it's as if the memory of Reese's face, shouting across at me in the restaurant, is forcing all the other things I'm meant to be remembering out of my brain. I must have left it on the coffee table.

Pushing open the door into the living room, I'm not surprised to find that the sofa cushions Xavier was eyeing up have been assembled into some kind of pillow fort, a cloud of smoke surrounding it like a moat even though he's nowhere to be seen. I reach down to pick up the final page of my script from the coffee table, red pen marks circling different sections, hurried scribbles climbing the margins. I begin to scan the words until I realise that it's not a page from the script, but a page from my contract with Sloane Star, which I haven't moved from the table since the morning it arrived. I haven't even taken it out of its manilla envelope again. And yet here it is, envelope-less and written across.

My eyes scan the scribbles at speed. Were they always here? Had I just missed them? But no, the contract came clean as anything from the producers to me, *Marley*. I read the lines as if scanning a script, but the story remains far from clear. What the hell is going on?

Burden a third of the cost if unsuccessful? I make out the messy handwriting before deciphering the next note: *No security for M to be in second series? W to have 80% of income accrued as male lead and co-author of the work?* The room spins as my legs collapse into the nearest armchair. Who wrote all of this? What does it mean?

'You found it,' Xavier says as soon as he emerges into the

room. I have no idea where he's been but judging from his spaced-out smile, his dilated pupils and the fact that he's now wearing a top hat alongside his cape, I surmise he's still high.

'You did this?' I say, unable to stop the quiver from my voice.

'Yeah I...'

'Xavier this is an *important* document,' I say, my volume rising.

'It's a *bogus* document,' Xavier says, slumping down on the cushion-less sofa and looking from me to his pillow fort with pride, removing his top hat and cape as he does. It's then that I see red. How am I still living with this moron? He may be able to pillow-fort his own life away, but I need more, I was made for more. I was made for *this*.

'This document is the single most important thing that's ever happened to me,' I say, waving the annotated contract in his direction. Xavier doesn't flinch. 'You've wrecked it. And now I'm going to have to ask for a clean copy...'

'You should ask for a *different* copy,' Xavier says, sitting up a little straighter, his height dwarfed by sitting on the cushion-less settee.

'That's what I'm saying...'

'No, Marley,' Xavier says, seeming to sober up a little. 'Different *terms*.'

'What's wrong with...' I begin, before realising that I'm arguing about contract terms with a grown man who has just made a pillow fort. What does he know about this kind of thing? Will is good at this stuff. Reese said so. But looking at Xavier now, considering what I now know about Reese, considering all the things *I've* lied about, I'm not sure who to trust.

'It's not a good contract for you,' Xavier goes on, my anger stretching between us.

'And you would know this how?'

'A blast from the past,' Xavier says, a little shyly. What? For a moment, my anger morphs into confusion; he must clock the change as soon he's adding: 'I kind of used to be a lawyer.' Xavier shrugs again, before standing and reaching for one of the cushions of his pillow fort, beginning to reassemble our sofa as my mind struggles to figure out how this latest fact about Xavier fits into my perception of him.

'What do you mean, kind of?' I ask, the contract still in my shaking hand. I need to know how much weight to give his words.

'I was an Associate at a magic circle law firm.' Xavier says this like it's a guilty confession. If one of the Bride Tribe wasn't a lawyer and always banging on about *magic circle this* and *silver circle that* I'd honestly think he was admitting to being in some kind of magicians' network. It would make more sense than this.

'What happened?' I ask, stunned by his sentence. He must have got fired.

'I got promoted,' Xavier says, still nonchalant. 'And I was richer and more respected than I ever thought I would be, and do you know what?' No, clearly, I know nothing. 'I was really miserable,' Xavier says, sitting on the now fully reassembled sofa. 'So, I quit. I wanted to take some time to actually enjoy all of the money I made rather than be the kind of miserable old man whose only kick in life is cheating on his wife...' I can't help but think of Jake. 'Plus, I wanted to take some time out to work out what makes me happy.'

Juggling. Plaster of Paris. Bonsai. Flute playing. The

bagpipes. Xavier's list of hobbies runs through my mind. I thought he was drifting, not able to stick at one thing or commit to something when the going got tough. I never for one moment thought that this exploration would be intentional. I never even cared enough to find out.

'So that's why you could afford to pay our rent,' I whisper out loud to myself, the knot in my stomach showing no signs of unravelling. Xavier wasn't who I thought he was, and I didn't even slow down long enough to get to know him properly. But what about Will?

'Uh-hu.' Xavier nods. 'And I know you'll pay it back, when things start going better with your work.' He smiles broadly, his faith in me unwavering. It makes me feel worse.

'I thought it was,' I say, a lump catching in my throat as I do.

'Well, I don't remember everything from my days looking at contracts,' Xavier begins, looking down at the papers in my hand. 'But I know enough to know that this contract is not the best thing for you.' He holds a hand out to me and I surrender the document, watching him flicking back over the pages again. How had I got him so wrong? 'Whoever negotiated this for you is not your biggest fan.'

'What do you mean?' I say, my palms starting to sweat.

'You mentioned that the production company is paying for the pilot,' Xavier says, motioning for me to come and sit on the sofa beside him. 'But here it says that the production company *only* pay for the cost if your pilot is successful in winning the competition.'

'Who pays for it if we lose?' I ask, knowing the answer before he says it.

'You do,' Xavier says, turning to fix his eyes on mine. 'Well, not just you, this Reese Priestly as well and...'

'But we've already booked stuff for the filming,' I say, trying to keep up with Xavier's explanation but worried about where it might take me. 'I've not paid for that.'

'Not yet,' Xavier says, and my stomach flips. 'You see here?' He points to a clause in the contract, circled with red biro rings. 'Will Hunt has named a third party as responsible for covering his third of the costs, which that third party has agreed to pay upfront.'

'A third party?' I ask, tears threatening to spill from my eyes.

'That's why you haven't been asked for any money yet,' Xavier goes on. 'This third party is shouldering all the burden upfront until the producers decide who has won, but after they do, and *if* you don't get through, they'll invoice you and Reese for your thirds.'

The room spins again as I try to make sense of this. Sure, I don't know Will that well, but I never thought he'd do something like this, after all the moments we'd shared together.

'Plus, it names Will Hunt as the co-writer here, so he gets a bigger cut of the earnings if you do win,' Xavier goes on, as if what he's already told me isn't bad enough. 'I assume from your face that he doesn't deserve that?'

No, and I don't deserve this, I think before my mind flips through all the people I have lied to: Cameron, Reese, Anna and Jake. Maybe I do deserve this after all. But Will and I connected, we *slept* together, we woke up together, lying and joking in his bed together.

'I'm not sure why you even signed this,' Xavier says.

'I didn't,' I say. Will said not to until I'd spoken to Reese.

'Isn't this your signature?' Xavier flicks to the final page before pointing down at my own signature, the one I'd practised every day of my childhood; the one I'd given to Will as we sat in bed together, wrapped in lust and last night's sheets.

'No,' I whisper, feeling sick to my stomach. 'It's my autograph.'

CHAPTER TWENTY-THREE

This isn't okay. Nothing is okay. Even the positive mantra I've been holding onto for so many years, preached to myself after every failed audition, has admitted defeat. Thanking Xavier and forcing my heavy legs to my bedroom, my feet feel like they're sinking into treacle and my heart feels like I've just downed ten energy drinks in one go. Collapsing onto my bed, I try to think straight but the room is spinning. Was Will always planning to do this or was it just when he found out I'd lied about being Anna? Either way, he slept with me knowing that he was going to screw me over. I hold on to my stomach to stop me from being sick but all it does is remind me of the moments I spent in his bed, his fingers feeling the curves of my body before I marked his diary with the curves of my signature.

With shaking hands, I pick up my phone to find an empty screen and those damn James Dean lines telling me to dream as if I'll live forever. I finally felt like I was able to, like the little girl who grew up with hope in her heart. Reese may have been wrong about a lot of things, but she was right about one: sometimes it hurts to hope. I click on his number.

'Hey gorgeous,' Will says down the line and against all my better judgement my body softens slightly. But no. He can't be trusted. He never should have been trusted.

'Will, where are you?' I ask, trying and failing to keep the quiver out of my voice.

'You need me?' he says flirtatiously.

'Will, I'm serious,' I say. Before, I may have played up to it. But not now, not today.

'What's up, Marley?' he says, and I strain to make out the background noise. Low music and chatter; it sounds like he's in a bar. Or at a restaurant on a date?

'Where are you? I need to talk to you about something.'

'I'm kind of tied up right now,' he says, lowering his voice. Oh crap, he's really on a date. 'Can't it wait until tomorrow?'

'No, it's about the competition; it's serious,' I say again, my hushed tones growing louder, angrier, until Will cuts me off again.

'Calm down, Marley,' he says, and I finally see a glimpse of the patronising man Reese was always rolling her eyes at. 'I said, I've not got time for this right now.'

Will's words sting me in places that are already sore, bruised by Reese, by Anna, bruised by myself. A silence stretches between us as he waits for me to respond. But it's not silence; it's chatter and activity and it's Pete from the bar's band filling my ears. He's at the Hyde Out. And though he may not have time for this, he's going to have to *make* time.

Rushing down the corridor and out of the house, I hear my name called behind me.

'Marley, is everything okay?' Xavier asks again, increasingly concerned. This time I don't want to jump down his throat, the days of being on my high horse long gone.

'No,' I say, unable to stop angry tears from tracing their way down my face. If I thought things were bad before, they've managed to become a whole lot worse.

'Are you going to talk about the contract?'

And the rest, I think, unable to say the words, unable to admit them to myself.

'I could come with?'

'You've already done enough,' I say and watch his face fall. Just because he brought the truth to light doesn't make him the bad guy here. 'I mean,' I correct as he takes a step closer to me, 'I think this is something I have to do alone.'

'I'm here if you need me.' Xavier stands in our front doorway, hands on his hips. I never dreamed of a moment where I'd want him to be wearing that cape he was wearing before but right now, it feels like he might have just helped save me. That's if I can speak to Will and change things before it's too late.

Running down the street, I try to flag down the next bus, but it rushes right past me. *Screw it, I'll run to the next one*, I think as my feet pick up pace on the pavement.

A bus finally stops on the brink of Tower Bridge and soon this bus is flying over it as fast as it can in one of the most congested cities in the world. I could have taken the tube, but I don't want to risk being without phone signal, not when there's so much that needs to be said. London is lit up with window-lights and illuminations dancing along the water and though it would usually fill me with wonder, tonight the city feels too big, like the size and pace of the place might just swallow me whole. I always knew London was the kind of city where you could feel surrounded by people but still feel alone. I just wish I didn't have so much first-hand evidence of that. Being Anna, being with Reese and Will, I'd finally started feeling less lonely.

The bus swerves around a corner to reveal the first glimpse of the Hotel Hyde off in the distance. It's only then that I remember that Will *isn't* alone. The only time I've seen him drinking in the Hyde Out is when he is there with Reese. But Reese isn't working tonight. If he's there with her, they've purposefully not invited me. That, or they actually are on a date. I figured the moment I found out about Reese and Jake that my suspicions about her liking Will were a thing of the past. But what about those messages? The ones nestled in there right next to Jake's. Was I that naïve to think that Reese would limit herself to one love affair? That Will would? Clearly, fidelity isn't high on Reese's agenda, and I guess that would explain how angry she was to find out that Will and I had slept together. How could I not have pieced all the shards of this situation together by now? Reese and Will are a team and I was just a pawn in their plan.

Clambering off the bus, I run the best part of a mile to get back onto my normal route, walking the last few metres to the Hotel Hyde. Standing outside its iconic entrance, I stop still. Can I really go in there and accuse Will of being the bad guy when I've been far from good? I may have taken a name, but he has *signed a contract* in my name; the reason the two of us got so close is because I drew the line at that. Even so, I struggle to find the strength to go charging into the hotel. This place made me feel like something. After I confront Will, I will be left with nothing. Perhaps I never really had it in the first place.

Walking into the glorious reception room, I try not to make eye contact with any of the staff. As far as they know,

I'm Anna Adams and my fiancé and I are the most indecisive venue-viewers to ever walk into this place. I try not to think about Cameron and all the explanations I owe him as I walk over to the Hyde Out, but I see him there, leaning against the bar, almost instantly. As I stand there at the entrance, our eyes meet, and he reaches his hand to give me a welcome wave. I'm just about to walk towards him when I notice Will's familiar shoulders. He is sitting with his back to me, and an even more familiar face is talking back to him. I freeze on the spot. *It can't be.*

Taking a step back from the entrance, I try to remain out of view whilst looking closer at his face. It's Jake. But what on earth would Jake be doing here? With Will? My cheeks drain of colour as I try to make sense of it. Are they friends? Does Will know about Reese and Jake too? Has he been keeping it from me all this time? I feel the betrayal rush through my body and my legs beginning to chatter beneath me. But this is nothing compared to how Anna will feel when she finds out all of us have been keeping this from her. I watch on as Jake reaches a hand out across the table and Will puts his on top. *What the...?* I had every intention of storming in there, of finding out the truth, but right now, I know the one person I should be talking to is the reason I stepped foot in here in the first place.

I had so many reasons for not telling Anna the truth about Jake earlier but right now, none of them make any sense. *I don't want to hurt her. I shouldn't have taken that note. What have I even got to tell her? What about the competition?* None of them work. Ever since we found that scrap of paper with Reese's number on it, I should have told Anna every scrap of truth I came across until we could finally put the pieces together. Together. That's what Anna and I should have been. That's what we'd always been. Until she met Jake. I rush from the bar entrance into the Hotel Hyde and back across the reception room as the tears start to flow. I don't have all the answers, I don't have all the words, but I know I need to start talking to her.

'Anna, wait.'

I'm almost at the main doors when I hear her name called behind me. I turn around to see Cameron standing there, his shirt sleeves pushed up high again, a little out of breath.

'What's wrong?' he asks, his beautiful face marred with concern. I don't deserve it.

Everything, I want to say. I want him to hold me in his arms and let me cry, the way I had with Will the morning that Billie Forester had called to dump me. The way I had when I had let him in. But no, I can't. I need to be with Anna.

'Is it the wedding?' he asks, taking a step toward me.

'I just need some more time,' I whisper through my tears and Cameron puts a hand on my arm, willing me to go on.

'Anna, I can't,' Cameron says, his face falling, looking guiltier than he needs to feel. He's already shown me far more kindness than I deserve. 'I tried to hold the date, but another couple were offering the payment upfront and I—'

'It's okay.' I cut his sentence in two. I've already wasted too much of his time. And if I look at his sad face for a moment longer, I'm not sure I'll be able to keep my heavy heart from wanting him, my weary limbs from throwing themselves around him and holding on tight.

'If there's another cancellation I can try again...'

'No, it's okay.'

'You don't need it anymore?' Cameron asks unsurely. 'Is

it things with your fiancé? Anna, please. I know we're not friends, but I thought that maybe...'

'No,' I say, wiping a tear from my eye, somehow stung by his words. 'We're not friends.' Nor are Reese or Will or anyone else I met here. Anna is my real friend.

I don't turn back around to see Cameron's expression but hop in an Uber as quickly as I can. My mind races with thoughts as the car crawls through the city streets but only one thing is clear: I have to tell Anna about Jake and Reese. It's gone 11 p.m. by the time I'm running up the stairs to Anna's apartment, but I know Jake won't be in, because I've just seen him with Will. Why the hell have I just seen him with Will?

'Marley?' Anna opens the door bleary-eyed and ready for bed. 'What's wrong?'

'Is Jake in?' I ask; I already know the answer.

'No, he's out at work,' Anna says, far from convinced, still standing in the doorway, blocking my way from coming in, still keeping up her protective barrier. But it's time for the barriers to come down, all of them. 'Marley, it's really late.'

'Anna, can I come in?' I ask, still on the verge of tears. 'I need to tell you something.'

'Can it not wait until the morning?' Anna asks, as a tear escapes and starts making its way down my face. Am I nobody's priority? I shake my head as more tears fall.

'Is it things with that Will guy?' Anna says, like she's not surprised, and all the memories of how annoying Anna has been lately come rushing back in. Maybe once I let my guard down, she'll let hers down too and we can go back to being *us*.

'A little,' I admit, the understatement of the century. 'But it's more than just him.'

'Okay,' Anna says slowly, walking down her corridor and into the living room. I know to follow and take a seat on her sofa whilst she gets a glass of water. I wish she'd choose something stronger, but something tells me that there's not enough alcohol in the world to soften the blow of this. 'What do you want to talk about?'

'It's a long story.'

'Jake will be back soon,' Anna warns as my mind jolts back to seeing them together, as thick as thieves, in the Hyde Out; I wouldn't be so sure.

'Can you remember when I went to that appointment at the Hotel Hyde for you?'

'Yeah, of course,' Anna says, trying to stifle a yawn.

'Well, I went *as* you,' I say, and Anna's confused expression tells me she's none the wiser. 'There was this really snobby receptionist, and she was acting like she couldn't believe I'd be able to get married at the Hotel Hyde and well, I just said I was you but then one thing led to another and that night I met someone at the bar, still using your name.'

'Let me guess, this Will guy?' Anna says, a stern edge to her voice. She's too tired for this. And not just because she's ready for bed but because we're too old for drama now.

'Not exactly,' I say, inhaling deeply. 'I met a woman called Reese, who I entered this television show competition with.'

'Using my name?' she says, her body inching away from me on the sofa.

'Yes, but not... officially,' I add quickly.

'Okay, is that everything? That you used my name with these strangers?'

'Well, that's the thing, they're not strangers,' I say, but

after today I wouldn't say I know them. 'And she's not a stranger to Jake.'

Anna stiffens as soon as I've said his name. 'What are you insinuating?' She narrows her eyes in my direction.

'Look Anna, please don't be mad, but after we found that note...'

'Marley, what is it with you and that damn note?' Anna says, getting to her feet. 'We were having a blip and then we got over it. We're happy now.'

'Yes, but that's the thing,' I say, choosing my words carefully. Lord knows I should have done that more over the past few weeks. 'It wasn't a blip.'

I watch as Anna's cheeks flood pink and she begins to pace the floor before me.

'That evening I let myself into yours, the night where you were busy with an open house, I heard Jake on the phone to someone, saying he needed to see her.'

Anna stops still to look at me, her arms crossed but curious to hear more.

Into the silence, I carry on. 'And so, I took the note. I know I shouldn't have but you're my best friend and you are marrying him in *weeks* and I couldn't just watch you mess up your life...'

Her eyes widen in something like realisation as she uncrosses her arms; I think she's starting to soften.

'And so, I called the number, and I couldn't believe it, but it went through to this Reese girl's phone, the one I entered the competition with.'

'I don't believe it,' Anna says, under her breath.

'Neither could I,' I say, rising to stand before her. 'But it's true.'

'No, Marley,' Anna shakes her head. 'I actually *don't* believe it.'

'I know it's hard, Anna,' I say, taking a step towards her. She takes a step back. 'But we'll get through this together. Like we always do.'

'I don't believe *you*.' Anna's words cut to my core. 'Why should I? You've been lying about being me all this time, to this Will guy and now "Reese". Is she even real?'

'Is she real?' I echo Anna's words back to her. 'What do you mean?'

'Well, everyone knows you love the drama,' Anna snaps back.

'That's not fair,' I say, my cheeks burning red.

'Isn't it?'

'Reese is real. I was even with her earlier and checked her phone and there's all these messages from Jake on it. Recent ones.' *And messages from Will.* I force the thought away.

'Marley,' Anna is shouting now. 'Stop lying.'

'I'm not, Anna, I promise. Jake is cheating on you with a woman called Reese.'

'He's not,' Anna says as if the idea is almost laughable, but it was her idea in the first place. 'I'll tell you what's going on.'

'Please!' I say, exacerbated.

'Jake is out with a work contact.' He's out with Will. 'You pretended to be me and now you're trying to lie yourself out of *your* mess by messing up things for me.'

'That's not true,' I say, hot tears running down my cheeks.

'I'll tell you what's true,' Anna says, tears running down

her face too. 'You're jealous of me and Jake and what we have. That's why you're trying to derail it...'

'You're the one who told me he was cheating,' I object, willing her to listen to me.

'Yes, and then I told you he wasn't.' Anna shakes her head. 'You just won't let it go.'

'But why would I make it up?' I cry.

'I don't know,' Anna shrugs dramatically. 'The same reason you pretended to be me?'

'And what is that?'

'That you're unhappy with your own life?'

'At least what I have is *real*,' I say, instantly feeling the bitterness of the words. Nothing about these last couple of months have been real. Not the friendships, not the opportunity. They were always too good to be true.

'Then you'd best get back to it,' Anna says, walking purposefully towards her front door and holding it open for me.

'Anna, please,' I begin. It isn't supposed to end like this. But as Anna forces me out of the door, I can't help but feel like what's left of our friendship is finally over.

CHAPTER TWENTY-FOUR

I stare at the ceiling until the night turns into the morning, every limb feeling like a tonne, weighing me to the mattress. I can't move. And even if I wanted to, where would I go? My mind races through the last twenty-four hours. My confrontation with Reese. Reading through the contract with Xavier. Seeing Will and Jake together. Seeing Cameron. My horrific fight with Anna. I'm not sure which punch to the gut delivered the final blow. Right now, I wish it had finished me off.

Turning over on my side, every inch of me hurts. I feel my phone jut into me from somewhere beneath the covers and I risk reaching for it and looking at the screen. The Bride Tribe is alive with chirps and chatter. Maybe the silver lining of this whole thing is that I'll be kicked out of the group and never have to witness their WhatsApps again. Oh God, I'll actually be kicked out of the group. But not just the group. The whole bloody wedding – if it goes ahead. And the rest of Anna's life as well.

I look down at the screen at the most recent message:

How about Never Have I Ever? They're discussing games we could play on the hen party, not one of them aware that anything might be going on with Anna and Jake. I click open their chat and scan through the messages, all going above and beyond to make Anna's big weekend the best. Who am I to say whether she's confided in any of them about her relationship? I figured after the last time she turned up at my doorstep that she'd always turn to me but was I really that supportive? I didn't even believe her until she stopped believing that Jake could cheat herself.

I think Anna really likes that game Lauren has written on the chat. *I'll send my Never Have I Evers ahead of your big trip with a little gift as well.* Just reading it back makes me feel worse; how can everyone else be content just being there from a distance when I'm trying to build a bridge back to what we were, whilst the bricks fall from beneath my feet?

Lauren is right; Anna does like that game. I used to like that game too, but something tells me I wouldn't fare well this time around. Never Have I Ever gone to an appointment even though I should have just said no. Never Have I Ever pretended to be my best friend. Never Have I Ever embarked on the greatest opportunity with the worst of people. Never Have I Ever tied myself in so many knots that I've become the worst of people myself.

I look down at my phone screen, just willing someone to call but I know no one will. Not my agent, who has dropped me. Or my parents, who have given up on me ever applying for a real job. I thought I'd prove them all wrong when we won this competition, when I could finally pay off every debt I've accrued. This was meant to be my big break, but now everything is broken. And even without Will's shitty contract, I'm really bloody broke.

I throw my phone onto the floor and hug my pillow to my chest, the tears coming thick and fast, the same way they did last night at Anna's as she showed me to the door. The same way they did as Cameron caught me leaving the Hotel Hyde for the final time. What must he think of me now? I hold the pillow tighter as my shoulders start to heave in time with my sobs. Assuming by now that Will has told Reese everything, Cameron will know I'm not Anna; that I've been lying to him this whole time. Either that, or they both still think I'm Anna and that I've cheated on my fiancé with Will. Right now, I'm not sure which is worse.

My phone buzzes on the floor and I peer down past my pillow, still clutched in my weary arms, and see the name flashing across the screen: *Reese's mobile.* I don't have the strength to speak to her, to hear her lay into me about sleeping with Will again.

I turn over on my side and sob even harder. Everything is such a mess and it's all my fault. Maybe Anna is right? Maybe I did want the drama? Maybe I did want something to happen that day I walked into the Hotel Hyde to shake up the monotony of *waiting* for something to happen. Lying here now, feeling more rejected and alone than I ever have before, I know what people mean when they say you should be careful what you wish for.

'Marley?' I hear Xavier's voice on the other side of my bedroom door. I roll over on my side again to face the door, firmly closed shut.

'Are you 'k?' It's the same question he asked me yesterday when I was still reeling from my dinner with Reese, back when I thought things couldn't get any worse. I wasn't okay then and I'm not okay now. And although Xavier may have wanted to save me from walking blindly into a 'bogus contract', neither one of us can change the fact that it's already signed. Xavier can't save me. He shouldn't have to.

'Marley, can I come in?' he asks again, his voice barely above a whisper. I look at the door between us, keeping me inside, keeping Xavier out.

'No, I'm just...' I begin, unable to keep from crying. Xavier and I are not friends, we're just two people who live together. I didn't even know he used to be a hot-shot lawyer. Because I never asked, because I never let him in.

'Is it okay if I come in?' he says, louder this time.

'I'm a bit of a mess,' I say, pushing myself to sitting, tears still rolling down my face.

Before I can object, Xavier's bearded face is floating in the gap between the frame and the door, now pushed ajar. He smiles at me and I crumble even more.

'Marley,' he says, sitting on the edge of my bed precariously. 'You may be messy, but I've already wrestled you into my bed when you were so drunk you couldn't walk, and you've seen me high as a kite and trying to play the bagpipes.'

'You were actually okay,' I lie through my tears and he raises his eyebrows.

'And you need to stop bullshitting,' he says with a grin, moving his body a little further onto my bed. 'If you can't be a mess in your own home, where can you be?' He grins again and before I can stop myself, I'm flinging my arms around him and sobbing into his shoulder. The past year we've lived together this place has never felt like home; I've always been too busy running off to Anna's to make it one. 'What's this all about?'

'I think she might be right,' I sob, still held in his arms, and what's weird is that after yesterday, this feels like the most normal thing of all.

'Who?'

'Anna,' I say, pulling away from our hug to look at him.

'The one who turned up here crying a few weeks back?'

'I thought you were too high to notice that,' I say, wiping the tears from my face.

'You also thought I was stupid,' Xavier says with a kind smile.

'I didn't think you were stupid.'

'Well, you didn't think I was smart.' He smiles again. 'I saw how surprised you were yesterday,' Xavier continues, 'and not just about that contract.'

'Okay, I might have thought a lot of things, but I was wrong,' I admit, trying to keep the conversation as far away from the contract as possible right now. With Anna not talking to me, thinking I'm a liar, it suddenly doesn't feel like the most pressing thing of all. Even with the pilot filming still set for tomorrow.

'I didn't even bother to find out what was true about you,' I go on as Xavier listens. I was always too busy to take an interest in his latest fancy. I didn't realise we were both just trying to find ourselves. 'And you're right,' I say, managing my first smile of the morning. 'You're not very good at the bagpipes.'

Thankfully, Xavier laughs too.

'But I know you'll find what makes you happy soon.'

'I know I will too,' he says confidently, as if this was never in doubt. I like that about Xavier; he backs himself even when the world thinks he's crazy. 'What I don't know is why you've been crying all night.' He strokes his bushy beard thoughtfully, like a detective trying to work out a crime; the massacre I've made of my life. 'Is it the contract, was Anna warning you against that?'

'She didn't know about it.' I shake my head, my voice shaking too.

'Then what was she right about?'

'Not everything, that's for sure,' I say, thoughts of Reese and Jake, and Jake and Will swirling around my head. 'We had a fight last night, and loads of things were said,' I explain, knowing that right now I've not got the energy to explain it all but that in time, I'll tell Xavier everything. He's here for me when I'm upset; he's trying to prevent me from harm without me needing to ask him to; he's even covering my rent and not lording it over me. Of all the things I never thought I'd be this year – Anna, faux-engaged, an almost-successful actress, Will Hunt's plaything – I didn't expect to become Xavier's friend.

'Anna accused me of being jealous of her and I think I she's right,' I say. 'I have been jealous of her. Of her perfect partner and her perfect apartment and her perfect life.'

'Things didn't seem that perfect when she turned up here.'

'No, they weren't, and do you know what's awful?'

'My bagpipe-playing. You've made your point,' Xavier says without pause and I can't help but laugh out loud – smart *and* funny.

'I kind of enjoyed her needing me again,' I whisper, any laughter returning to tears.

'That makes sense if you guys used to be really close.'

'Yeah, used to be,' I say, brushing another tear away, beginning to wonder when they might dry out. 'If I thought drifting away from a friend was hard, having them tear your friendship into threads is worse. I was trying to help her,' I say, not sure why I feel the need to convince him. 'But it was too little too late.'

'It's never too late,' Xavier says, and it sounds like he's speaking from experience. 'I've seen commercial deals dissolve completely before the parties patch it up again.'

'She doesn't trust anything I say anymore,' I say, searching Xavier's face for answers. 'But she needs to know that what I'm telling her is the truth.'

'Well, you know what the solution is,' Xavier says, as if it's simple.

'I promise you I don't.'

'Homer's *Odyssey*.'

'Huh?' Just when I thought he was starting to make sense.

'Remember what I told you when you'd taken what didn't belong to you?'

His note. Her name. And here I was, convinced he wouldn't even remember that encounter.

'The lesser of two evils,' Xavier reminds me again. 'Which is worse: letting Anna walk away and risking that she may never find out the truth? Or trying to get her to listen to you again and again and risking that you might get hurt in the process?'

'I would take a hit for that girl any day of the week,' I say, realising that although our trains might be on different tracks there will always be a turntable bringing us together again.

'Drug-hit or bullet-hit?' Trust Xavier to have to ask the question.

'Bullet-hit,' I nod as Xavier's smile spreads across his face.

'Then I think you've found your answer.'

I call Anna's phone at least once every five minutes but she's not picking up, which is precisely why I'm already on the way to her flat. I know she doesn't want to see me; is it still breaking and entering if you have a spare key?

Pushing my way into Anna's building, I take the stairs up to her floor. Waiting for the lift may have been quicker but at least going straight for the stairs keeps me moving. I don't want to give myself any more time to decide to turn back around. Xavier was right. Out of the host of screw-ups and betrayals that these past few weeks have seen, my friendship with Anna – our entwined history, our indeterminate future – is worth the fight.

Xavier: I hope it all goes okay. I look down at his message, lighting up my phone. I quickly type one in return: *Thanks. I'll be home soon x*

Standing outside Anna's front door, I decide to knock. Even if I need to shout my apologies through the wooden panels, I will.

'Anna, open up. I need to speak to you.' I hammer hard on the door.

'Marley?' It swings open quicker than I thought it would, and I see Jake standing there with swollen eyes and furrowed brow.

'Jake? I...' I begin. I have a thousand things I want to ask him. About Reese, about Will. About how he could be so knee-deep in his affair with another woman that he's even having pints with her uni friend. Or more than friend? I don't know that for sure but the temptation of telling Jake that his other woman has *another man* is almost too much to bear. But right now, it isn't about them, it isn't about anything other than Anna.

'What are you doing here?' Jake asks again. Isn't it obvious?

'I need to talk to Anna,' I say, pushing all of my anger at

him deep beneath my surface. Right now, he's the person standing between me and my best friend.

'I thought she...' Jake begins, and his muddled expression makes me snap. I know she doesn't want to talk to me right now but if he loves her, he shouldn't get in the way of her friendships. If he loves her, he shouldn't have ever accepted another girl's number.

'Jake, you need to tell her the truth,' I explode. 'About Reese.'

His mouth hangs open in shock.

'I already have,' Jake says, apology written on every inch of his face. 'At least some of it. She ran out before I could explain it all. I thought she'd be with you. Has she not called? I have no idea where she is...' The tempo of Jake's sentence speeds up with every thought. He's told her about Reese? 'Why has she not called you?'

Because she doesn't trust me. Because she thinks I'm jealous of her.

'I need to find her.' Jake steals the thought from my mind.

'No, you wait here,' I say, putting a hand up to stop him from taking another step toward me. 'You've already done enough.'

'Marley, I'm so sorry, I—'

'Save it, Jake,' I say, and he looks like my words have just slapped him across the face. 'I'm going to find her.'

Jake nods, his cheeks ghost-white, his eyes brimming with tears.

'Just let me know if she turns up here.' We both know that she won't.

Rushing back down the stairs, I mentally run through all the places she could be. If she's not at hers and she's not at mine, then where is she? As soon as my feet hit the pavement outside Anna's building, I decide to head to her office. It's just around the corner and no matter where her open houses are, she always has to head back there.

'Marley?' Arabella looks up from her desk as soon as I bustle into the estate agency.

'Have you seen, Anna?' I say, no time for niceties.

'She's not working today.' Arabella shakes her beautiful, bouncy hair. 'Marley, are you okay? Do you want me to call her for you?' She stands up, her heels click-clacking over to me. She puts a hand to my shoulder and steers me to a nearby seat. 'Can I get you a coffee, honey?' she offers softly.

'Thanks,' I say, as I feel my emotions getting the better of me. 'And sorry I've not got back to you about your latest idea on the Bride Tribe group,' I say, feeling guilty again.

'Oh, don't you worry about that,' Arabella waves the apology away. 'It's all just suggestions, anyway. I know provided we're all there Anna will have a great time.'

I look at her now, her beauty shining on the inside and out and realise that I may have judged her too. Could it be that my envy was clouding everything? That being annoyed by the Bride Tribe was about being annoyed at myself?

'I do think the Best Investment bikini was a good idea though,' she adds.

Okay, so maybe they are a little annoying. But like Xavier, I never really gave them a chance.

'Yeah maybe,' I say, as I watch her swipe to Anna's number.

'She's not picking up,' Arabella says, shaking her head again. 'You take milk?'

'I really need to find her,' I say, getting up and making my way to the door.

'Just let me know if there's anything I can do to help,' Arabella calls behind me.

'Thank you.' I turn to her with a smile. 'I really appreciate it.'

Back outside, I try to call Anna again but see Reese's name filling up my screen. I can't deal with her right now. Now that Anna knows the truth, it's time to show her where my loyalties lie. Walking aimlessly through Greenwich, I filter through the places she could be. I pop into Grind, our favourite coffee shop in her neck of the woods, but she's nowhere to be seen. Our favourite places are all around Central London, all closer to mine.

Realisation washes over me: in the years that we've lived here, we've spent plenty of time near mine, or on mutual ground; when did I start thinking that it was always me coming to her? When did I start thinking that where we were had to mean something?

It's then that I realise – she'll be by the water; we used to always sit on a bench looking out at the Thames, remarking on how we didn't need to spend a fortune to enjoy the city. I walk as quickly as I can to the benches scattered along the water outside the Old Royal Navy College. There's no sign of her. *Come on Anna. Where are you?*

I walk further down the Thames, the Shard growing marginally clearer as I do. My phone continues to buzz with Reese's calls, which I ignore, and Anna still refuses to pick up. She could be anywhere by now. In Leicester Square listening to the buskers play, as we have done so many times together when we've decided to enjoy the city as tourists. She could be in Tayyabs in Aldgate, eating her emotions away with the best Indian food in town; it's where we used to head after every break-up or bad workday one of us had survived.

She could be standing on London Bridge, looking over to Tower Bridge, tracing the same circuit we used to run at least once every week together. Or she could be wandering through Hyde Park looking up at the Hotel Hyde, dreaming about the man she may or may not want to marry there.

It's then that my heavy legs draw to a halt. Why would Anna run to a happy place she's shared with me when I've been struggling to be happy for her? Anna may have become obsessed with building her perfect life over the last couple of years, but haven't I been obsessed with the fact mine isn't perfect? And hasn't she tried to invite me into it all as much as possible? What if she wasn't trying to make me jealous but simply make me a part of it; the way we have with every relationship and break-up and milestone we've had before.

Trudging to the bus stop, I finally admit defeat. I'm not going to find Anna today. She's not going to call. And I'm not going to sort any of this out before the pilot filming tomorrow. It's not like I can go and be with Reese and Will now. Not now that everything is out in the open. Well, almost everything. I look down at Reese's number still trying to get through to me, remembering her face when she found out about Will. What would she say if she found out the truth about me, the truth about Anna?

As the bus pulls up on Tower Bridge Road, I begin to walk back to my flat, the five-minute journey feeling like five hours. I thought I'd be walking home with Anna, arm and arm and laughing about how stupid we'd both been. But no, this isn't a fairy tale, this is real life: messy and complicated and entirely off-script.

Opening the front door into our living room, I expect to find Xavier surrounded by his familiar cloud of smoke, baking something or making something or adding more details to the contract stipulating my demise. But I never imagined this. He's sitting bolt upright in the middle of the sofa, sandwiched in between two other faces looking up at me like thunder. To his left is Anna, arms folded, face tear-stained. And to his right, sits Reese.

CHAPTER TWENTY-FIVE

'Hi erm...' I begin, walking into the room slowly and taking a seat in one of our scrubby old armchairs, not even knowing whether I'm welcome to take a seat in my own home anymore. But I couldn't keep standing even if I wanted to. What are they both doing here? *Together?* I look from one stone-cold face to the other, neither one happy to see me.

'Xavier, why didn't you call me?' I say, looking to him with accusation in my eyes.

'You said you'd be back soon,' he says with an unsure smile, and I remember the message I sent him just hours before when I was standing outside Anna's door, mere seconds before Jake admitted that he'd told Anna about Reese. I look at her now, a single tear-mark making its way down her pretty, pinched features.

'Anna, I've been trying to call you...' I say, looking to her and trying to ignore Reese completely even though our last encounter makes the frost between us impossible to thaw. What is she doing here? Coming back for round two? 'Are you okay?'

'Of course I'm not okay,' Anna snaps back at me, her head still fixed forward, refusing to look in Reese's direction too. But Anna did come here. That's got to be a good sign. I sit back in my seat, bitten and bruised by every word that's been flung between us.

'Anna came here looking for you,' Xavier says slowly, his head oscillating between the two women on either side of him. Weeks ago, I would have thought he was too wrapped up in his own world to notice anything going on outside his pillow fort. Now, I know better.

'I was looking for you too,' I say, leaning further forward. 'I went to yours. Jake said that he'd told you about...' I look to Reese, who is busy studying her bashed-up biker boots.

'I know,' Anna says, her tears coming thicker now. 'I came straight here. I didn't know where else to go.'

'I'm glad you did,' I say, just wanting to hold her close, to tell her everything's going to be okay. Even if I don't believe it for myself. 'You're always welcome here. Anna, I'm—'

'And is *she*?' Anna spits her interruption, finally looking across to Reese.

'Well no... she...' I look at Reese too, and she's a far cry from the confident badass I met on my first night in the Hyde Out. She looks broken and open, like the woman who cried to me on that bench in the park; the woman I was starting to consider a friend, or at least 'Anna' was. 'Hang on, how do you even know where I live?' I ask her with trepidation.

'Surprising, right?' Reese says, with a smirk. 'Seeing as I didn't even know your *name*.' Oh crap. No, no. 'Marley, is it?'

'I can explain...'

'I think *she's* got some explaining to do too,' Anna snaps in Reese's direction.

'Who's *she?* The cat's mother?' Reese gets to her feet as I flinch.

'No, the *bitch* who—'

'Stop!' Xavier shouts into the room, standing as he does and towering over us all. 'You. Sit,' he says authoritatively, putting a hand out in Reese's direction. For once, she does as she's told. 'I don't know who you are, but you came here asking for Marley, saying you *know* her, that you've worked together. And I know Anna and Marley have some erm... catching up to do,' Xavier says, looking between our two tear-marred faces. 'So, if you can please enlighten us all as to why I've let you into my house...'

'I read the contract,' Reese says, turning to me. 'I kept pushing Will for it, and he kept saying that he'd let me look at it soon.' She goes on; not one of us interrupts her. 'But after our fight, after I found out you were screwing each other,' Reese spits the words; it was one night, but right now, I don't think that matters. 'I called up Tanya Moore at Sloane Star and asked her to send me a copy of the contract directly.'

'*You're* Reese Priestly?' Xavier says, eyes scanning her concerned face.

'Yes...' Reese is slightly taken aback by the question. It's not like her identity is the one in question. Did he really not ask for her name before letting her into our home? 'Why?'

'You're just prettier than I imagined.' Xavier brushes a hand through his beard.

'That's not the...' both Anna and I begin in unison and our eyes lock. I will her to smile but she doesn't and right now, who can blame her?

'I, err... thanks,' Reese says, trying to get back on track. 'So, I receive this bullshit contract and as if that wasn't bad enough, Will has found some way to be able to sign it on my behalf, a contract between me, a third party and some woman I'd never heard of.' She looks at me, her cheeks blushing red. 'So, I thought I'd go to her address and find out who the hell she is... And then I meet *Anna* here.'

'Reese, I'm so sorry,' I say, and even though she's the other woman I know she deserves an apology. 'That day we met at the hotel, I wasn't in a good place,' I begin to explain, glancing to Anna who is biting her nails nervously; she's heard it all before.

'I told you about the audition I got rejected from the day before we met?' I ask and Reese nods, remembering how we'd bonded over our shared experience of our crazy industry that makes everyone feel like they're missing the mark. 'Well, times that by a thousand and that's what my last few years have been like. That, and the feeling that everyone's striding into adulthood, whilst I'm stuck in the same place unable to move forward but not knowing what direction I'd go in if it wasn't the one I was already taking...'

I look to Anna who is now crying fully, her eyes still fixed on me.

'I went to the appointment *for* Anna,' I continue, all three of them listening on. 'But then when I told the receptionist I *was* Anna, things started to change. She started to treat me differently, Cameron started to treat me differently,' I go on, his name and the memory of where we left things like another punch to the gut. 'So, I was Anna for the day, and I didn't think it mattered but then I met you and we applied to the competition and I just never thought it would go this far... I never thought *we* would get this far...' I say, a lump catching in my throat again. 'I felt like things were coming together for the first time in ages.'

'Me too,' Reese whispers.

'I know,' I say, my eyes fixed on hers, Anna's eyes burning into my side. 'And I was going to tell you everything but then I found out who *you* really were too.'

'The bitch who shagged my fiancé,' Anna cries across at her, wanting to break off any heart-to-heart between me and the woman who has just broken hers.

'I didn't shag your fiancé,' Reese says, the edge in her voice softening. 'I promise. And you didn't cheat on yours?' She turns to me now, her features softening too.

'I don't have a fiancé,' I say. 'I'm single. I'm Marley,' I finally confirm the basics. 'And I'm really sorry for lying to you. Both of you.' I look to Anna again.

'What do you mean you didn't sleep with him?' Anna says, the bite from her words melting into exhaustion, her sentence laced with hope. 'He said the note was from you.'

'It was,' Reese says. 'And I'm sorry. I didn't know he had a fiancée.'

'You need to tell me everything,' Anna says, her throat hoarse with heartache.

'I don't even know you,' Reese says, her defiance forcing its way to the fore.

'Please,' Anna whispers, almost leaning over Xavier now sitting in the middle of them again.

'*Please*,' I echo, and as Reese turns to me, I see a glimpse of warmth in her eyes.

'Okay,' Reese says, her shoulders relaxing. 'I did meet Jake a few weeks ago when he was drinking with some colleagues at the Hyde Out.' She says this to Anna, whose face is fixed on hers, fearful but fascinated. 'He seemed pretty out of it and ended up staying late, coming to sit with me and Will for a drink after hours. We were flirting and I ended up giving him my number, but I had no idea he had a fiancée, I swear.'

'He didn't tell you?' Anna asks, the hurt in her voice evident for all to hear.

'Not at first,' Reese explains, her voice soft; I know she doesn't want to make this harder than it already is. She knows what it's like to have a broken heart. 'We messaged for around a week. He said he was stressed, that he had made some pretty bad investments at work and that he was struggling for money, to keep up with some big payments coming up.'

I look to Anna, the tears running down her face. We know she means the wedding.

'Then we met up for dinner,' Reese says, looking sorrier still. This is awful, devastating, but I know Anna needs to hear it. 'And about five minutes in, Jake told me about you, said he had a fiancée, and that she was wonderful and more than he deserves. He said that messaging me that week, even entertaining betraying you, was the worst mistake he'd ever made.' Reese looks sad now, sad and sorry. I think she might have actually liked him.

'And then what?' Anna asks, now sat on the edge of her seat.

'Then nothing,' Reese says. 'Honestly. The second I knew about you, it was over.'

'You didn't sleep together?'

'We didn't even kiss,' Reese says, and it sounds like she's telling the truth.

'But what about those messages on your phone?' I say, somewhere between indignation and guilt. I know I shouldn't have been looking through them, but I remember what I read: *I know neither one of us saw this coming, but you have to let me take care of you, you have to let someone take care of you...*

'What messages?' Reese looks genuinely confused.

'The ones you received at dinner,' I say. 'They were signed off from J and he called you beautiful. He called you *bella...*'

'I knew there was more to it than you're telling us,' Anna says, shaking her head. 'Jake has been acting weird for weeks,' she finally admits, looking in my direction. 'You were right about that; I just didn't want to face it.'

'I know—' I begin sensitively before Reese cuts me off.

'And *I* know that I haven't sent any messages to Jake since he told me about you.' Reese scrambles for her phone and out of the corner of my eye I see Will's name at the top of the screen. If things were over between her and Jake, then why did I see Jake with Will? 'Oh,' Reese says, flicking through her screen. 'These messages are from Will.'

'But what about the unsaved number?'

'They're from him too,' Reese says, turning her screen around to face me. 'Will had so many ideas for our script that I asked him to use his old phone to message me any suggested amendments. I told him that it was so I wouldn't miss them, but really, it was so I could filter them out from anything *important* about the competition.'

I read the messages again, the lines growing all the more familiar.

'These are lines from the script?' I ask, still unsure who to trust.

'Suggested ones,' Reese confirms. 'He wanted Jack to call Ella, Bella, as a pet name.'

'I hate that,' I say, knowing that's not the point.

'Me too,' Reese says, a timid smile turning up the corners of her mouth.

So 'J' was *Jack*, not Jake?

'But then why did I see Will and Jake together at the Hyde Out yesterday?' I ask.

'*What?*' Both Anna and Reese snap together.

'I was trying to find him, to confront him about the contract.' I can't help the anger from surging through my veins; how has everything got so twisted? 'And I saw him there, having a drink with Jake.'

'But that doesn't make any sense,' Reese says, looking from Anna to me.

'I thought they might have become friends when you were dating?' I say to Reese quietly, even though I know Anna is hanging on our every word.

'I've told you, we didn't *date*,' Reese says. 'They did meet at the bar that night, they seemed to be getting on really well, but I didn't know they'd kept in touch. Will never mentioned anything.' Will didn't mention a lot of things.

'What did they talk about?' I say, not knowing what they'd be doing together.

'I told you, Jake mostly talked about his work, about the highs and lows of being an investment banker,' Reese confirms again. I don't know about Anna but I'm starting to believe her. It still doesn't make Jake innocent, but I know it's a lot better than the scenes that have been playing through Anna's mind – and mine – ever since we found out about the note.

'And we spoke about our script, the competition,' Reese continues, remembering out loud. 'Will was bragging about how we had the chance to make one hundred thousand pounds easy, far more if the pilot got picked up...' Reese goes on, the size of the opportunity only emphasising the size of this mess. 'Jake kept on joking that he'd invest in us.'

'What if he wasn't joking?' Xavier says, reaching forward for my copy of the contract, the pages still sitting with all his scribbles on the coffee table before us.

'What do you mean?' Reese asks.

'This contract may screw you two over,' Xavier says. 'But it screws up this third-party investor the most.' He scans down the paper as the thought settles in my mind. *No way.* Is that what Will and Jake were meeting about? Reese looks to me, her mouth hanging open as the penny begins to drop. 'Anna, whose address is this?'

She holds the contract in her shaking hands, her bent legs chattering against the chair.

'Jake's,' she confirms, a look of horror on her face. 'That's his parents' address.'

'Shit,' Reese whispers, practically humming with rage.

'But Jake wouldn't have signed this, not with Marley's name on it.'

'He didn't need to,' Xavier says, shaking his head. 'The way it's drafted...it gives Will the power to... I told you it was *not* a good contract.'

'What does this mean?' Anna asks, her red face flushing white.

'It means Jake is paying for our pilot,' I say, a wave of sickness washing over me.

'But Jake's money is my money,' Anna cries.

'It means Will is screwing us all,' Reese says into the space between us.

'How the hell are we going to get out of this?' I ask, sweat prickling on my palms.

'I think it's time we start working together,' Reese says, looking to Anna for something like permission.

Reluctantly, she nods. Reese isn't the enemy right now.

'And I think it's time,' Xavier says, 'for me to start acting like a lawyer again.'

CHAPTER TWENTY-SIX

'Okay, I've managed to get hold of the studio space that Will booked,' Reese says down the phone. 'Do you want the good news or the bad news?'

'There's more bad news?' I ask, and I hear Reese let out a little laugh down the phone. It feels good to be speaking again, for everything to be out in the open. I know it sucks that Jake messaged Reese for a whole week, but right now, that betrayal feels like nothing compared to Jake going into business with Will without telling Anna.

'The good news,' Reese continues, with no time to waste, 'is that I've been able to cancel the studio; the bad news is that there's a cancellation fee,' she says. 'But it's nothing compared to what it was going to cost.'

'Thanks Reese,' I say. I really mean it. Soon after we found out that Jake and Anna were the ones fronting the cost of our pilot, Reese was on the phone to Tanya Moore again to work out what the terms for the pilot filming really meant, managing to do it without letting on that anything was amiss.

It's not like they're going to let us stay in the competition with a cheat.

'I think that's every ludicrously expensive thing Will purchased cancelled and replaced with a cheaper option, but it's still costing us a bomb.'

'Xavier's working on the contract, on what he's going to say to Will,' I explain, looking over to him now, sat with his laptop open in front of him at our dining table. He looks happy; maybe it wasn't the work he disliked, just the environment? 'But even with Will getting his fair cut and shouldering his fair share of the risk, it's still going to bankrupt me if we don't win... more than I already am.' As helpful as Xavier is being, I can't ask him to lend me any more money; he's already done enough.

'I've chatted to my parents,' Reese says. 'They can give me some.'

'Mine too,' I say, feeling the warmth of their support shooting through me.

'But it's not enough,' Reese whispers down the line. She's already lost a good friend, now we're going to have to say goodbye to the competition too.

'We'll take your script elsewhere,' I say, knowing it's time to bow out.

'*Our* script,' Reese says down the line. 'I'll call Tanya and explain we're pulling out. Then I'll call up and cancel the space I've managed to get hold of for this afternoon – it's not like it's in high demand.' She sighs. 'I have half a mind to let Will find out for himself.'

He deserves that and more. But we both know what it's like to lose yourself in chasing after the thing you think will make you happy. Plus, we still wanted to see whether we can win this thing and pay off everything, for Anna and Jake. But it's too risky.

'Let's just tell him the truth,' I say. 'But call everything off first, leave it to the last minute.'

'I'll tell him I'll let him know the details *soon*,' Reese says, a hint of venom in her voice; we both know it's what Will has been telling her all this time.

A knock on the door interrupts our moment and soon Reese and I are saying goodbye, both knowing that her next call to Tanya Moore will see us say goodbye to our dream for good. Walking to answer the door, I pray that it isn't Will. He's been trying to call me and Reese since yesterday, ever since our silence started to make him nervous. But as I swing open the door, I find Anna there, clutching a bouquet of flowers.

'Can I come in?' she asks sheepishly.

'Of course!' I say, stepping aside. She gives Xavier a little wave, but I know from the look on her face that she'll want our next conversation to stay private.

'What are these for?' I say, as soon as we're in the safety of my bedroom.

'To say good luck,' Anna says, with a little smile. 'For today.'

'Thanks,' I say, genuinely touched even though the luck is no longer needed, not for filming our pilot at least. 'But it should be me buying these for you,' I say softly. 'Anna, I'm so sorry. For *everything*.'

'Me too,' she says, snuggling further into the headboard of my bed.

'What have you got to be sorry for?' I ask, following suit. Right this moment, Reese is cancelling everything and forgoing our chance of winning the equivalent of an *actual* salary, but sitting here with Anna right now, raw and real, feels priceless in comparison.

'For some of the things I said to you, for a start,' Anna begins slowly. 'For saying you were jealous of me.'

'I am jealous of you, Anna,' I say. Or at least I was. 'These last few years you've really got your life together whilst I've felt like mine's been falling apart. But I'm sorry. I should have known you being messy too wouldn't have made my mess any better.'

'That's okay,' Anna says, weary and relieved. 'I've been jealous of you too.'

'Jealous of me?' I say, sitting up straighter. '*Why?*'

'Because you're still having all of these adventures and auditions and chasing your dreams,' Anna says, and I can't believe I'm hearing this. 'Having my own apartment is fun and being in a relationship with someone you love is...' She stutters on this last line. *Someone you loved?* I can't help but think. 'It's great and everything, but sometimes it's really hard,' she says, looking more sincere than she has in weeks.

'Then why didn't you say anything?' I ask quietly.

'Because I could see you were struggling,' she says, reaching for my hand. 'And I didn't want to be the kind of friend who moaned about my mortgage or my partner when I knew you were beating yourself up for not having those things. I wanted to seem grateful.'

'You seemed a little smug,' I confess softly, and Anna doesn't look offended.

'I know,' she admits. 'But it's a hard thing to get right. Too happy? You seem smug. Too down? You seem ungrateful,' she goes on, and I can appreciate how that could be tricky. 'Meanwhile you just got to be whatever you were feeling. You could be real with me. Cry about your auditions, about living with a stranger. I had to self-regulate, keep it all together, until I couldn't do it anymore.'

'I'm sorry,' I say, every meltdown of mine flashing through my mind.

'But I know I went too far,' Anna goes on. 'I began to resent you for being able to be yourself whilst I had to be the grown-up one, the stable one, then I thought screw it, if I'm going to play this role, I'm going to make it as perfect as everyone thinks it is... the perfect house, the perfect partner, the perfect job. Somewhere along the line, I started to care more about what everyone else thought my life was like, rather than what I did.'

'And what do you think about it?'

'I thought it was pretty good by my standards before I started measuring it by everyone else's. *Anna's life is so amazing. Anna's job is so cool.*' She begins to mock the voices I know she's heard, the sentences I've said myself. '*Anna and Jake are perfect...*' She struggles to even mock the words now that that's so far from the truth. 'I never wanted us to be perfect until I convinced myself we *should* be. But before long, I let the pressure of living up to everyone's perceptions make a caricature of me – one I started to believe was true.'

'I'm sorry I made you feel like you had to be perfect,' I say, holding her hand in mine.

'I'm sorry I made you feel like you had to *be me*,' she says, tears in her eyes. 'I know I lost myself there for a bit.'

'Me too,' I whisper and right now they feel like the two most powerful words in the world. 'How about I be me and you be you?' I say; it feels as cheesy as it sounds.

'Okay,' Anna begins slowly. 'But whilst we're being honest?'

I gulp, not sure what she's about to say next.

'Sometimes I feel like in being *us*, we're trying to be who we used to be,' she says, choosing her words carefully. 'Like maybe you're trying to shoehorn us back into a time when things were a bit simpler or something? I just don't think we can be those people we were ten years ago anymore, Marley,' she says, a sadness in her voice.

'But I miss those girls,' I say, my voice cracking.

'I know, me too.' Anna smiles. 'But I think the women we are now could be pretty good friends too, if we just relax and stop trying so hard to *be* something.'

I know Anna's right. I've been trying to hold on to who we were so tightly that I've unintentionally confined our friendship to the history books, clinging onto a scrap of the people we used to be. But we could be something now, something else in the future.

'You're right,' I say. 'I feel like I've screwed everything up.'

'Well, yeah.' Anna's laugh fills the room. 'You're human. We make mistakes but that doesn't mean it derails everything.'

Suddenly, I'm not sure we're talking about us two anymore.

'How did things go with Jake?' I ask, still clutching her hand in mine.

'We talked all night,' Anna says, the dark circles under her make-up-less eyes evidence enough. 'About everything,' she continues, and I nod her on. Unbeknownst to Anna right now we quite literally have all day. 'Don't get me wrong, what he did is inexcusable. He should have told Reese he had a fiancée the second he met her, *never* should have messaged her, never should have dreamed of going for *dinner* with her, should

have never gone into business with Will without telling me...'
she goes on, the list of offences against him almost as long as
my own. 'But he started opening up to me about how bad
things at work have been, how a few wrong investments have
landed him in a pretty awful place. Then with all the pressure
I was putting on us to be perfect, to have the perfect wedding
so quickly, I think something inside him kind of cracked.'

I listen to Anna speak. Despite everything, there's real
empathy in her voice. She's not being lax with him, but she is
being fair. She's being patient, she's being kind; love might
get complicated sometimes, but I know in my gut that it
should always be these things.

'We're calling off the wedding,' Anna says, and I throw
my arms around her.

'Oh Anna, I'm sorry,' I whisper into her hair.

'For now,' she says, her voice muffled by our embrace and
I pull away to look at her. 'I was only rushing our wedding
because I felt like it was another thing I *should* be doing,'
Anna goes on. 'Jake is going to get some help, you know, for
his mental health and we're going to take some time, see if we
can rebuild the trust again,' she says, her sadness tinged with
grace. 'And we're going to sort everything out with this Will
guy.' She smiles at me. 'We sure know how to pick 'em, eh?
Anna manages to laugh though a stray tear runs down her
face.

'We sure do,' I say. 'But for the record, I think Jake's actually a good one. A stupid one, sure,' I add quickly. 'But you
know, a good one at the core.'

'I think so too,' Anna adds, with a soft smile. 'He says the
hardest part was keeping a secret from me, but once he'd
gone into things with Will, he knew he couldn't tell me about

Reese. And Will threatened to, you know, if he pulled out of the investment.'

'What a dick,' I whisper. 'But don't worry, we've sorted things with Will.'

'You have?' Anna asks, genuinely surprised; everything seemed so complicated last night.

'Yeah, we're dropping out of the competition,' I explain. 'There's a few cancellation fees we have to pay, but Reese and I can cover them... with some help from our parents.'

'But you're not even going to try and win it?' Anna asks, suddenly animated.

'Even with the cheapest studio fees we can find, it will still be too much for us to cover without Jake's investment – and we can't risk losing your wedding fund.'

'No, you can't,' Anna says, with a tiny grin. 'But *we* can.'

'What?'

'Jake and I talked about it, last night,' Anna says. 'Now we're postponing the wedding, we have this big pot of money just sitting there.'

'Yeah, until you have a wedding to pay for,' I object. I know they'll rebuild things.

'Which could be in a year or it could be in ten...' Anna muses. 'But right now, we have an investment opportunity and we kind of like the odds.' She smiles at me.

'You can't do that,' I say, shaking my head, heart in my chest. 'It's too risky.'

'You know what they say?' Anna grins again. 'High risk, high reward.'

'It's too much,' I object once more, but Anna reaches for my hand, holding it tight.

'Marley'– she looks at me, tears still in her eyes – 'I'll always bet on you.'

CHAPTER TWENTY-SEVEN

I arrive at the empty warehouse to find Reese standing there, leaning against one of the boarded-up windows dressed head to toe in black, her smile beaming white.

'I can't believe this is actually happening,' she says, slinging her arm around my shoulder as we make our way down the side of the building in search of the door, wheeling a large suitcase in her other hand.

This is actually happening. I repeat her sentence under my breath, rolling the words around my mind. I've been saying them to myself ever since I found out about Reese, ever since I knew the truth about Will. And yet looking from Reese to the decrepit old showroom where we're about to film our pilot, the words still seem fitting.

'I'm so glad you didn't cancel this place,' I say, just as Reese uses her full weight to barge open a suspiciously blacked-out door, the confidence in my words wavering as I look around the dingy, open-place space. I called Reese as soon as Anna's generosity confirmed we could go ahead this afternoon. But is this really the sort of location a competition-winning episode is filmed? But what other choice do we have? Even with Anna's investment, I wouldn't have wanted her to cover the eye-watering costs that Will had managed to rack up.

'Well, I'm so glad you have a best mate like Anna,' Reese says, smiling back at me. It's a sentence I never imagined her saying but I guess after last night, everything's a little clearer. Jake will be in the doghouse for a long time but if these past few months have taught us anything it's that anyone can make mistakes – especially when all the *oughts* and *shoulds* of adult life make the walls feel like they're caving in.

I hear Reese fumbling in the dark, holding her phone high like a torch. Then I hear a click and the expansive room floods with light.

'It's *perfect*,' Reese says softly. It was her idea to reach out to the ex-businessman who often props himself up at the Hyde Out bar, bemoaning the closure of his furniture stores.

'Since when have you been an optimist?' I say, as she turns to see my eyebrows soar.

'Okay, so I know it's not high spec,' Reese goes on; it's the understatement of the century. 'But look, we've got the bathroom,' she says, holding a hand out towards a tiled corner of the showroom, with no less than three dust-covered bathrooms to choose from. 'And the bedroom.' She grins again, pointing over to four beds spanning the length of the warehouse, each one set in its own decorated square. I am not in a rush to lie on a mattress that has been left here for God knows how long. Thankfully, our pilot doesn't have any in-bed action – just the shower scene. For all our practice, now we'll have to do it for real. Now I'll have to do it knowing who Will really is.

'Have you heard from him?' I ask, as Reese bends to her knees to open the suitcase.

'He hasn't stopped calling,' Reese replies, not needing to ask who I'm talking about. 'Haven't answered though. How about you?'

'Same,' I say, feeling the familiar buzz of my phone through my back pocket; he hasn't stopped calling me back ever since he blew me off when I needed to speak to him. From his increasingly frequent, increasingly frantic calls, I assume he doesn't enjoy this taste of his own medicine. 'He's going to freak when he finds out what we've done,' I say, before Reese can glare my guilt away. What we've done is *nothing* compared to what he's done.

'I think we're being pretty damn fair given the circumstances,' Reese says, still on her knees and lining the contents of her suitcase along the exposed concrete floor, from some kind of cleaning spray to an extra pair of clothes. What has she got in there? 'We'll text him the address in plenty of time before he sets off for the studio he booked, so that he arrives just as our crew does.' 'Crew' feels a bit of a stretch given that we've hired two camera operators and a sound engineer. But we have one more special guest coming that makes me feel that Will might actually keep it together until we've wrapped. 'But until then,' Reese says, picking up a pair of marigolds from off the floor and thrusting them in my direction. 'We've got work to do.'

We've just finished cleaning our chosen show bathroom and dusted down Jack and Ella's 'bedroom', when people start to arrive. First our camera crew, friends of Reese's who have agreed to charge us mates' rates. Then, the sound guy who has offered to double up as our gaffer, even though he might know nothing about lighting. Turns out people are pretty happy to pay you favours when you're real with them, when you cut the crap and show them your passion, tell them the truth. Once the lights are up and pointing at our selected spots, things start to look a bit more professional. It's still a far cry from what Will had in mind.

'What the hell is this?'

I hear his voice ring from behind me, and I turn to see him red in the face.

'I've been trying to get in touch with you for *ages* and all I get is one message with a new address to *here*.' He spits the last word, thrusting his hands wide open to indicate his indignation at our surroundings. 'What's going on?'

'Chill, Will,' Reese says, striding across towards him as I follow behind. The last time we saw each other I thought we were more than friends, I thought he cared. Seeing him now, I'm not sure I ever felt anything other than a buzz of adrenalin, the buzz of winning; nothing built to last. 'We've got everything covered,' she says with a smirk, mocking his habitual tone.

'But I didn't even know whether we were going to film today, whether something had happened to either of you,' he says, eyes darting to the crew behind him. 'I had... no, I *have* no idea what's going on.'

'I can't imagine what that's like,' I say, looking from Will to Reese with a shrug. Will takes a step back, like we're now as unfamiliar to him as the mystery crew behind us.

'Why are we *here?*' Will says, worry reverberating through his words. 'We need to get to the studio in the next twenty minutes, it'll be tight but...'

'There is no studio,' Reese says, shaking her head.

'But I *booked* the studio,' Will objects, his confusion palpable.

'Yes,' Reese says, exasperated. 'And I *cancelled* your studio. A friend of mine offered me this place on the cheap, complete with bathroom.' She beams, killing him with kindness. 'I thought you'd be pleased,' she adds, smiling sweetly, and I follow suit; we still want him to follow through with the filming; he's clearly a good actor, one of the best.

'Why would I be *pleased?*' Will says, pushing a shaking hand through his floppy hair. 'This place is a dive.' He should have seen it before we cleaned up. 'This isn't my vision at all.'

'You're right,' I say, taking a step forward as I see a familiar figure walk into the warehouse behind him. 'This isn't *your* vision.'

'Sometimes you have to spend money to make money,' Will says, as I glare back at him; *yes, but whose money?* 'You know as well as I do that the producers will take one look at the quality of this pilot and laugh us out of the competition.'

'I think the producers are smart enough to find quality in the right places,' Tanya Moore says loudly behind him. Will turns to see her standing there, dressed down in ripped jeans, T-shirt and an oversized cardigan. Her stern face stops his tirade in its tracks just like we knew it would.

'Thank you for coming, Tanya,' Reese says, reaching an open palm to her.

'Thanks for inviting me,' Tanya replies, shaking Reese's hand before turning to me. 'You're the first team in all the years of this competition to actually *ask* for our input.' Not their input, but *her* input; I imagine that's at least half the reason she's actually turned up at such short notice. 'I haven't got long, I'm afraid,' she adds as my mind fills with all the ways a producer like her must spend her workdays. 'When do you start filming?'

'Now,' Reese replies, beaming.

'But I...' Will begins to object, his cheeks still red, his hands still shaking.

'What's the matter?' I say, looking Will dead in the eye. 'Unprepared?'

Will's eyes widen again, like he can't comprehend the scenes unfolding before him. There's so much we need to have out with one another, but right now, we need to film this thing. Anna and Jake are banking on us. I'm banking on us too.

'Of course, I'm prepared.' Will laughs nervously, casting a glance in Tanya's direction. She nods, content. As far as she is aware, nothing untoward has happened between us, but as she strides across to the show-bathroom, every inch the woman we hoped she would be, something tells me she's smart enough to know at least some of what's going on.

Scene after scene, we bring the pages of our pilot to life until we come to the final scene, the one that got us into the competition in the first place.

'We've only really got one shot at this,' Reese says, as soon as we're in position. I know she's talking about the shower scene, about the fact that as soon as water is pooling all over the bathroom space, it'll take too long to mop up and start again, but I still feel like she could be talking about the competition. Despite all that has happened, this is our chance.

I nod, and even though we've now been acting together for the last few hours, Will is still looking dazed and uneasy between takes but before he can object, Reese is turning on the water we've managed to hook up to the show-bathroom. We've made holes in the shower hose and patched them up in a way that the owner of this place suggested when Reese described our scene to him. They'll hold the water in for a few seconds whilst Will says his first lines and I pretend to be fixing the shower, but then the water will burst through, spraying everywhere, so there's no time to think twice.

'Ella,' Will croaks as he fixes his eyes on mine, the sound of the water now gushing through the hose and out of the shower head I'm holding into the base of the shower. 'You don't have to have it together all of the time.' It's at that moment that the patches fail and water sprays between us.

'But if I don't, who the hell will?' I recite my line, trying not to think about the first time I said it, back when Will was just another gorgeous stranger in the Hotel Hyde.

'I will,' he says, reaching his hand to my waist and pulling me into him with force. *Liar*. Ella might not need to keep it together, but I do. For Reese. For *me*.

Will moves in closer to me, the shower-spray soaking through my white T-shirt, making it see-through. There's no time to feel self-conscious about that when I know Will is about to peel it off.

'But only if you let me,' Will says, as I step toward him. His hands are on my sides, lifting up my top, his fingers searching me hungrily as thoughts flood my mind: our first kiss, the embrace we shared when I was crying, the sex we had back when I still believed in him. I take all the emotion, use it all, and force it back into his kiss. Turns out I can use him too.

His familiar mouth touches mine but he feels like a stranger, I know he feels it too. He lifts my sopping shirt over my head and then I do the same to his. We stop undressing there; the pile of clothes we shoot in the puddles on the floor later will tell the audience what they need to know. As he pulls away, I keep my eyes on his, he smiles broadly, the way he did when we first played out this scene, back when the chemistry of our kiss seemed to leave him stunned. But Will's not the only one with surprises up his sleeves.

'Cut,' Reese shouts, and someone somewhere switches off the water. Will and I just stand there, our bare torsos still inches apart. I hold onto him tightly.

'You're such a good actor,' I whisper, just loud enough for him to hear. I feel his body soften slightly, as if he might be able to put our behaviour earlier down to nerves. His eyes search mine, the way they often have and it's as if he's trying to work out whether I'm back where he wants me, whether I'm still putty in his hands to manipulate or whether my silence since our last phone call is proof that he's been found out. He looks down at my hand, still lingering on his torso and I see the corners of his mouth turn up. He broadens out his chest as if re-inflating his ego.

'Not so bad yourself.' Will smiles down at me. 'You worried me for a second there, keeping me out of the loop like that.' He laughs to himself as if the fact that he could be blindsided by two little girls is preposterous. I feel my muscles tense up as he holds my waist tighter. 'I thought we told each other everything,' he whispers softly, but after what Reese, Anna and I have just managed to pull off I feel too strong to melt this time. 'Marley.'

He whispers my name like a secret, like it's the very thing that is holding us together. And here I was thinking that it was attraction or affection, or maybe even more. His eyes dart to Reese who is too busy chatting to our makeshift crew to overhear.

'Reese knows,' I say, still holding him tight, my eyes tracing his over to her, the one person he wants to keep me away from so he can keep fooling me into thinking that he has everything in control. But he's not in control anymore. Not of this. Not of me.

'She knows?' Will looks surprised. 'And she's still here?'

'I know too.'

'What do you mean, you know too?' Will says, his body stiffening even more. 'It's your *name*. That Anna thing was your secret to begin with,' he whispers, eyes darting to the people around us, looking for someone to tell him what is going on, but they're all busy reeling in wires and positioning our tops and some spare jeans into a puddle beside us.

'No.' I smile, holding him closer still, whispering the words onto his neck, glistening with shower water and sweat. 'We know *your secret*.'

'What secret?' Will says, using his hands to gently push mine away. He doesn't want to touch me if he's not doing the holding, if he's not the one in control. But I am in control now. And not just of this situation, but of my whole damn life. I may not have 'made it' or have ticked that many milestones off my win-at-life bingo card, but if winning means losing myself, if winning means behaving like Will, I don't want any part of it.

'Marley?' Will hisses my name, more anxious still. Marley. *Marley.* He can say it as loud as he likes because all my secrets are out now. I'm unashamedly myself. 'What secret?' he asks again, his forehead crinkled in confusion.

'The contract,' I say. Now that we've got what we need from him, we've got nothing left to hide. 'I know all about the contract. The unfair terms, your mystery third party, my signature you *forged*.'

'I sorted it for you,' he says, clutching at straws, his face falling with fear. 'I said I'd handle all of the contract stuff so that you didn't have to.'

'So, you admit it?' I ask again. 'That you forged my signature on the contract?'

'Of course, I admit it,' Will replies, reaching to hold me again, softening his voice and hoping he can seduce me all over again. 'But I did it for you.'

But I won't be seduced again. Not by him and his lies. Or the lies that tell me I can't be happy until I've made it or made millions. No more lies. I only want reality, with all its highs and lows. I only want *my* reality now.

I look into his eyes, my own reflection visible within them and smile.

'Oh babe,' I whisper, squeezing his hand in mine one last time, letting out a little laugh as I do. 'You may be a good actor – but you're not as good as you think you are.'

'That was wonderful,' Tanya says, as soon as I've turned my back on Will to arrive at Reese's side. I don't need to look back to know that he's following behind.

'Thank you,' Reese says, before adding, 'I'm sorry it'll be a bit rough and ready.'

I turn to find Will standing beside me and despite the bomb I've just thrown at him, his face seems to scream *you can say that again*.

'Please don't apologise,' Tanya says, scooping her hair to one side. 'We're looking for storytelling and talent – and you guys have plenty.' She smiles between me and Reese. 'Once you have your edited pilot, just send it across to us and we'll let you know in the next couple of weeks about the result – you do have an editor lined up, right?'

'We do,' all three of us say in unison. Will looks from Reese to me, more out of his depth with every passing second. It was his job to line everything up but surely, my last comment explains why he's been fired from his 'I've got it all covered' responsibilities.

'Great, well I look forward to seeing how it all plays out,' Tanya says. I catch Reese's eye; we're looking forward to seeing how our next scene plays out too.

Tracing our footsteps back across the warehouse floor and out into the open air, we know from Will's hurried stride that he's less than ten seconds away from exploding. But as soon as he's taken one step away from the building, he stops still.

'What the...' he begins, as he finds Xavier, Anna and Jake smiling back at him. I catch Anna's eye and she winks, as I reach my hand out to hold Reese's in mine. We both know it's the first time she's seen Jake since their meeting, the one that never should have happened, and right now, she could do with a friend – maybe even two. Out of the corner of my eye, I think Will is about to bolt before Xavier puts a hand on his shoulder.

'Good to see you, buddy,' he says as Will's expression morphs from confusion to disgust. I hold Reese's hand tighter in my own.

'I'm sorry,' Will begins, his voice a little shaky. 'Do I know you?'

'No, mate,' Xavier says, a manilla envelope grasped in his hands. 'But I know you.'

'What's going on?' Will says again, eyes searching the group and landing on Jake. 'Mate, what the hell are you doing here?'

'We're checking in on our investment,' Anna says, grabbing Jake's shaking hand in hers and taking a step forward toward Will.

'*Your* investment?' Will scoffs, as Anna stands there as strong as anything. I used to think she was wrapped around Jake's little finger, that Reese was the feisty one. Now I see that the strong girl I became friends with in the first place is still very much alive. It's just that this strength looks a bit different to how I thought it would; the strength to listen, to understand, to forgive. The strength to stand by your loved ones even when they've made mistakes, acted so out of character.

'Yeah, isn't that what your contract says?' Anna says again, and Jake just looks at her like she's the most incredible woman he's ever met. I squeeze Reese's hand again, but her eyes are fixed on Will, watching his entire body squirm. 'That we should pay for the filming of this pilot and only be reimbursed if it goes on to win the competition, whilst you shoulder absolutely none of the risk?' Anna takes another step forward; Will takes one back.

'Forging someone's signature on a contract seems a little risky to me, mate,' Xavier mumbles under his breath.

'No,' Will says above Xavier's mumbles. 'It says that *Jake* will.' He looks at him now and I can tell from the way Jake is struggling to look him in the eye that what Anna said about Will threatening him if he were to back out must be true.

'What's his is mine,' Anna says, and if looks could kill, Will would be a goner.

'You're still going to marry this eejit?' Will scoffs, shaking his head in disbelief.

'Yes,' Anna says defiantly before softening. 'Maybe, we're going to take some time to...' she looks between me and Reese before fixing her attention back on Will. 'Actually, I don't need to explain myself to you.'

'And if anyone's got some explaining to do...' Xavier mumbles again.

'Mate,' Will explodes, eyes shooting to Xavier accusingly. 'Who *are* you?'

'My name's Xavier.' He grins his goofy smile, putting one hand out for Will to shake, the other still holding the envelope. Will just stares on. 'And I'm Ms Priestly and Ms Bright's lawyer.' He's not. Apparently, there's some more hoops he needs to jump through before he can officially represent us, but Will doesn't need to know that.

'You're their *what*?' Will shouts.

'I'm their lawyer,' Xavier says. 'And we've got some questions about this contract.'

'Great, well, Reese, ask away, I'd be happy to explain them,' Will says, lying through his teeth; as far as he's aware she's still not seen the contract. 'But if *Anna* had any issues with them, she shouldn't have signed it.'

'Anna didn't...' I say, my anger impossible to control any longer; everybody knows about me pretending to be Anna now, there's nothing left to hide. '*Marley* didn't either.'

'Really?' Will says with a stupid smirk turning up the corners of his mouth. 'Because it sure looks like your signature on the contract.' Now that we know that Sloane Star insisted on having at least two signatories, the fact he only forged my signature makes more sense.

'That *you* wrote,' I say.

'No, I didn't,' Will says, narrowing his eyes on mine. 'Sounds like you signed it before realising that your best friend's fiancé was burdening the risk...' So, he did draw the dots between me and the real Anna? I wonder when the penny dropped. It's not like it matters now. 'And you've simply changed your mind.'

'That's not what you admitted earlier,' I say, holding my cool. 'After we wrapped.'

'Well, I guess it's your word against mine,' Will says, a cocky edge to his voice.

'Not exactly,' Reese says before Will's attention swings towards her.

'What?' Will snaps.

'It's just that...' Reese begins slowly, like she's unsure about what's happening even though I know she knows precisely what she's doing. '...after I called "cut" we left the sound recording rolling for a couple of minutes,' she says with a little smile. Will's face falls. 'So, we've actually got *your* words on the record.'

'Fine, call me out, lock me up.' Will throws his hands out, every bit the dramatist. 'But what's going to happen to our pilot and our chances in the competition then?'

'Oh, that part's easy,' Reese says, her eyes shining.

We've looked at whether we can kick Will out but he's as much a part of this team as we are; not more, just as much. Plus, we're smart enough to know this behind-the-scenes drama is hardly going to convince Sloane Star to take a chance on us.

'Xavier here has drafted a new contract for us, a *fair* contract,' she says.

'But I've already done all the negotiating with the producers,' Will objects.

'Yes, and we called them this morning to let them know we've had some second thoughts about the way we're going to distribute the reward and the risk,' Reese goes on. 'Around the same time, we thought to invite Tanya Moore to join us here today. She says provided we agree to cover the costs somehow that she doesn't mind how it's split.'

'Here's the revised contract,' Xavier chips in, opening the unsealed envelope to pull out the papers inside. 'A fair one.'

'So, let me get this straight,' Will says, trying to reclaim some kind of control over the situation; we all know he's acting in vain. 'If I sign this, we're still going to submit our pilot to the competition, and we're still in for a chance to win this thing, *together?*'

'That's right,' Reese says, as I nod.

'But why would you even *want* to do that?' Will looks a little shamed now.

'We don't, really...' Reese begins. 'But we do want to win this thing,' she adds. 'We've got some pretty cool people invested in it.' She smiles at Anna. 'Plus, the revised contract names me as the *sole* author of the work, so if you don't start playing by our rules, I'll write you out of the next part of the script quicker than you can say...'

'Cut!' Xavier shouts dramatically and Reese can't help but laugh at him. 'I've always wanted to say that. But yeah. Anyway dude, here's the contract...'

'And you're okay with this?' Will says, turning to face me now. 'Working together as on-screen lovers after everything that's happened?'

'I mean, it might take a while to get used to using other people to get ahead in my career,' I say. 'But I'm sure I'll find someone to give me pointers.'

CHAPTER TWENTY-EIGHT

'Top-up?' Xavier asks, as I thrust my empty glass up towards him, my tired legs hanging over one arm of the chair I'm sitting in, hugging one of the cushions we've just gone halves on in a bid to make the place a little bit homelier. I had an interview earlier – not an audition but an *interview*. For one of the executive assistant jobs my parents sent through. Needless to say, my heart wasn't in it, but it's been two weeks since we sent off our final pilot episode and we've still not heard from Sloane Star.

'And you?' Xavier turns his attention to Reese. I'm pretty sure it's been on her all evening. Even with the signed contract now back with the producers, Xavier's normal hobbies haven't resumed. Instead, I've been walking into our living room to find him sat at the kitchen table in one of our newly purchased chairs, reading some textbook on media law or watching a seminar online. He's not told me he's going to renew his certificate to practise law yet, but I can tell it's coming – a classic case of the right thing, the wrong circumstances.

I can't help but think of Cameron.

'That's the last of it,' Xavier says, topping Reese's glass up to dangerously high proportions as I take a sip of my own, washing all thoughts of Cameron away. It was much easier to do when my messy mind was momentarily hung up on Will. We haven't heard much from him in the past fortnight, neither good nor bad, and I'm glad. I know if our pilot gets picked up, we'll find a way to be professional, for the sake of the show, but right now, at least socially, I'm content for our trio to be down to two.

'You trying to get us drunk?' Reese looks up at Xavier with wide eyes and I'm not entirely convinced I'm part of the 'two'. Even so, it feels good to just be me, just Marley.

A loud knock fills the room and I rush to open the door before yelling back into the living room, 'Don't worry. Anna's brought more wine!' I grin back at her, accepting the bottle she's offering me and walking over to the kitchen cupboards to grab her a glass.

'Hey guys.' Anna plonks herself down on the empty armchair facing the one I've just been slumped in. 'Something's different.' Her eyes dart around the room.

'We've cleaned,' Xavier jokes.

'And added some personal touches,' I add.

'It's a bit like polishing a turd.' He smiles at me.

'But we're *trying*.' We both know it's our recent conversations and not just the cushions that are making this place feel like home.

'I like it. Any word from the producers?' Anna asks hopefully. Reese shakes her head.

'If we hear anything, you'll be the first to know,' Reese says, smiling over at her. It's weird that the two of them hanging out together isn't weirder; it turns out they have a lot in common. Plus, in the afterglow of all we've been through, we've got pretty content with weird, although I think we've all drawn the line at Jake being added into the mix for now.

'How did the interview go?' Anna asks, accepting her glass of wine from me.

'It went,' I say, letting Anna fill in the blanks. It's not the kind of job I expected I'd be applying for at this stage in my life, but I also never imagined I'd get to produce a real-life pilot for a producer like Tanya Moore. I guess we never know what's around the corner.

'It's only temporary,' Anna adds, and I know she's right. It's the reason I applied for this job in the first place. That and the fact that it has such flexible hours, that I'll be able to spend a fair bit of time searching for auditions, maybe trying to find a new agent. I always thought temporary was a bad thing – temporary living, temporary times – like there was no point investing in something if it wasn't forever. Sitting here in my now-home with Xavier with an old friendship in new settings and a new friend that's starting to feel like an old one, 'temporary' sounds a bit more like 'flexibility', maybe even 'opportunity.'

'I really want to know what happens next,' Anna says, seeming more at ease than she has in weeks; not as high as she was acting before, but at least this sense of calm seems real.

'Yeah, we all do,' I say, as if that's obvious, as if we haven't all been checking our phones for calls and refreshing our inboxes for emails ever since we sent off our film.

'No, I mean for Ella and Jack,' Anna goes on. 'Now that I've watched the pilot.'

I smile at the memory of Anna watching it for the first time. Will was right: the quality of our filming was pretty poor. But Tanya was right too: the strength of Reese's writing and Will's talent really shone through. I could tell from Anna's reaction that she thought I was pretty good in it, too. 'Have you written anymore?'

'Not really,' Reese says, taking a swig of her wine, plum-red stains subtly circling her pout. 'I've been too busy at the bar.' I know Reese has taken on extra shifts at the hotel, preparing to pay Anna and Jake back for their contribution. It's the reason I went to the interview today – well, that and rent, and food, and being able to afford being a grown-up.

'How is the hotel?' I ask, as nonchalantly as I can; my days spent within it are over.

'The *hotel* is doing okay,' Reese says with a sly smile, as if she knows what I'm really asking about, who I'm really asking about.

'You've got those pages in my room,' Xavier says, responding to Anna's question about Reese's writing, characteristically out of sync with the conversation. Reese glares at him.

'That's interesting...' I say, putting a hand to my chin in contrived confusion. 'Why on earth would your notes be in Xavier's room?' I had my suspicious, but this is *news*.

'Not the reasons you're thinking about, Marley,' Reese says, narrowing her eyes in my direction teasingly, but her blushing cheeks suggest I might be closer to the truth than she's letting on. 'I was just hanging out there for a second before you arrived back from your interview,' she explains, getting to her feet. This feels like another half-truth, but I know *some* secrets are best left to brew for a while. 'I'll go and get them,' she says quickly, clearly sheepish. I catch Anna's eye and know we're both thinking the same thing.

'I'll help,' I say, even though it's completely unnecessary. Xavier is none the wiser.

'What is going on with you two?' I whisper, as soon as we're in the safety of his room. 'Is it a *thing*?' I ask and Reese rolls her eyes.

'Must you know everything?' She laughs.

'Well, after a while of feeling like I know *nothing*, can you blame me?' I laugh. In reality, this has nothing to do with the past few months and everything to do with a welcome distraction from thinking about Cam— the *competition*, thinking about the competition.

'Okay.' Reese puts her hands up in surrender. 'It's not *not* a thing.'

I squeal into the room.

'Shut up,' Reese hisses, reaching a hand to my mouth. 'He'll hear.'

'Xavier is as oblivious as...' I begin before I realise that that's not true anymore. Ever since I started letting him in, he's been smoking less, more present; it makes me wonder whether he was lonely before. I know I was. 'Yeah, you're right.'

'I'm always right,' Reese jokes, picking up the pages of her freshly written scenes from their position on the floor, suspiciously close to the bed. 'Anyway, what about you?'

'What do you mean?' I say. I know I'm not always right – far from it.

'Love-life wise?'

'Oh, I think it's fair to say any kisses with Will will be strictly on-screen from now on,' I say, actually feeling a little repulsed by the thought. He's still good-looking and talented, sure, but since when has that ever been enough without trust being thrown into the mix along with it? My stomach turns, remembering all the people I'd been lying to.

'I wasn't talking about that wanker.' Reese shakes her head, definitely a little tipsy. 'I was talking about Cameron.'

'What do you mean?' I shake my head, heart hammering at just the mention of his name. I've wanted to ask Reese about him but what's the point? He either thinks I'm Anna, about to get married. Or he knows I'm not, and that I'm a silly little liar.

'I saw the way you guys looked at each other,' Reese says, kindness in her voice. 'He said you two connected on some level or something.'

'He said that?' I ask. I had thought that too – before I convinced myself that was ridiculous, before he reminded me that we've never really been friends.

'Yes.' Reese nods.

'Then why didn't you tell me?'

'Because I thought you had a fiancé,' Reese reminds me. Oh yeah, that. 'But you don't anymore. You're single and *he's* single. So, what's stopping you?'

'He must think I'm so stupid, though,' I say, a small flicker of hope in my heart. 'You've told him that I'm not Anna, right?'

'No,' Reese says slowly. 'I haven't. You made that mess, I thought I'd leave it to you to clear up.' She laughs, but I know she's not being mean. Over these last couple of weeks, so much of it spent with her and Anna, I've started to laugh about it all too. I'm still pretty sure Cameron won't be joining in the laughter once I tell him the truth, but it's worth a shot.

'Right, who's up for a game of something?' Xavier asks as soon as we're both back in the room. 'I could fish out my *Lord of the Rings* jigsaw or something?' I look at his eager face and feel comforted by the fact that some of Xavier's whimsy will never fade.

'A jigsaw?' Reese says, turning up her nose. 'That's no fun.'

'Well, what do you find fun?' Xavier asks so flirtatiously that for a second I'm a bit fearful of the answer. Anna catches my eye, and I can tell she's trying not to laugh.

'I don't know,' Reese says. 'Something with a bit of competition?'

A loud hum from the coffee table interrupts their debate and we all glance down to see Reese's phone vibrating against it.

'Oh no,' Reese says, reaching down to hold it in her hands. 'It's Tanya.' She stares at her name lighting up the screen for a second that seems to stretch for minutes.

'Answer it, then,' I say, now perched on the edge of my seat.

'Hello, Reese speaking.' She finally swipes open the call and paces across to the kitchen in the corner of the room. We sit in silence, trying to gauge her monosyllabic replies until Anna stands up and walks the few short steps from her chair to mine, coming to perch on one of the arms, reaching one arm tightly around me.

'You do know that whatever happens, everything will be okay,' Anna whispers, and given what she's already been through this year, I actually believe her. 'It may seem make or break but it's not,' she goes on. 'There's always a surprise around the corner.'

'Thank you,' Reese says. 'Yes... ah-ha... uh-huh... thanks. We will. Bye.'

I see her hang up the call and come to sit on the sofa next to Xavier. I try to read her face, but I can't.

'So...?' I ask, unable to wait a moment longer.

'We didn't win,' Reese says, and I feel my shoulders slump. It would have been so exciting if we had. I know Anna's right, that it was never make or break but it would have been nice for our big break to have been now. Anna squeezes my hand in hers whilst Xavier reaches for Reese's. I can't help but wonder if this is another case of the right people, wrong circumstances. Well, the right *person*.

'At least now we don't have to keep working with Will.' Reese steals the thought from my mind, but I can tell she's gutted too.

'What else did she say?' Anna asks softly.

'She said it was really close,' Reese goes on. 'And that if Tanya had her own way, they would have gone with us.'

I listen on, holding that compliment to my chest.

'But when it came down to it, it was three against one.' If only Will had slept with that producer who fancied him rather than me, we might have won it. 'She also said that if we want to show her some of our work in the future, she'd be very happy to receive it.'

'That's amazing,' Xavier says, eyes darting to the jigsaw now on top of the coffee table, as if assembling a picture of Frodo and Samwise might piece us back together again. It won't but time will. Time can unravel big messes and bring impossible strands back together again; I know that now.

'And you got all this experience – and exposure,' Anna adds.

I've gone from feeling like I have no cheerleaders to having three. Four, if you count Tanya Moore.

'But no money,' I say, as the realisation sinks in. 'I'm sorry, Anna. I can't believe your wedding fund has gone.'

'Not all of it.' She smiles back at me kindly.

'Bloody hell, how expensive was your wedding going to be?' Reese asks and I can't help but laugh; *really bloody expensive.*

'And it was a risk we were willing to take,' Anna confirms again.

'Well, I'm going to pay you back every penny,' I say, her hand still in mine.

'I know you will,' Anna says. 'At least now you've got an amazing piece of work for your portfolio – and when you book a big job, you can start paying me back.'

Anna may not have noticed it, but she said *when* not *if*, and that means everything.

'We can start paying you back today, actually,' Reese says. 'Tanya says they're giving us each seven hundred and fifty pounds for getting to the final.'

'That's cool,' I say, not as cool as my share of one hundred thousand pounds but it's something. And we got to the final, that's something too. More than. 'I'll transfer it as soon as it lands in my bank account,' I tell Anna, who begins to shake her head.

'Why don't you hold onto that for a bit?' she says. 'It can pay for your room when, if... Jake and I do get married.'

I know Anna means *when* not *if* again.

'Okay,' I say, knowing that after all that's happened Anna probably won't be going near a £750-a-room wedding venue again. That it doesn't need to be perfect to be right – it just needs to be real. 'I appreciate it. I appreciate *you*,' I say, knowing when she does get married, I'll be there by her side, regardless of whether it costs my arm, my leg or my dignity to do so.

'If I knew you guys were going to be this cheesy, I would

have brought more booze,' Reese says and though I can't tell for sure, I think she's welling up.

'If I knew we were going to get rejected I would have got more in,' I say, but for the first time in a long time the word 'rejected' has lost its sting.

'Hang on,' Xavier says, standing to his feet. 'I think I've got some boxed wine in my room we could drink.' He disappears, and I clock Anna crinkling her nose at the thought. Moments later, Xavier returns with a black box with small font engraved into its side, which he discards on the coffee table as he proceeds to pop the bottle and pour bubbles into our already slightly red-wine-stained glasses.

'Xavier,' Anna says, studying the box. 'This isn't wine, it's Dom Perignon.'

Xavier looks at her like he has no idea what she's on about.

'How did you have a high-flying legal career without knowing what Dom Perignon is?' Reese says, looking at the glass he's just handed her with wide eyes. 'This is like, one hundred and fifty a bottle.'

'Well, it may surprise you, ladies,' Xavier says, handing Anna a glass before passing one to me, 'but I didn't really fit with the high-flying lawyer types.'

'Well, you fit in with us,' Reese says, as he comes to sit beside her.

'And you told us off for being cheesy.' Anna rolls her eyes. 'To you guys.' She lifts her glass into the air and we each do the same.

'To falling at the last hurdle,' Reese says, with a laugh.

'And the messy bit in the middle.' I clink my glass against hers.

'And all that's left to come,' Anna adds, before taking a sip.

'Any good?' Xavier asks, looking down at the bubbles with suspicion.

'Uh-huh,' Anna says, unconvincingly. 'I think it's better chilled.'

'And out of clean glasses,' Reese says, looking at the slightly pink hue of her own.

I take a sip, and let the bubbles evaporate on my tongue. This whole competition journey started with a glass of this stuff in one of the fanciest hotels in town, full of promise but tangled up in knots – and I know there's one twist left for me to unravel. But right now, rejected again and drinking warm champagne from an unwashed glass in the shit-tip Xavier and I now call home, I don't hate where it's ending up; it has notes of new beginnings.

CHAPTER TWENTY-NINE

This will be okay. Everything has to be okay. I look up at the entrance to the Hotel Hyde and it feels every bit like the first time I found myself standing outside it. Except this time, it's worse. Because not only am I the kind of girl who would never fit in here – now, I'm the very girl who has spent the last couple of months pretending to be the kind of woman who does.

I walk past the open iron gates, still scattered with seasonal flowers all year round. I hold my head up high. All that *this kind of girl* stuff is bollocks. Anna may like coming to these fancy places, but it doesn't mean she's perfect; she doesn't even want to be anymore. Reese might work here but that doesn't mean she can't rub shoulders with producers and businesspeople and knock back Dom Perignon with the best of them. We can morph and change and grow and be any kind of women we want to be.

'Anna?' Cameron says, as soon as I've walked into the hotel. But I can't be Anna. Not for another minute longer. Not even if Cameron hands me a vat of champagne or whisks me off to Borough Market. Not even if he rockets me to the moon.

I look up into his kind eyes and wish I had just a moment longer to absorb the beauty of our surroundings, which clash so clearly against my jeans and T-shirt combo.

'No,' I say softly and watch his gorgeous face twist in confusion. 'I'm Marley.'

'I err...' Camron's brow crinkles as he reaches a hand to his jaw. 'Is that some word the cool kids are saying that I should know?'

'I think you're thinking of gnarly,' I say, and he nods in recognition until he realises that leaves my last utterance unexplained. 'It's a long story. When do you go on your break?'

'Anytime I like really,' he replies, humouring me completely even though my last sentence is pretty stupid given that I know he's the manager here. I don't think he's going to find my next sentence any less confusing.

'Great,' I say, my heart beating fast, my mind scrambling to work out how best to explain the worst of mistakes; I feel like I should be more used to it by now. Cameron begins to walk in the direction of the bar but then hooks a right just before the entrance into the Hyde Out. He steers us deeper into the belly of the hotel until he comes to a standstill before a lift and presses the button. For a moment, I wonder whether he already knows the truth about me after all, whether he's going to take me into some kind of punishment chamber and make me pay the hard way. But that's what I'm here for; I'm here to pay Cameron back for every penny on 'Anna's' Hotel Hyde tab. That, and to say sorry.

'Where are you taking me?' I ask, as soon as we're in the lift together. In the confines of the space, Cameron's body feels incredibly close. I wish I didn't like him so much. It makes what I'm about to tell him even harder.

'I'm taking you to where I usually have lunch,' he says, as I feel my ears pop. How high does this lift go? Just then, it comes to a halt and the doors open onto the roof. 'You enjoy the view, I'll go and get some food,' he says, as soon as I've walked out onto the concrete space, scattered with flowers and colour, the horizon visible from all sides. I turn around to tell him not to go to any effort – any *more* effort – but the lift doors are closing and Cameron disappears out of my sight entirely.

Oh crap, I'm actually alone now. Is he going to leave me here, never come back? Or worse, get someone to push me off? Either way, I know the outcome of my confession is not going to be good. I may as well enjoy this whilst I can.

I walk further towards the edge of the rooftop and realise that the mismatched flowers I'm walking past must be discarded wedding flowers. Who doesn't make sure that every last bunch of these babies are taken home?

I edge closer to the wall lining the drop, perfect leaning height. I look around to see that part of the roof is cornered off, sheltering a gorgeous rooftop pool, lined with sun-loungers in front of a fully decked-out bar. I remember that on my first visit to the hotel Cameron had told me about it but had not shown me, as it was completely booked out. Standing here, in the slightly shabby 'back office' section of the rooftop, the peace of the place seems to make the view even more breath-taking.

'Like it?' I hear Cameron's voice behind me, and his face reminds me what I'm doing here; ten pounds says he won't be smiling when I share what I've come here to say. I look down to his hands to see that he's holding a slightly squished pizza box.

'The chefs always make me some lunch – perk of the job,' he says, offering the box for me to take. 'We'll have to share, though.'

I open the box and even though the pizza looks great, I've suddenly lost my appetite.

'Ready to tell me this long story?' Cameron asks as we lean against the wall and look out across the city. 'What's a marley?'

Why didn't I just tell him in the lobby? Refuse to follow him to such a vast, high, *secluded* space? I never know when to stop. Except I do: I know it's time to stop now.

'I'm a marley,' I say. 'I mean... I'm Marley.'

Cameron looks at me, his head tilted in curiosity as he leaves space for me to go on.

'The first time I came here, that first appointment, I was here for my best friend Anna, who is getting married...' I go on and watch Cameron's face for changes, for the reddening of rage or the downward stare of disgust but there isn't any sign of either, so I take that as my cue to go on. '...I was in a bit of a strange place and needed an escape and one thing led to another and I pretended to be Anna for the day, but then I met Reese...' I breathe, remembering again all that we've been through together. 'I wanted to tell you the truth, I was going to tell you the truth, but then we got through that competition and there was just never a good time to tell you and...'

'So, you're not Anna?' Cameron says, his eyes searching every inch of my face.

'No, I'm not but...'

'And you're not getting married?' Cameron says, putting

down the slice of pizza he's just picked up. Oh crap, I'm making him lose his appetite too.

'No, I'm not,' I say, grabbing his stunned silence as permission to go on. 'But everything else I told you about me was real, I swear,' I say, a lump rising in my throat, tears forming in my eyes. 'I'm a currently out-of-work actor with a crippling inferiority complex, I like a laugh and a drink and have honestly never heard of Pete's band...'

I watch Cameron's lips and in a glimmer of hope or naïvety think he might be struggling not to smile.

'I am not good with spice and cannot handle my wine, and sometimes I can be smart, but sometimes I can be really, really stupid. And I think...'

I hesitate, not sure that Cameron even wants to hear this next sentence, or anything about what I think.

'The kindness you show your staff is beautiful and your hard work and the fact you've built your career from the bottom up is admirable, and I am so sorry that I ever lied to you...'

Cameron doesn't say anything, looking from me to the view surrounding us on all sides.

'I have spent the last few weeks wondering why it was so hard to just be me, and I guess I didn't think I was enough; I wasn't where I wanted to be...'

Cameron's face seems to soften; I know he knows what it's like to always feel behind.'

So, I started thinking I wasn't *who* I wanted to be.'

'I see...' Cameron says slowly.

'It was stupid and immature and honestly, after pretending to be Anna for a while, after seeing that even her life isn't perfect, I think I just want to be me from now on.'

'You're right,' Cameron says slowly, as I prepare myself

for the onslaught to come. 'Pretending to be someone else is pretty stupid.' He shakes his head.

'I know, and I'm sorry—' I begin before he cuts me off.

'Because it was the imperfect moments, the vulnerable moments, that I thought were kind of great.' He gives me a small smile, it's not much but for now, it's enough. 'I did suspect something was going on, but I just thought you weren't happy with Jake.'

'Yeah... I'm not,' I say, and I wonder if Cameron will ever see the funny side of this.

'Is he even real?' Cameron says, and I can't blame him for asking. 'Are you single?'

'Yes, I am,' I say quickly. 'And yes, he's real. He's my friend Anna's fiancé.'

'And will *they* be getting married here?'

'Maybe one day.' I nod, knowing that Anna and Jake are now far more likely to get married in a local town hall. 'But not in the near future.' I watch his face fall. 'So, I'm here to settle up her tab, *my* tab,' I correct. 'Honestly, Cameron, I am so sorry. I never meant to waste your time or anything and had I not met Reese that night and entered the competition I would have found a way to tell you sooner because I really like you and I started to think you might like the parts of me that were actually *me*, and well, yeah... I can't give you your time back but I'm here to settle up every single penny.'

I know I can't write my debt off completely, but I can transfer it from the Hotel Hyde to the bank of Mum and Dad for now. I can cut off all my ties to Cameron and this place and let him waste his time on someone else.

'Don't worry,' Cameron says softly. 'I understand how not being where you want to be and the pressure to get there can make you do some crazy things.'

'Thanks Cameron,' I say, with a little smile, his kindness making it hard for the tears not to fall. 'So how much do I owe you? For all of it, everything.'

I watch as Cameron takes in my sorry expression once again. I hope he knows I mean every word. He holds my eye contact for just a while longer before he shakes his head again.

'It's on the house,' Cameron says, a smile crossing his face.

'No, it can't be... that's too much, and it doesn't even account for your time.'

'I *chose* to give you that time,' he says, as memories of our day-long tour and our hours in Borough Market fill my mind. 'You must have known that I didn't spend hours and hours with every single client, that I didn't need to do all those shifts in the Hyde Out.'

'I thought you said it reminded you of who you used to be?' I ask. 'How far you've come?' I'm hardly in a position to challenge him for not telling the truth.

'It does,' Cameron says quickly. 'I needed to remind myself that although I spend my days with the kind of people who think money can buy them out of their responsibilities, their commitments...' He breaks off to look down at his shoes for a moment before placing his gaze back on me. 'I'm not the kind of guy to fall for a soon-to-be married woman,' he says kindly. 'I needed to remind myself of that.'

'What? Why?' I say, something like lightning shooting through my veins.

'Why do you think?' Cameron says with a little laugh.

No, what, wait? Does this mean... Cameron reaches for my hand.

'Marley?' Cameron asks and it feels good to hear him say

my name. 'If the hotel writes off your tab, does that make our time in Borough Market a date?'

'Well... I mean, technically...the hotel would be paying so...' I watch as Cameron's eyes widen, cuing me in for my next line. 'Yes,' I say. 'Yes, that would make it a date.'

'Great.' Cameron smiles fully. 'That means I can ask you on a second...'

CHAPTER THIRTY

I walk through Greenwich Park in the direction of Anna's flat. Looking up at the green expanse, to the top of the hill, I watch the increasingly silhouetted figures of tourists, friends and lovers up there watching the sky turn from blue to black. It's beautiful, and far from being reserved for this city's elite like I once imagined, it now feels open to all. So does Anna's. Now that over three months have passed since we got to the bottom of what had gone on between Reese and Jake, now that Jake and Anna are safely back on track, not even hanging out at their place all together feels wrong. The fact that until recently Reese and Xavier have only had eyes for each other no doubt accelerated that.

I turn through the gates out of the park and walk closer and closer to Anna's place, my legs tired from a day of running around after the children. Not my own, obviously. But at the school I've recently started to work at as a TA.

I walk past a line of shops and cafes, at locals drinking and joking outside the pub on the corner of Anna's street. The only thing I enjoyed about school when I was there was my friendship with Anna and the fact that one day we'd get out, we'd be able to get our dream jobs and live our dream lives. But now, being back in the place where those dreams are made isn't half bad – especially now that I'm taking on more and more responsibility in the drama department. Plus, it's not like I've stopped dreaming either. I still take the odd audition from time to time, it's just not the be all and end all anymore, not since I started recognising how full my life already is. And I'm writing now too; I have Reese to thank for that.

'Hey!' Jake beams as he opens the door to find me standing here. 'Come in!'

He looks healthier and more rested every time I see him. Apparently, his work's still difficult, up one second, down the next, but he's sharing the highs and lows with Anna now; she's sharing her highs and lows with him too. It seems to be working for them.

'Jake, is that Marley?' I hear Anna shout from the living room. 'Marley! Get your arse in here now, I want to hear this script!'

'I think that's your cue,' Jake says, with a subtle wink.

'And yours,' I joke. 'Please tell me you have somewhere else to be on Girls' Night?'

Jake nods. 'Going out with the work lot. And before you say anything, no I will *not* be drinking myself blind and accepting notes from random crazies.'

'I heard that!' It's now Reese's turn to shout from the living room. Jake's coy face tells me he meant her to – for both her and Anna to. Sure, it was awkward at first when we started hanging around here, but we've all talked about it enough, healed enough, *grown* enough in the last three months to be able to laugh about it by now.

'About time,' Anna says as I walk into the room to find her and Reese sitting on the sofa sipping what I *think* is their first glass of wine.

'I was at work,' I say before they roll their eyes. I've been talking about the kids ever since I started the job, about my favourites, about the ones with promise, about the ones who have come the furthest – all the while maintaining that it's a temporary role. But just because something doesn't last forever doesn't mean it isn't good. Speaking of which...

'How are you doing, darling?' I ask Reese softly.

'No, not you too!' she says, looking from me to Anna. 'Less of that sympathetic head tilt. I'm good, honestly,' Reese says, and I believe her. 'Xavier's found the perfect job up North and I'm loving my writing course down here.' No wonder she's loving it, it's one of the most prestigious in the city and agents are already sniffing around her, offering to take her for dinner. And I know from phoning Xavier that he's settling in to being a lawyer again too, this time in a slightly more down-to-earth firm. My new housemate, a friend-of-a-friend of Xavier's, is settling in well too – and there's been no bagpipe sightings from him, *yet*. 'You do know *boy meets girl, lives happily ever after* isn't the only storyline that matters?' Reese asks, every bit the strong woman I know and love.

'Yes, I do,' I say. Even though things with Cameron have been going from strength to strength, I know it's not the only thing that matters, not when I have friends like these.

'Is that a spoiler?' Anna asks, a telling grin covering her face. Reese and I started working on a new script, the scribbled pages she left on Xavier's bedroom floor, almost as soon as our pilot was rejected by the producers at Sloane Star. The character of Jack in the last script was quite literally written for Will and now that there's nothing holding us together anymore, it felt like it was time for a fresh start.

'Not entirely,' Reese answers coyly, taking another sip of her drink.

'Well, what's it about?' Anna asks, somewhere between excitement and exasperation. 'It's killing me.' Anna is my biggest fan now, maybe she always has been; I was just too hung up on our differences, too jealous of her, to see it.

'It's about a woman in her late twenties,' I begin, as Reese scrambles to grab a copy of the freshly printed script from her bag, handing it to Anna. 'Who goes to an appointment for her best friend but in a bid to impress this absolute *babe*,' I go on, and I can't help but smile as Cameron's face fills my mind, 'pretends to be her best friend—'

'Then, she meets this super-hot, razor-sharp stranger and the two become friends,' Reese interrupts, as we both watch Anna's smile grow wider still.

'What the protagonist doesn't know, is that they're about to get their big break and it's going to be a lot harder than she thought to wriggle out of her lie,' I go on.

'It's a story of friendship and forgiveness,' Reese continues, trying her best to keep a straight face. 'Where the men may seem central at first but are a sub-plot at best.'

'A nice added extra,' I joke, and Anna is laughing now, eyes scanning the script.

'It's essentially about how screwed-up your life can get when you're trying to stick to the narrow script you wrote for yourself way back when,' Reese adds as we both search Anna's slightly messy post-work make-up for her reaction.

'It sounds great,' she replies. 'But don't you think it's a little bit *unrealistic?*'

'Unrealistic?' Reese asks.

'I mean who would be stupid enough to pretend to be their best friend?' Anna says again, her eyes narrowed in mock sincerity.

'I hear it happens to people all the time,' I say with feigned nonchalance.

'Only you, Marley.' Anna laughs again. Reese is laughing too. 'Well, it's original, that's for sure,' she adds. I'm not sure if we're talking about me or the script. 'One of a kind.'

'Right, let's send it off,' Reese says, reaching into her bag again for her laptop and opening it up on her lap.

'What?' I ask quickly. 'I thought we were just running through it for Anna tonight?'

'No, that's what we told you.' Reese laughs. 'We knew you'd overthink it.'

'I preferred it better when you guys hated each other,' I joke.

'You're not a very good liar, Marley,' Reese says.

'It doesn't have to be perfect, remember?' Anna says, and I smile back at her.

'Right, that's it. Tanya Moore's email address is in, the script is attached,' Reese says, her eyes scanning her screen. 'All we need to do is press send.' She takes another sip of wine, turning to face me. 'You want to press it?' she asks me. 'I did it last time.'

'I don't know how you even remember that...' I laugh; it's all still a blur.

'You press it, or I will,' Reese threatens. She knows I'm stalling for time; it's just the script feels messy, the story half written, but it's fun and it's exciting and it's getting there – and if we keep editing and polishing and striving for perfection, it might never arrive.

'I'll do it,' I say, and Anna squeals with glee. 'What's the worst that can happen?' They both laugh as I click the 'send' button and the email flags as sent. Our script has just landed in Tanya Moore's inbox, full of opportunity. Just like last time. Except not entirely.

This time, the opportunity has *my* name on it.

———

Were you desperate for Marley to untangle the mess she'd made and finally end up with Cameron? Then make sure you don't miss **The Spare Bedroom** by Elizabeth Neep, another hilarious and heartwarming rom-com about an unfortunate mix-up and forging your own path.

Available now!

A LETTER FROM ELIZABETH

Dear reader,

I want to say a huge thank you for choosing to read *The New Me*. If you did enjoy it, and want to keep up to date with all my latest releases, just sign up at www.bookouture.com/elizabeth-neep. Your email address will never be shared and you can unsubscribe at any time.

This story, like the others I've written so far, began with a real-life mix-up (side note: let's hope ridiculous things don't stop happening to me if you're in the market for more of my books. I for one, hope to keep writing them).

The weekend away was set; a large group of friends of friends of friends were heading out of London for a couple of days of 'escaping to the country' (or you know, to some random hotel just off junction 15A). The only snag? One of my best friends' ex-boyfriend was part of the group. Oh, and so was the new girl he was seeing.

Needless to say (and with suitable amounts of shame) Instagram stalks of said girl were had. 'She looks pretty young,' I said. 'Yeah, I think she's a few years younger than us,' said my friend. More than a few, I thought, before remembering that my own back-in-the-day dating profile swam dangerously close to catfishing. So, on the weekend away we went and, on the first night, I made a new friend out of the friend-of-friends-of-friends. We got on so well that we hung out on the second night too. Then, on the last morning, having brunch with my bestie, chatting about whether she'd crossed paths with her ex's new girl, who should show up but the ex's new girl who – you – guessed it, also happened to be my new bar-buddy. Turns out I had social media stalked the wrong person and accidentally befriended the 'other woman' in my bestie's relationship. Naturally, it wasn't that dramatic given that we're all grown-ups and no one was actually cheating on anyone (me and the two girls are now in the same friendship group and the guy is long forgotten). Still, the seed of an idea was sown: what if you accidentally befriended your best friend's worst nightmare?

Of course, stories are a bit like onions (and ogres, apparently) in that they need layers – and it was my wonderful editor who wondered whether I could 'pull on the thread' of Anna's wedding and the obvious tensions this highlighted in Marley and Anna's friendship. This wasn't hard for me to do. Not because I've witnessed many bridezillas but because I've had times of feeling like a bit of a bridesmaid-monster myself. The more I learn about marriage, the more I realise that it's no walk in the park but a couple of years ago, thanks to some unmet (and unrealistic) expectations and a period of low mental health, I started seeing marriage as a destination. To me, marriage had somehow slipped into meaning so much more than two people bravely choosing to commit to one another: it meant you were loved (publicly), chosen (publicly) and that you'd passed all the necessary milestones to be seen as a grown-up (publicly). This warped way of thinking, leading me to secretly (and sadly, sometimes not-so-secretly) resenting the brides – as if their happy-ever-afters (see, dangerous destination thinking!) lessened the chance of me finding my own.

Despite Marley's unravelling lies in this book, I have tried to fill these pages with truths, all of which I believe in my heart, but frequently need to remind my head: joy is not in scarce supply. In fact, the more you share, the more you feel. Relationship statuses, mortgages or bank balances do not a grown-up make. And as much as static social media squares make milestones look like destinations, they're actually a marker on the journey, every single step on the way (and after) counts too.

Oh, and I truly love my brides, Sophie Ingram-Smith, Emma Cottier, Rachel Sadler and Grace Baxter-to-be: thank you for choosing to make me part of your day.

I hope you loved *The New Me*, and if you did, I would be very grateful if you could write a review. I'd love to hear what you think, and it makes such a difference helping new readers to discover one of my books for the first time.

I love hearing from my readers – you can get in touch on my Facebook page, through Instagram, Twitter, Goodreads or my website.

If you take one thing from this book, I hope it is this: you are on your own journey, may it be full of twists and turns and grace and grit and may we all learn to love the ride. Oh, and if you are going to be someone else for the day – maybe ask them first?

Love,
Elizabeth x

www.elizabethneep.com

facebook.com/Elizabeth%20Neep

twitter.com/elizabeth_Neep

instagram.com/elizabeth_Neep

ACKNOWLEDGEMENTS

If you've followed me on social media for more than ten minutes, you'll know that my favourite place to write is in independent coffee shops, powered by flat whites, pastries and background noise. Instead, thanks to national lockdown number two thousand and twenty (I'm dramatic, go figure), almost every page of this novel was written from the same corner of the same room, locked down with the same man. Thankfully, this man was Nick Stevenson Steels who had the good sense to buy his first flat (complete with writing desk by the window) during a global pandemic, which meant that we could 'bubble' together. Nick, thank you for that well-timed purchase but more than that, the well-timed coffees, cuddles and cheerleading that I've needed now more than ever. You are extraordinary.

Speaking of extraordinary...

Mum, Dad and Tom, the best thing about this pandemic has been spending more time with you. Rachel, the worst thing has been not seeing you more, but you've handled it like you handle everything else in life, with confidence, determination and grace. Neeple People, you are my team, and I couldn't love you more.

To Emily Richardson, Corina Straub and Audrey Schneider, thank you for reading my early chapters and cheering me on.

Nathan, Tom, Rick, Jenn, Nancy, Kevin and Aimee, thank you for loving me through the sunshine and the muddy puddles during the writing of this book. To the friends who have Zoomed and FaceTimed and messaged until we can meet again, I can't wait to see you.

To Sallyanne Sweeney, thank you for being nothing like the agent in this book and every bit the smart and sensitive champion you are. Cara Chimirri, for making every page of this novel infinitely better (I'm so glad we managed to squeeze in one real-life coffee between lockdowns). To the team at Bookouture, I'm genuinely learning so much from you. And to the early book reviewers and bloggers, your time means more to me than you know.

Finally, to God for sustaining me and giving me the words. And to you, dear reader, for giving me the chance to write for you again – I'll forever be grateful.

CPSIA information can be obtained
at www.ICGtesting.com
Printed in the USA
BVHW080348030721
611060BV00002B/355